Alan Furst, who has often been compared to Graham Greene and Eric Ambler, is widely recognised as a master of the atmospheric spy thriller. It was a journalistic assignment, for *Esquire* magazine, that inspired him to write the first of his highly original novels about espionage in eastern and western Europe before and during World War II. He now lives on Long Island, New York.

RED GOLD

Sequel to THE WORLD AT NIGHT.

Film producer Jean Casson has been reluctantly drawn into the dark world of espionage — until he is discovered and forced to flee France. He returns to Paris under a new identity, knowing that for him nothing will ever be the same. As a fugitive from the Gestapo, he must struggle to survive in the shadows — among the pimps and whores, anarchists and thieves. This time, he is determined to stay clear of trouble. Yet, as the war drags on and he witnesses the suffering of his fellow citizens, Casson drifts back into the dangerous world of resistance and sabotage . . .

Books by Alan Furst
Published by The House of Ulverscroft:

THE WORLD AT NIGHT

ALAN FURST

RED GOLD

Complete and Unabridged

ULVERSCROFT
Leicester

First published in Great Britain in 1999 by
HarperCollins Publishers, London

First Large Print Edition
published 2000
by arrangement with
HarperCollins Publishers Limited, London
and Random House Inc., New York

The moral right of the author has been asserted.

This is a work of fiction. Names, characters, places
and incidents are the product of the author's
imagination or are used fictitiously. Any
resemblance to actual events, locales or persons,
living or dead, is entirely coincidental.

Jacket Photograph © Sabine Weiss/Network/Rapho

British Library CIP Data

Furst, Alan
   Red gold.—Large print ed.—
   Ulverscroft large print series: adventure & suspense
   1. World War, *1939 – 1945* —Underground
   movements—France—Paris—Fiction
   2. Paris (France)—Social conditions—20th century
   —Fiction
   3. Spy stories
   4. Large type books
   I. Title
   813.5'4 [F]

   ISBN 0–7089–4253–9

Published by
F. A. Thorpe (Publishing)
Anstey, Leicestershire

Set by Words & Graphics Ltd.
Anstey, Leicestershire
Printed and bound in Great Britain by
T. J. International Ltd., Padstow, Cornwall

This book is printed on acid-free paper

'What will become of us in twenty years' time?' we asked ourselves one evening. Thirty years have passed now. Raymond was guillotined: 'Anarchist gangster' (so the newspapers). I came across Jean again in Brussels, a worker and a trade-union organizer, still a fighter for liberty after ten years in jail. Luce has died of tuberculosis, naturally. For my part, I have undergone a little over ten years of various forms of captivity, agitated in seven countries, and written twenty books. I own nothing. On several occasions a Press with a vast circulation has hurled filth at me because I spoke the truth. Behind us lies a victorious revolution gone astray, several abortive attempts at revolution, and massacres in so great a number as to inspire a certain dizziness. And to think that it is not over yet.

VICTOR SERGE,
Memoirs of a Revolutionary,
1901 – 1941

PLACE CLICHY

PARIS. 18 SEPTEMBER, 1941.

Casson woke in a room in a cheap hotel and smoked his last cigarette. The window by the bed was open and the shade, yellow and faded, bumped gently against the sill in the morning breeze. When it moved he could see fierce blue sky, a bar of sunlight on the lead sheeting of the roof across the courtyard. Something in the air, he thought, a ghost of something, and the sky was lit a certain way. *So then, autumn.*

A knock at the door; a woman came in and sat on the edge of the bed. She had a room down the hall and came to see him sometimes. He offered her the cigarette, she inhaled and gave it back 'Thank you,' she said. She stood up, pulled her slip over her head and hung it on a nail in the wall, then climbed in next to him. 'Tell me,' she said, 'what is it you see out there?'

'Sky. Nothing much.'

She pulled the blanket up so it covered their shoulders. 'You live in a dream,' she said.

'You think it's wrong?'

He felt her shrug. 'I don't know — why bother?'

She felt settled next to him, so the tips of her breasts brushed the skin of his back, ran a finger down the line of hair from his chest to his stomach, and slid her hand between his legs. He stubbed the cigarette out carefully in a saucer he kept on the windowsill, then closed his eyes. For a time he stayed like that, adrift.

'Well,' he said, 'maybe you're right.'

He turned to face her, she rested a knee on his hip, opening her legs. After a moment she said, 'Your hands are always warm.'

'Warm hands, cold heart.'

She laughed, then kissed him. 'Not you,' she said. He could smell wine on her breath.

His mind wandered. It was very quiet, all he could hear was her breathing, long and slow, and the yellow shade, bumping against the sill in the morning air.

* * *

Place Clichy. He sat at an outside table at a café and sipped the roast barley infusion the waiter brought him. *Coffee*, he thought, remembering it. Very expensive now, he didn't have the money. He stared out at the square, Clichy a little lost in the daylight, the cheap hotels and dance halls gray and crooked in the morning sun, but Casson didn't mind. He liked it — in the same way he liked deserted movie sets and winter beaches.

On the chair next to him somebody had left a damp copy of yesterday's *Le Soir*. He spread it out on the table.

. . . the low hills of Lokhvitsa, brooding at nightfall, the steep banks of the river Dnieper, the grumble of distant cannonade. Suddenly, white Very lights fired from flare pistols, sputtering as they float to earth. A signal! Guderian's Third Panzer has linked up with Kleist's Sixteenth Panzer! The Kiev pocket has snapped shut like a trap: 300,000 Russian casualties, 600,000 taken prisoner, five Soviet armies obliterated. Now, Kiev must fall within hours. Victorious Wehrmacht columns burst into song as they prepare to march into the defeated city.

Casson shook his head — *who writes this shit?* His eyes wandered to the top of the column. Oh, from their foreign correspondent, Georges Broux. Well, that explained it.

5

Once upon a time, when he'd been Jean Casson, producer of gangster films, with an office near the Champs-Elysées, Georges Broux had sent him a screenplay. *Morning Must Come*, something like that. Maybe it was *Dawn* that had to come, or *A New Day*, but that was the general idea. La Belle France brought to her knees by decadence and socialism. 'Dear Georges, thanks for letting us have a look; unfortunately . . . ' And did, Casson wondered, the Wehrmacht actually burst into song? Maybe it did.

He searched in his pocket until he found the cigarette stub and lit it, sipped his barley coffee, turned to the movie page. Playing at the Impériale, over on the Champs-Elysées, was *Premier Rendezvous* — first date — with Danielle Darrieux and Louis Jourdan. If you'd seen that, the Gaumont had 'a frothy romantic comedy.' Or, if you were really hard to please, you could go out to Neuilly for 'a little jewel, bubbling over with mirth! A sly French wink!' Casson read through the listings for the smaller theatres, sometimes they ran revivals and his old films showed up. *No Way Out* or *The Devil's Bridge*. Maybe, even *Night Run*.

He heard the engine — tuned to a perfect hum — and forced himself to look up casually. A black *traction-avant* Citroën, a

6

Gestapo car, had pulled to the curb in front of the café. Casson's heart hammered against his ribs. He bent over the newspaper, concealing his face, and turned the page. A goalie leaped toward the edge of his net as the ball sailed past his hands, a jumble of print, this team 2, that team 1. He had an identity card, *Marin, Jean Louis*, and a ration book. Nothing more. It wasn't a quality fake, he'd bought it from a taxi driver, one phone call and that was the end of him. Casson was wanted by the Gestapo; taken in for questioning at the rue des Saussaies office three months earlier, he had crawled out an unbarred window and escaped over the roof. Dumb luck, Casson thought, the kind that doesn't come a second time.

The driver got out of the Citroën and held the back door open. A tall man in a dark suit, a raincoat worn over his shoulders, came out of the little hotel next to the café. He was young and fair, very white, very drawn. There wasn't much, really there wasn't anything that you couldn't buy on the place Clichy. Perhaps the German officer had bought something he hadn't liked — or maybe it was just the next morning he didn't like it. He paused at the door, put one hand on the roof, leaned forward. Was he going to be sick? No, he climbed into the car, the driver slammed the door.

Look down. That was barely in time. Casson stared at people — who were they? It was just something he could not stop himself from doing. And the man who'd held the door for his superior had caught him at it. *Nantes O, Lille O. Caen 3, Rouen 2. Please.* The Citroën idled, then the front door closed, the driver put the car in gear and drove off, turning onto the boulevard Batignolles.

★ ★ ★

His room at the Hotel Victoria. Six floors up, under the roof. Ten by ten, narrow iron bed, a chair, a washstand. Ancient wallpaper, the color of oatmeal, and bare wooden boards. Faint smell of sulfur, burned to get rid of the bugs, faint smell of black tobacco. And all the rest of it. Casson took an overcoat down from a hook in the wall. Not so bad. He rubbed his thumb idly across a small stain above the pocket. He'd bought it back in August, when he still had a little money, from a peddler's cart in the place République. For winter, he'd thought, but he wasn't the one who was going to wear it this winter.

He hunted through the pockets, made sure

8

the Goddess of Luck hadn't left a fifty-franc note in there for him. No, nothing. He rolled the coat up tight, held it to the right side of his body. It was his one possession and La Patronne knew it. He owed three weeks' rent, if the owner caught him taking it out of the hotel, she'd stop him, would make a great scene, would probably call the police. Like a mythic beast she stood behind the hotel desk, keeping guard on the door. Draped always in black, wearing broken carpet slippers for her sore feet. Flabby face, eyes like wet stones. She could smell money in the next block. She truly could, Casson thought.

He closed his door silently, went downstairs one cautious step at a time. On the landing of the second floor he became aware of conversation in the lobby, something not right in the tone of it. Halfway down the final flight he stopped. He could see black shoes, blue trousers, the bottom of a cape. *Merde.* Police. Not an exotic moment in the life of the Hotel Victoria, but Casson could have done without it. He stood still, held his breath, listened intently. *About forty years old. Was last seen. If by chance he should.*

He went cold. Tried to swallow. The police voice stopped. A long moment. Casson could hear people talking in the street outside the door. Then, finally, the patronne. *Mmm, no, she didn't think so. It wasn't anybody she'd seen. Of course she would notify the préfecture if.* Jesus, they were looking at a photograph. He counted to three, then clomped down the stairs in a hurry, making all the noise he could. The policeman turned to glance at him as he went by, the patronne looked up from the photograph. '*Bonjour, madame,*' he muttered — busy, tense, angry at the world. She started to say something to him, he could feel her mind working, but he was through the door in three strides and that was that.

He went around the corner, slowed down, got his composure back. Then headed south, toward the 3rd Arrondissement. A bright day, the little ghost of a chill still hung in the morning air. Early autumn this year, he thought. Which meant: early winter. *Well, good.* Maybe he'd get a few francs more for the overcoat.

★　★　★

He took backstreets, crossing into the 10th Arrondissement. Turgot, Condorcet, d'Abbeville. Then the rue des Petits-Hotels — Yes, there were some. On rue Paradis, too many Germans, milling around the Baccarat salesroom. Then, a choice: to cross the boulevard you could take either the rue de la Fidelité or the passage du Désir — street of fidelity or alley of desire. Which? He took the alley, but noted that it ran downhill. Next, he hurried across the broad boulevard Magenta. Too wide, too open. That fucking Haussmann, he thought, rebuilding Paris a hundred years earlier, designing open boulevards to facilitate field-of-fire, cannon shot, against the revolutionary mobs of days to come. A visionary, in his way. He had destroyed the medieval rat's nest of Paris streets, anybody, even a lumbering German, could find his way around. Real Parisians, even those, like Casson, who'd spent their lives in the Passy district of the snob 16th, knew the value of a good maze, rank with crumbling drains and metal *pissotières* on the corners.

Head down on the narrow streets. Baggy flannel pants, suit jacket with the collar up, three days' growth of beard, workman's peaked cap tilted to one side, shadowing the face. Someone who belonged in the quarter if you didn't look too hard, if you missed the melancholy intelligence in the eyes. He was dark; dark hair, coloring like a suntan that never really went away. A small scar on the cheekbone. Lean body, forty or so. Something about Casson had always made him seem a little beat up by life, even in the old days, on

11

the *terrasses* of the good cafés — knowing eyes, a half-smile that said it didn't matter what you knew. He liked women, women liked him.

Two *flics* pedaled by on their bicycles, one of the wheels squeaked each time it went around. Casson watched them. *Sooner or later*, he thought. He would be taken. Sad, but there wasn't much he could do about it, life just went that way. He knew too many people in Paris, at least a few of them on the wrong side. Or maybe it would be some German version of Simenon's Maigret: self-effacing, unprepossessing, looking forward a little too eagerly to lunch. Taking his pipe from clenched teeth and pointing it at his assistant. 'Mark my words, Heinrich, he will return to his old haunts, to the city he knows. Of this you may be certain.' And, in fact, when all was said and done, that was the way it turned out. He'd gone home — the *romans policiers* had it just right. Why? He didn't know. Everywhere else felt wrong, was all he knew. Maybe to live the fugitive life you had to start young, for him it was too late. Still, he didn't want to make it easy for them. *Sooner or later*, went that week's motto on the Casson family crest, *but not today*.

★ ★ ★

3rd Arrondissement — the old Jewish quarter. Cobbled lanes and alleys, silence, deep shadow, Hebrew slogans chalked on the walls. Rue du Marché des Blancs-Manteaux, the smell of onions frying in chicken fat made Casson weak in the knees. He'd been living on bread and margarine, and miniature packets of Bouillon Zip when he could afford the fifty centimes.

Between two leaning tenements, the municipal pawnshop. Massive stone portals; *Liberté, Egalité and Fraternité* carved solemnly into the granite cap above the doors. Inside, a municipal room: flaking gray paint, the fume of disinfectant rising from the wood floor. A few people scattered about, looking like dark bundles forgotten on the high-backed benches. At the front of the room, a counter topped with frosted-glass panels. Casson could see the shadows of clerks, walking back and forth. He took a brass token from a *gardien* at the door and found an empty bench in the back of the room. An official appeared at the wire grille that covered the cashier's window. He cleared his throat and called out, 'Number eighty-one.'

A woman stood up.

'Yes, sir.'

'Will you take thirty francs?'

'Monsieur! Thirty francs — ?'

This was as much argument as he cared to listen to. He waved a dismissive hand and pushed a crystal serving dish out onto the counter.

'Well,' the woman said. A change of heart, she would take whatever they offered.

'Too late, madame.' The voice polite but firm. Really, he would *not* be subjected to the whims of these people. 'So then, eighty-two? Eighty-two.' A bearded man carrying a copper saucepot shuffled toward the counter.

Casson began to worry about the overcoat— unrolled it, tried, surreptitiously, to fluff it up a little so it didn't look so much like a bundle of dirty rags. Remember, he told himself, it's important to make a good impression, confidence is everything. *A fine coat! Cosy for winter.* God he was hungry. He had to have fifty francs from this coat. He stared up at the lights, yellow globes with shimmering halos, it hurt to look at them. He closed his eyes for a moment, the back of the wooden bench in front of him banged him in the forehead.

A hand gripped his elbow. 'Unless you want to see the cops, you better wake up.'

Casson shook his head. Apparently he'd fainted. 'I'm all right,' he said.

'No sleeping allowed.'

A hard voice, Casson turned to see who it

was. A man perhaps in middle age, not so easy to say because one side of his face had been burned, skin dead white in some places, shiny pink in others. In an attempt to hide the damage he'd let his hair grow long and it hung lank just above a knob of remaining ear. '*Ça va?*' he said.

'Yes.'

'Done this before?'

'No.'

'Well, if you don't mind advice, you'll get more out of them if you wait until the afternoon. After they've had their lunch and their little glass of wine. That's the only time to do business with the government.'

Casson nodded.

'I'm Lazenac.'

'Marin.'

Lazenac put out a hand and Casson shook it. It was like gripping a rough-finish board.

'Let's go somewhere else,' Lazenac said. 'This place . . .'

★ ★ ★

Deeper into the Marais. Paper-white men in black coats, women who kept their eyes lowered. To a tiny café in what had been a store. Lazenac ordered a flask of Malaga, cheap red wine, and black bread. 'It's good strength,' he told Casson.

Whatever that meant it was true. The sour wine jolted him back to life. Chased down with a chunk of the mealy bread it made him feel warm.

'Don't mind the neighborhood, do you?'

'No.'

'Funny thing, since I had my face blown up I like the Jews.'

'What happened?'

'Just the war. Chemin des Dames at Verdun — the second time we tried it, November of '16. My corporal got hit, I turned to see if I could do anything and one of those fucking *Nebelwerfers* — mine-throwers — got me. But, turning like that saved my eyes, so I suppose I should be grateful.' He paused for a sip of wine. 'Were you in that?'

'With a film unit,' Casson said. 'Air reconnaissance.'

From Lazenac, a certain kind of smile — *the fix is in.* 'Sweet job,' he said.

Casson shrugged. 'It wasn't my idea. I just signed up, they told me where to go.'

'Way of the world, if you don't mind my saying that.'

'No, I don't mind.'

Lazenac stared out the window. 'I'm not so bad off. With the girls, it's okay as long as you don't ask them to touch it. And I have to keep

16

the conversation on my good side. But then, my grampa did that for twenty years.' They both laughed.

Lazenac poured some more wine in Casson's glass. 'Go ahead, it's the only way to deal with those assholes on Blancs-Manteaux.'

Casson raised his glass. 'Thank you,' he said.

Lazenac shrugged it off. 'Don't bother. I'm rich today, tomorrow it's your turn.' He looked around the little room. A very old man in a yarmulke turned the page of his newspaper, squinting to see the print at the top of the column. 'The worst of it is,' Lazenac said. He paused, shook his head. 'Well, what happened to me really didn't matter, if you see what I mean.'

'Because, in June of '40, they got what they came for the first time.'

'Yes.'

'Maybe it isn't forever,' Casson said.

'No. It can't be. Of course, we both know people who'd like to ignore the whole thing — just try to get along with them. But you know the saying, *le plus on leur baise le cul, le plus ils nous chient sur la tête.*' The more you kiss their ass, the more they shit on your head.

'Some people used to say that even before

17

the war,' Casson said.

Lazenac nodded. 'Yes,' he said. 'Now and then they did.' He poured himself some more wine. 'Where are you from, Marin?'

'Paris.'

'I can hear that, but one of the *bons quartiers*, right?'

'Yes.'

'So what are you doing down here?'

'No money.'

'No friends?'

Casson shrugged and smiled. Of course he had friends and some of them — one or two of them anyhow — would have helped. But if he went anywhere near his old life he was finished, and so were they.

'I'm doing a job tonight,' Lazenac said. 'We're going to take something from the Germans and sell it. There are three or four of us, but we can always use one more. I'm not sure about the money but it'll be more than you're earning now. How about it?'

'All right.'

'We'll meet at the porte de la Chapelle freight yards, the rue Albon bridge, about eight. Have a shave, and give your jacket a brush.'

Casson nodded. Was Lazenac just being kind?

'Some of the people we talk to, maybe you

18

can do a better job than we can. Want to try it?'

Casson said he did.

★ ★ ★

'Number one hundred and thirty-eight.'

By now the room was warm, a fly buzzing against the grimy window. Casson walked up to the counter, eyes down. The clerk behind the grilled window had a small face, pink scalp, the eyes of a terrier. He looked at Casson a moment longer than he needed to. *Well well.*

Casson slid the coat across the polished counter. *No rueful smiles, no jokes.* The urge was powerful but he fought it off. He trudged back to the wooden bench, let his mind wander, tried not to watch the clock on the wall.

'One hundred and thirty-eight?'

Casson stood.

'Monsieur, will you take a hundred and eighty francs?'

What?

'Yes,' he said, headed for the counter before they came to their senses. What in the name of heaven — maybe the thing actually had value. His wife, Marie-Claire — they'd been separated for years — used to suspect the

19

little paintings they bought at the flea markets were lost masterpieces. *You don't know, Jean-Claude, poor Cézanne may have paid his laundress with this, see how the pear reflects the light.* But a coat? Was it llama, chamois, something exotic?

The clerk pulled a pin from the corner of a packet of ten-franc notes and, using a practiced thumb and forefinger, snapped eighteen of them into a pile. As he slid the money and the pawn ticket across the counter his eyes met Casson's: a sad day for us, monsieur, when a gentleman of our class is forced to pawn his overcoat.

Outside, Lazenac was leaning against a wall, smoking a cigarette.

'Let's go have a little something,' Casson said.

★ ★ ★

Another liter of Malaga, then he headed back to Clichy. He would eat. A bistro around the corner from his hotel had fried potatoes and the smell drove him crazy every time he went past. With the dinner you got a piece of stewed chicken, called *coquelet,* a polite way of saying the rooster got old and died.

Shit, he thought, *I'm rich.* He could pay a week on his hotel, sixty francs, and thirty for

20

a meal. And then there was Lazenac's 'job' out at the porte de la Chapelle. If he didn't get thrown in jail, he'd have even more. *From there, he went on to become one of the wealthiest men in Europe, and today, his portrait hangs in every lycée in France, this beloved entrepreneur who —*

Oh the Malaga.

He hadn't felt this good for a long time. In July, on the run from the Germans, he'd been about to leave the country when love — and love was hardly enough of a word for it — had driven him back to France. Pure madness, a *folie de jeunesse* at the age of forty-two, and he'd gotten just what he deserved. Because, when he went looking for her, she was gone. Why? He didn't know. She hadn't been arrested, and she hadn't fled in the middle of the night. She had packed her bags and paid her bill and left the hotel. *Fin,* like the end of a movie.

June 1941, off the Normandy coast, just at the moment of escape, as the fishing boat turned toward England, he had jumped into the sea and swum for the shore, British special operatives waving their Stens and calling him names. Walking all night, he'd made his way to a cottage he owned at the edge of Deauville, rented to an oil-company lawyer and his wife. But they were gone and the Germans had fixed lead seals to the doors, with tags stating that the house, in a strategic area, had been declared off-limits to civilians.

Too bad, but maybe it didn't matter. He'd had a thousand francs, faked papers, and love in his heart. Had crossed the line into the *Zone Non-Occupée*, the ZNO, then south to Lyons, then up the hill to 'their' hotel. Then, a clerk: 'I'm sorry, monsieur . . . ' She had gone. No mistake in identity possible, she was well known; the film actress called Citrine, not a star exactly but certainly not somebody who could simply fade away. She was just — gone. Did she know he had escaped Germans? Did she panic when he disappeared? Had she simply fallen in love with somebody else? He didn't think so, but what he did know was that with her — a life of highs, lows, tears, chaos — anything was possible.

He survived it — maybe he survived it. Wandered north for a time, to Bourges, to Orléans, to Nantes. Where he'd been a stranger. Always a bad thing in France, and now a dangerous thing — just waking up in these places felt wrong.

So he came home to Paris to die.

★   ★   ★

He was tired, sat on a bench in a little park. A woman strolled over, gave him a look. He shrugged — sorry, I'd like to, but I can't afford it. She was heavy and matronly, like the headmistress in a school. Fine theatre to be had there, he thought. 'Maybe next time,' he said. She looked sad, went off down the street. The sun was low, orange flame in a puddle of dirty water on the cobblestones. What was it, Friday? Maybe. September — he was sure of that, anyhow. He should have asked how much, maybe they could have struck a deal.

★   ★   ★

8:10 P.M. Porte de la Chapelle freight yards. Casson stood on a pedestrian bridge above the tracks. Rails crisscrossed into the distance, a dull sheen in the last of the twilight. Below him, a train of empty boxcars was being made up by a switching engine. A long whistle echoed off the hillside, a cloud of brown smoke drifted over the tarred beams of the bridge. From where he stood he could see Lazenac and his friends, gray shadows in workers' clothing, heads down, hands in pockets.

At the end of the bridge Lazenac introduced him to Raton — small and wiry, with sharp eyes and a clever smile — and Victor. He was simply Jean. They walked east, along the edge of the yards. Not taking it easy, exactly, but not in any hurry; going to work, there'd still be plenty left when they got there. Across the street, a row of warehouses, rusty iron gates chained shut. As they passed an alley, Lazenac made a small motion with his hand, a truck's engine sputtered to life and backed away, deeper into the shadows. Another hundred meters and they reached the main entry to the railyards: a striped barrier bar lowered across the road, an Alsatian shepherd in the alert prone position. Wehrmacht military police lounged around a guard-hut. Nobody said anything, nobody's eyes met, but the feeling was like Friday night in a workers' bar — the fight had to happen, the only question was when.

Five minutes later, well out of sight of the guards, they stopped by a wall. Ten feet high, old plaster cracked and peeling. Two hand-made ladders lay flat in the weeds. Raton and Victor set one of them against the wall and braced the bottom. Lazenac climbed to the top, took the second ladder as it was handed up, and lowered it carefully down the other side of the wall. He put one foot across, then shifted his weight gracefully and stood on the second ladder. 'You're next,' he called to

24

Casson in a stage whisper. Casson worked his way up the awful thing — barely wide enough to get a foot on each rung. He was scared now, not so much of the Germans, but of being asked to do something he wouldn't be able to do.

As he neared the top, Lazenac said, 'Watch your hands.' A moment later he saw why: broken glass — wine bottles had been cemented into the cap of the wall. Casson took a deep breath, got one foot over, balanced, then swung across. He did it wrong — he knew it an instant before it happened — and began his backward tumble to the ground. Only he didn't fall, because Lazenac saw it coming, reached up and grabbed him by the belt and forced his weight back on the ladder. '*Merci bien*,' Casson said, breathing hard.

'*Je vous en prie*.'

On the other side of the wall, Casson knelt by some kind of storm sewer, the open end of a drainage culvert. Over time, the outflow had cut itself a channel, some three feet deep, into the hillside. When the others were down the ladder, Lazenac led them single file, crouched low, along the gulley. 'Stay close to the ground,' Raton whispered to him. 'If the *schleuh* catch you in here they'll break your head.'

At the foot of the hill, they waited. A busy night: in the distance, the sound of yard engines chugging up and down the tracks, and the steel clash of boxcars being coupled. Directly in front of them were flatbed cars stacked with peeled logs, probably cut in the forests of the Massif Central and now en route to Germany. After what seemed to Casson like a long time, the red glow of a track lantern moved toward them and Lazenac said, 'At last, the *cheminots.*' Railwaymen.

There were two of them. They shook hands all around, then the one with the lantern said, 'It's about two hundred meters up ahead. Third track in.'

'An SNCF car,' the other said. '7112.'

'All right,' Lazenac said. 'We're on our way.'

'Keep an eye out for the yard security.'

'Thanks for everything, we'll settle up on the weekend — same as before.'

'See you then. *Vive la France.*'

'Yeah,' Lazenac said. They both laughed.

The lantern faded away down the track, Lazenac led them in the other direction. Casually, without stealth — *every right to be here.* The SNCF car stood high above its cast-iron wheels. A wire seal secured the door handle. From inside his jacket Lazenac produced an iron bar about two feet long. He worked it through the loop and put his weight on it until the wire snapped. Standing on the metal rungs beside the door, he pushed it open and ran the beam of a flashlight up and down the stacked cargo. Cotton sacks piled to the ceiling, stenciled with the name of the company and the label SUCRE DE CANNE. Sugar.

Lazenac swung inside and reappeared a moment later carrying a sack. Victor stood below him. Lazenac dropped the sack on Victor's shoulder and Victor then headed back toward the hillside. Casson was next. 'Don't worry,' Lazenac said. 'You're stronger than you think.'

Who *was* strong was Lazenac. He swept a sack into the air and lowered it onto Casson's shoulder. Casson felt his knees buckle and said '*Merde*' under his breath. Raton, leaning against the freight car, laughed, then patted him on the arm.

He moved off, swaying at every step, but he *wasn't* going to fail. Up ahead, Victor was plodding along at a steady pace. Casson went about ten steps, then, the sour voice of authority: 'All right — just where do you think you're going with that?'

Casson turned to look. Some kind of railroad guard — an official armband, a whistle. He was tapping his palm with a long, wooden *bâton blanc*, a policeman's club. 'Put it down, you,' he said to Casson.

I'll never be able to pick it up again. Lazenac leaned out of the open doorway and rapped the man on the head with the iron bar. For a moment there was dead silence.

'More?'

Indignant, the guard rubbed furiously at the spot where he'd been hit. 'Are you crazy?' He grabbed the silver whistle around his neck and put it to his lips. Raton kicked him in the stomach and he folded in half. Lazenac jumped down off the boxcar and tore the whistle off his neck, then the two of them beat him senseless. When he lay full length on the cinders and didn't move, Casson adjusted the sack on his shoulder as best he could and headed for the wall.

Somehow, he got himself up the ladder. How he did it he would never know, but he reached the top, using both hands to haul himself up a rung at a time. When he stopped to rest, panting like an engine, he discovered that Victor was waiting for him at the top of the ladder on the other side. 'Now, just lift it across — I'll help you — and try not to break the glass.'

Casson looked puzzled.

'Why let them know how we did it? There's a war on, you never know when you might want to get into a railyard.'

★ ★ ★

The truck was waiting for them a little way up the street. A small Citroën delivery van — *camionette* — with a shutter in the back instead of doors and the name of a bakery painted on the side. Victor rolled the shutter up and tossed his sack in. Casson did the same — secretly very proud of himself when the weight made the truck bounce on its springs. A minute later, Lazenac and Raton showed up. 'You know where you're going?' Lazenac asked the driver.

'The rue Hennequin. In the seventeenth.'

'Out by the Ternes Métro.'

'What's it called?'

'Ma Petite Auberge.'

The driver snickered — my little country inn. '*Mon petit cul,*' he said. My little backside.

Lazenac laughed. 'Well, when you have a restaurant, that's what you'll call it.' He leaned into the cab of the truck and said, 'Keep a cool head, Michot. There'll be Gestapo cars, Germans, a real circus.'

'We'll be fine.'

★ ★ ★

Casson and Lazenac rode the Métro out to the 17th. It was sad on the train. Before the war, that time of night, there would have been waiters going home in their black jackets and white aprons, lovers who couldn't wait to get into bed, and the strange old birds one always saw — Sanskrit professors, stamp collectors — going out to eat cassoulet or heading up to Montmartre to give the girls a bad time. Now, people stared at the floor, their spirit broken.

'For us,' Lazenac said, 'getting hold of the stuff is the easy part.'

'I'll do what I can,' Casson said. 'What's the price?'

'Oh, maybe three hundred francs a kilo — but not for the quantity we've got. Tonight we'll try to sell a hundred kilos.'

'So, two fifty?'

'*Tiens!*' Lazenac said with a grin — *wouldn't that be nice.*

The train stopped at Abbesses, idling for a time in the empty station. Casson smoothed his lapels, trying to make them lie flat. His face burned like fire, he'd shaved close, using a three-month-old razor blade. Cleaned his shoes with a rag, borrowed a tie from the old man down the hall, and that was about the best he could do. At least, he thought, looking down at his feet, his socks were still in decent shape. It was the socks that went first. A whore he knew said she only took customers whose socks were in good condition. One of Casson's fellow lodgers had shown him how he used a pen to color in the skin that showed white in the holes.

Lazenac dropped a heavy hand on his shoulder. 'Don't worry too much,' he said, as though reading Casson's thoughts. 'It's all in your face — who you are.'

'Once upon a time, maybe, but now . . . '

Lazenac smiled, only one side of it really worked. 'No,' he said, 'life's not like that.'

★ ★ ★

10:30 in the evening in the rue Hennequin. Some restaurants lived secret lives, others spread out into their streets. This was the second kind; a green-and-gold façade, a line of handsome automobiles. A Horch, a Lancia Aprilia. In the back seat of an open sedan, a redhead with a dead fox around her neck was smoking like a movie star. On the street: German officers in shiny leather, boots and belts and straps; their girlfriends, wearing plenty of rouge and eye shadow and black stockings; and the strange tidal debris — the

Count of Somewhere, Somebody the art dealer — that flowed into conquered cities.

'We go around the back,' Lazenac said.

Down the alley the door to the kitchen was propped open with a chair. The air was thick with clouds of garlicky steam, frying fat, old grease, and lye soap. Lazenac spoke to one of the cooks and a waiter appeared a moment later. 'Oh, it's you,' he said to Lazenac. 'You have something for us?'

'Sugar,' Casson said. 'As much as you like.'

Their eyes met, the waiter stared at him.

'The *patron* around?' Casson said.

'I'm the one you see.'

'Maybe we'll come back when he's around.'

'Don't be smart.'

'Thursday? How would that be?'

'Now look — '

'*Au revoir.*'

It took a minute for the waiter to run off and get the owner. A true *beauf*, Casson thought — from *beau-frère*, brother-in-law. Stocky and pink and mean. He framed himself in the doorway and put his hands on his hips. 'So, what's the big problem?'

'No problem,' Casson said. 'What's the price for sugar tonight?'

'I don't know. What do you want?'

'Lebec is offering two fifty. And next week we'll have butter.'

'Butter.'

'Yes.'

'How much sugar?'

'A hundred kilos.'

'Hmm. That's, ah, twenty-five thousand francs.'

'That's what Lebec said.'

'Then go see Lebec.'

'If you like'

'No, wait a minute, I'm only kidding. Save yourself the Métro ticket — I'll give you twenty-two five for the whole thing. That's fair, isn't it?'

'How about twenty-three. C'mon, be a good guy.'

'You're talking advantage of my good nature, you know.'

'I know. But, what the hell.'

'All right. Where is it?'

'Out in front.'

'Have them bring it around.'

* * *

Le Diable Vert. Midnight.

Twelve hundred francs!

In times gone by he'd spent more than that on a suit, but life changed, didn't it, and by moonlight mathematics he was richer than he'd ever been. And, oddly enough, people — some people anyhow — seemed to sense it. Certainly the working girls knew — smiles, whistles, coats thrown open from every doorway on the rue Moncey — but it was their vocation to see into men's souls and on the way they would naturally stop to count what was in their pockets.

Le Diable Vert.

He'd always liked a good hellhole and it was surely that. A tiny bistro, set a half-story below the street, through the open door of which he could see feet hurrying through the rain. *Diable Vert* — a leering green devil with a pitchfork and a splendid tail on a sign that swung on its chains and creaked in the wind. Ten tables, brick floor cured in wine, a sign by the cash register had a photograph of a funeral and the legend LE CREDIT EST MORT. And, packed in, wall-to-wall, what seemed like the whole neighborhood — laughing, shouting, arguing, and knocking back half-liters in a dense fog of cigarette smoke.

Twelve hundred francs.

So the death of credit was no problem for Casson — not tonight. Tonight he was the local sultan. Lazenac had laid it all out, plainer than any of the merchant bankers Casson used to deal with in the movie business. The twenty-three thousand francs

34

was to be split with the railwaymen, the remainder shared out by Lazenac and his crew. The man who drove the *camionette* received a share, and so did his van, that was traditional. Then there was a handsome slice carved out for a certain Monsieur X, nameless but clearly important.

'Marin, may I join you?'

It was a man named Bruc. Casson wasn't sure exactly what he did, but he worked nights and headed for the Métro wearing green rubber boots.

'Please,' Casson said.

Bruc took the empty chair, Casson filled his glass and offered him a packet of Gauloises Bleues, a luxury in that part of town. Bruc drew a cigarette from the pack with care, holding it in his mouth with thumb and forefinger while Casson struck a match and lit it for him. 'Thank you very much, Marin,' he said formally.

The crowd surged around them. Two girls wearing the neighborhood dance-hall uniform — satin shirts, suspenders holding up wool trousers, and tweed workers' caps — gave Casson a glance over the shoulder.

'My night off,' Bruc said. 'I like to be where people are.'

'What's your work?' Casson asked.

'I'm part of the crew on a pumper truck.

Out in the old quarters on the edge of the city. We pump out the cesspools.'

'I thought it all went in the sewers.'

'No. Not out there it doesn't. Some nights we do apartment houses, some nights the office buildings. They take a lot longer.'

'Really?'

'Oh yes, a lot longer.'

Bruc took a sip of wine and a long drag on his Gauloise. A man had jumped up on a table and started to sing, people were clapping to keep time.

'Why does it take longer?' Casson said.

'Well, the cesspools are the same size, but the stuff in the office buildings is harder, really hell to pump out.'

Casson stared. A peculiarity of office life?

The owner worked his way through the crowd, a full *chopine* in his hand. He poured the last of the old flask into the two glasses.

'You'll take a little more?' he asked Casson.

'Yes,' Casson said. 'Certainly we will.'

'Generous of you,' Bruc said.

'Monsieur Bruc,' Casson said. 'How is it different?'

'The water, monsieur. In the apartment buildings they are forever cooking and cleaning and washing the laundry.'

* * *

Casson wandered out the back door to a courtyard, unbuttoned his fly, and stood over an open drain. *Drinking all day*, he thought. Well, so what? Above him, a fine starry night; with the city under a blackout the sky had returned. Autumn heaven — *les Poissons* up there somewhere, his birth sign. Somebody had once tried to show it to him, but all he could see were drifts of stars.

It was late. Up in Passy, his former life went on. Marie-Claire and Bruno, the Arnauds and the Pichards, would be chattering over after-dinner drinks. Good talk, witty and dry — life was irony. No doubt they would be talking about the *affreux* — dreadful — Germans. Not so *affreux*, of course, that one refused to get rich off them. Maybe they talked about the war, maybe not. Like any other inconvenience it would go away when it was ready. In the meantime, *x* was broke, *y* was sleeping with *z*. Then, a glance at a watch, kisses all around, and home they'd go. Home, where they hung their clothes on quilted hangers in closets with mirrored doors. Home, to bed.

Casson fumbled at his fly, getting the buttons done. *Jean-Claude, you are drunk.* Well, yes, I am, it's true. But I have a theory about that, if you'd like to hear it. I believe it may result from drinking a lot of wine. As observed by Doctor Vinkelmeister in his paper read before the *Académie Nationale*. Casson laughed out loud. Doctor Vinkelmeister.

Back in the Diable Vert it got louder and louder. Monsieur Bruc had wandered off somewhere. The man who had jumped on a table to sing a song was now crawling around on hands and knees and barking like a dog. People shouted at him, 'Down, Fideaux! Roll over! Shake hands!'

Two men wearing sharp suits came to Casson's table. Brothers, he thought. They had the same face. Thick shoulders, heavy throats, chins dark only hours after shaving. Casson could smell the hair oil. Pimps. From the south, he thought, the Midi. Come up to Paris to make their fortunes. 'Won't you offer us a drink?' This one was fatter than the other and wore an expensive black shirt.

Of course. With pleasure.

They were sniffing at him. And the drink wasn't optional. The fat one took the flask and filled both their glasses to the rim. 'See?' he said to his brother. 'I told you he was a good guy.'

He was glad when they left. The dance-hall girls came back. The dark one with curly hair dropped into the empty chair and said, 'What a crowd!'

'*Et alors*,' her friend said, hands on hips, playfully indignant. 'Kind of you to take the chair.'

'Don't mention it. I could tell you wanted me to have it.'

'Well.' She looked around, then shrugged and settled herself delicately on Casson's lap. 'With your permission, monsieur.'

'More than welcome.'

'There, you see?' she said to her friend. 'Some people still know how to be polite.' Then, formally, to Casson: 'How are you called, monsieur?'

'Marin,' He said. 'Jean Marin.'

'I am — Julie.'

As with all English names taken into French, it sounded exotic, the *j* soft, the accent rolling to the second syllable: Ju-*lee*. She caressed the name as she said it, clearly relishing the identity it suggested. *Who are you really*, he thought. Juliette, at best. More likely: Hortense. From some wretched little village somewhere. Ran off to Paris, leaving Albert the butcher's son heartbroken.

He could see why. She was one of those lethal girls, with the small face and the big ass, white skin, angelic pout. The hair pinned up under her cap was a strange shade of red, God only knew what had been done to it in various hotel sinks. She wriggled around to

39

get comfortable, then settled in — a warm vee against his thigh — gave him a playful nip on the earlobe and made a brat face. *Bit you!*

The friend looked grim and shook her head in mock despair — oh that Julie. She rooted around in her purse, found a small mirror, and went to work repairing the kiss curl on her forehead, wetting her index finger on her tongue and poking at the hair until it was plastered against her skin. For no particular reason that Casson could see, this operation was accompanied by a fierce scowl.

Julie hummed to herself, took Casson's glass and finished his wine. He pulled her against him and gave her a kiss. 'Mm,' she said, against his mouth. He could smell her lipstick, waxy and sweet. Big, heavy kisses, she moved her head from side to side, arms tight around his neck. He was fifteen again. She drew back and said '*Tiens*,' hanging on to her cap so it wouldn't blow away in the big storm they were brewing up.

Casson laughed, then fished a handful of francs from his shirt pocket. 'Another *chopine*, I think.'

'Let me,' she said, taking the money from his hand. He watched her as she moved through the crowd, richly curved in her thin wool trousers.

The din grew, and grew again — in the

40

Diable Vert it was time to sing. A group in one corner began the *Marseillaise*, a crowd of men across the room tried the one about the Breton housewife, her underdrawers eaten by a bull. The man who was a dog stuck his head out from beneath a table and bit somebody on the ankle. A tray of glasses smashed, a woman shrieked with laughter, a man shouted at a friend that only he could see.

In the middle of it, Casson brooded. *Where, where?* He'd seen a tiny storeroom off the corridor that led to the courtyard, that was one possibility. Ju-*lee*, bent over a plank table, pants around her ankles. Primitive, but not such a bad idea. Or, maybe, actually *on* the table. No, that was to invite comedy. In his room? Easily the best solution, but La Patronne would be guarding the hotel door. So, was there another way? Yes. Pay. This was double occupancy, not the end of the world. Ah, he thought, the old Casson, the 16th Arrondissement Casson.

What if she asked for money? No, it wasn't like that. Or, at least, not quite like that. She returned with the wine, sat down again on his lap, and ruffled his hair. At some point she had put on more perfume. Casson refilled their glasses, Julie raised hers in a toast. 'Mud in their eyes,' she said in English.

Like a rocket on Bastille Day, the

Friday-night mood. It climbed to the top of the sky, slowed, froze a long instant at the apogee, then burst, a thousand stars floating back to earth. For a time, the crowd in the Diable Vert felt good. Oh, maybe the last few years hadn't gone so well but it wasn't really their fault. Now everything was going to be different, they could see it, around the next bend in life. Justice at last, their rightful place, finally some money. Then the moment passed. They remembered who they were and they knew what was going to happen to them — the same things that happened to everybody they'd ever known. So, *fuck this life they handed me.* A little more wine, anyhow, you couldn't go too far wrong with that.

Casson felt it coming. Arguments, tears, fights, somebody sick in the middle of it. He pulled the girl against him, clung to her. A moment of surprise, then she put her arms around him and held him tight. Her back was damp beneath the satin shirt. 'Maybe it's time for us to go,' he said.

He felt her nod against his shoulder.

'Just across the square,' he said. 'The hotel where I stay.'

Again she nodded.

* * *

Cold outside, but the air felt good after the bistro. She took his arm as they walked. Clichy was busy and raucous, the Paris night rolling along toward the dawn. A fat man with a wildly rouged woman came down the street. He tipped his hat to Casson — *good evening, mon vieux.* Here we are with our girls and what fine fellows we are. Casson gave him a nod and a smile. Then, panic. Did the man actually know him? Old somebody he'd once met at the somethings' house?

Julie squeezed his arm. 'Look at the moon,' she said. Half a white disc just north of the river. From a dance hall on the other side of the square, *le swing jazz,* a trumpet, a saxophone, a spill of yellow light from the open door, then darkness. Behind them, a man laughed.

'The lovebirds.'

'*Coucou.*'

Casson turned his head halfway, the two men from the bar, about ten feet behind them.

'Just ignore them,' Julie said.

'*Gonzesse.*' Cunt.

Half a block. They walked quickly despite themselves. Then a turn into the side street and the Hotel Victoria. The men came up close, the one in the black shirt put a hand on Casson's elbow. 'I think we better have a talk,' he said, voice low and charged.

Casson pulled away. 'Leave us alone,' he said.

It was the other one who hit him first, threw Julie out of his way and punched him in the side of the head. Julie screamed, Casson found himself on one knee. Was it even possible he'd been hit that hard? One side of his face had gone dead. Black-Shirt kicked him — meant to kick him in the head but hit his shoulder, spun him halfway around, and he fell on his back. Julie started to scream again but Black-Shirt said, 'Shut up or we'll cut your face,' and she was silent.

Casson tried to stand up, got to his knees but that was the best he could do. He felt hands going through his pockets; Black-Shirt was excited, breathing hard, Casson could smell sweat — something like sweat, but much worse — and hair oil. When the man was done he stood up, then kicked Casson in the ribs. Casson heard himself cry out. He fell forward, tried to roll up to protect himself, saw the two men walking away, back toward place Clichy.

Julie knelt by his side, touched his face, her hand was trembling. She took a tiny handkerchief from her purse and held it against his mouth. There were blood drops on the pavement.

'No police.' He tried to say it but it came out a mumble.

'Your mouth is hurt,' she said.

Somehow he got up. Very shaky, but on his feet. He had to get off the street. She took his arm, helped him walk. In the lobby of the hotel, a night clerk was behind the counter.

'I'm taking him to his room,' Julie said.

The clerk hesitated a moment, then said, 'The patronne comes in at eight — just be out before then.'

They started up the stairs. Casson said, 'My key.'

'I have it,' she said. 'And your papers. They only wanted money.'

He held the little handkerchief against his mouth so he didn't bleed on his shirt. She took his arm, helped him up each step.

It took a long time to climb to the sixth floor. She got most of his clothes off, he fell onto the bed, faded out. He woke later, she was sitting on the bed in the dark room. He reached out, rested a hand on her knee. 'Are you all right?' he said.

'Yes,' she said. But she had been crying.

'I'm sorry,' he said.

'You couldn't help it.' She paused a moment. 'Somebody like you . . . '

They were quiet for a time. 'They should be shot,' she said.

'You know them?'

'They are always in that place. You see them next week, they'll smile at you. Up here, nobody goes to the police, that only makes it worse.'

He turned toward her. His side throbbed, his face was numb. She smoothed his hair back. 'Go to sleep,' she said. 'I'll be here.'

He didn't want to sleep but he couldn't stop it. For a few seconds he came back awake, felt how warm she was, sitting on the bed. Sometimes jagged and plummeting, sometimes about Citrine. Just before making love, when together they took her clothes off. She had once said that when a woman goes with a man, and for the first time he sees her with nothing on, that it is the best at that moment that it will ever be. Later he tried to turn in his sleep and a sharp pain under his arm woke him up. He reached out, felt nothing, opened his eyes. The first gray light of dawn was in the room and the girl was gone.

★ ★ ★

An hour later, the knock on the door.

'Police, open up.'

My revolver, he thought. Drawing it from beneath his pillow, firing through the door, pounding down the stairs. In the lobby, the patronne, eyes wide with horror. 'No! Please! Have mercy!' Shots ring out in the Hotel Victoria.

'I'm coming,' he called out, struggling to stand up. There was no revolver. When he got the door open he saw it was the same *flic* from the day before. So, he thought, it had been his photograph after all — he had been betrayed. By the patronne? Somebody else? He didn't know.

'Is your name Marin? Jean Louis?'

'Yes.'

'You're wanted for questioning.'

★ ★ ★

Not arrested, not handcuffed. He thought about making a run for it, but he was too banged up — the *flic* had to wait for him as he worked at getting dressed.

'Let's go, eh?'

'I'm trying.'

'Have you been fighting, Marin?'

He touched the swollen side of his face and winced. 'I was robbed. They beat me up.'

'Report the crime?'

'No.'

Probably that's a crime too, he thought. He managed to get into his jacket, looked around

47

the room one last time. Not so bad. Now that he'd never see it again he started to like it.

In the lobby, the patronne glanced up from the register she kept on the counter, then looked down, finding an entry, holding her place with a steel finger. '*Monsieur l'agent?*' she said.

'Yes?'

'Is this one coming back?'

'Couldn't say.'

The patronne's finger, stuck on Room 28, began to tap. Her eyes were shining with fury.

Small — a very small victory, he thought. But likely the only one of the day. Outside, a battered Renault police car. A detective sitting in the passenger seat was reading a dossier as Casson got in the back.

'You're Marin?'

Casson nodded. Closed his eyes for a moment. He was, more than anything, tired, in every way you could be. Tired of his life, of clumsy deception, of the world he had to live in. *Shoot me and get it over with.*

The old engine whined, turned over, and finally caught, missing and backfiring on the low-grade gasoline the Germans gave the police. The *flic* said, 'To the préfecture?'

The detective turned, rested his arm on the top of the seat, and looked him over. He was an old man, heavy, with a head of thick, white

48

hair and deep lines carved in his face. He had a big nose with a dent near the bridge and very pale blue eyes, wore an ancient black suit beneath his overcoat, a loose wool muffler, and a weatherbeaten hat with the brim snapped down in front.

'No. The rue Rondelet.'

Casson looked out the window as the car drove off. In May of 1940, recalled to military service, assigned to a *Section Cinématographique*, he'd seen the streets of eastern Paris through the windshield of a truck. *Different than the back of a taxi*, he'd thought then. Now, the same streets, from the window of a police car.

Blood will tell. It was a deep Gallic conviction, especially among women over forty. Casson's father had been a rogue, and his mother had been employed full-time as the wife of a rogue: long-suffering, humiliated by unpaid butchers, terrified of the phone. But, often enough, his father's shield. Casson *père* had more than once been spared by creditors who could not bear to hurt 'his poor wife.' Wealth had always been just around the corner; shares in Venezuelan lead mines, a scheme to import herring from Peru, a powder that kept lettuce from spoiling, tonics, treasure maps, mechanical pens. And, late in life, one honorable and very productive venture — a wool brokerage — which he'd been done out of by men he called 'licensed thieves who work in paneled offices.'

The rue Rondelet was a little street in a factory district with a small *poste de police*. Not the kind of place Parisian detectives usually worked. 'Go back to the préfecture,' the detective told his driver. 'If anyone asks, tell them I'll be in later.' The *flic* touched the visor of his cap with two fingers and drove off. Inside the station, a desk sergeant wearing a knitted green sweater under his uniform jacket greeted the detective like an old friend.

Upstairs, a small office used for interrogation — two chairs, a desk scarred with cigarette burns, tall windows opaque with dirt, a floor of narrow boards. The station backed up to a schoolyard, it was recess, and Casson could hear the kids, playing tag and yelling. The detective leaned on his elbows and read the dossier, now and then shaking his head.

'Casson, Casson,' he said at last, with a sigh in his voice. Casson flinched despite himself. The detective seemed not to notice. He turned the pages slowly, sometimes puzzling over the cramped handwriting. Suddenly he looked up and said, 'You're not going to insist on this Marin business, are you?'

'No.'

'*Grâce à Dieu* — I already fought with my wife this morning.'

'Will you turn me over to the Germans?'

'Worse than that, Casson, worse than that.' The detective read further. 'Here's your concierge,' he said. 'Kindly old Madame Fitou, in 1933. Hmm. Secret doings, something buried in the cellar.'

'*What?*'

'That's what it says here. Imagine, a man like you, a cat murderer.'

'It's madness, monsieur.'

'So, you deny it! Seems there was quite a ring operating back then. In league with the neighborhood baker, I see. And the priest.'

'She really said such things?'

'And more. You don't believe, I hope, that these women can actually live on what the tenants pay them?' He read on for a time, turning pages of handwritten paragraphs. '1937. Some considerable entertaining. Angélique, Françoise, Madame de Levallier.' He squared the stack of pages with his palms and closed the folder.

'What will happen to me?' Casson said.

The detective shook his head — *God only knows*. 'When I started to look for you, it gave me an excuse to see a movie or two. I must tell you that your policemen are a disgrace. Venal, brutal, and, worst of all, stupid. And when they shoot they don't hit anything.'

'It's just the movies.'

The detective leaned forward in his chair and spoke quietly. 'Tell me, Casson, why did you come back to France?'

'A woman.'

The detective nodded. 'Not patriotism?'

'No, monsieur.'

The detective smiled — somebody had told the truth! He glanced at his watch, went to a window, took the brass handles and shoved it up a few inches. 'The morning concert. Come and listen, Casson. It's the latest thing from Vichy — a hymn to Pétain.'

Casson went to the window. Down in the schoolyard, the children — eight- and nine-year-olds — were lined up in rows. Facing them, a music teacher, conducting with a stern finger: 'And one, and two, and . . . ' They sang with high voices, an angels' choir.

All the children who love you
and hold your years dear
to your supreme call
have answered smartly, 'Here!'

Marshal, here are we
before you, O savior of France.
We your little buddies swear
to follow where you advance.

For France is Pétain,
and Pétain is France.

They began the next song, the detective
closed the window, then went to the door and
started to open it, giving Casson a nod of the
head that meant *let's go*. 'Well, Casson,' he
said, 'perhaps you're in luck. You may not
have found patriotism, but it appears, God
save us all, to have found you.'

STALIN'S ORDER

The struggle against Germany must not be looked upon as an ordinary war. It is not merely a fight between two armies. In order to engage the enemy there must be bands of partisans and saboteurs working underground everywhere, blowing bridges, destroying roads, telephones and telegraphs, and setting fire to depots and forests. In territories occupied by the enemy, conditions must be made so impossible that he cannot hold out; those helping him will be punished and executed.

Stalin's Order of June 22, 1941

PARIS. 22 SEPTEMBER, 1941.

Ivanic came out of the Saint-Michel Métro in the early evening, turned right at the first street, then right again to the little *impasse* they'd told him to look for, and the small door with the ironwork frame. He had the key in his hand but it still took a long time. He had to try it this way and that way, had to stand there and jiggle the thing until the lock decided to open. It was dark inside, he could just make out a stairway. He climbed one flight to a door at the head of the stairs, found a second key left on the molding that let him into a tiny room that seemed to be used as an office. Down below, in the restaurant Agadir, he could hear people talking and laughing, and throbbing oud music played on a wind-up Victrola.

There was a swivel chair at the desk but he didn't sit down. He paced the office, checking his watch. Noisy outside, the rue de la Huchette, a North African souk around the steps of the church of Saint Séverin. It smelled like the old streets in Marseilles, he thought, sheep liver grilled on hot coals, burnt cumin, and the damp air that hung over the river *quais* at dusk.

Not so bad, he thought — the crowds, jostling and busy, the dark-eyed women. He wasn't in a hurry to try the food, but that was him. Food wasn't something he liked. He'd done his prison time east of the Oder: in Lodz — for pamphlets, in Esztergom — just because, and then, worst of all, the Lukishki, in Vilna. Abduction. The Lithuanian police had been waiting for them. Two years of that. And it could have been forever, but in August '39 the Hitler-Stalin Pact was signed and the NKVD came into the city and let Ivanic and his friends out of jail. Two years of that had done something to his appetite. He wondered if maybe it was the lentil mash they'd fed him in prison. Or maybe not. Maybe it was the work he did. He looked at his watch again, where were they? He was in his late twenties, tall and pale, with sleepy eyes. He'd grown up in Salonika but he wasn't Greek, he came from farther up the Balkans. It was a long story.

In Vilna, he'd decided that he wasn't going to prison again. But the people he worked for wouldn't let him carry a weapon in Paris. Only for work. That scared Ivanic — even with the finest passport and *Ausweis* and all the other paper the Germans thought up, things could go wrong. He heard somebody coming up the stairs and hoped it was the man he was supposed to meet and not the Sûreté, or the Gestapo.

A key turned in the lock, Ivanic backed against the wall. The door opened slowly. 'Hello? Ivanic?' Heavily accented French.

'Are you Serra?'

'Yes.'

They shook hands, both of them wary. Serra had dark hair, tousled and cut short, was perhaps in his thirties but he seemed much older than that. Ivanic knew he'd been a miner in Asturias — thus a specialist in dynamite — then, during the Spanish war, an operative for the Republican secret service. He had escaped over the Pyrenees, one of the last to get through after the fall of Barcelona in 1939, was arrested at the border, and spent the next year staring at an incomprehensible world through French barbed wire.

Serra had a little bag of tobacco. They tore strips off a page of *Le Jour* and smoked while they waited.

'Have you seen him?' Ivanic asked.

'Yes, I watched him. For a few days.'

'What is he like?'

'An athlete, perhaps. He stands very straight.'

59

'They all do.'

'Most of them.' Serra paused a moment. 'Were you in Spain?'

'No.'

'I thought perhaps I'd seen you.'

'No. I wasn't there.'

★　★　★

8:20 P.M. The phone in the office rang three times and stopped. Ivanic looked at his watch. Thirty seconds later it rang again. Ivanic raised the receiver from the cradle and put it back down. Another five minutes and they heard somebody coming up the stairs.

The man who stepped into the office was called Weiss. He had black and gray hair, combed back from the forehead, and wore a dark overcoat with the collar turned up. The world's plainest man, Ivanic thought. A salesman? Teacher? Editor of a technical journal, something esoteric and difficult? Perhaps he'd once done something like that. Or maybe it was simply that Weiss became what other people thought he was. In a smoky Berlin union hall, he was a labor official. Later on, a Milanese intellectual, or a Dutch civil servant. Ivanic had once been on the edge of a conversation where a senior Comintern operative had said, 'Of course

Weiss is Hungarian — like all spies.'

He said hello to them, put his scuffed leather briefcase on the desk, unbuckled the straps, and hunted around inside. '*Hauptmann* Johannes Luecks,' he said. He handed Ivanic a photograph, a clandestine shot taken from a first-floor window, slightly blurred, the blacks and whites faded to gray. The officer, a captain, had his head turned toward the camera. He was hatless, fair-haired, in Wehrmacht uniform. 'He commands a company of combat engineers,' Weiss said. 'Joined the army in '32, from Bremerhaven. Here is a list. Where he goes and what he does.'

Ivanic passed the photo to Serra and took the sheet of paper from Weiss. A twenty-four-hour schedule with daily headings. At the top of the page, an address. 'The rue St.-Roch,' Ivanic said.

'Yes, only the best. He's billeted with a French family.'

'St.-Roch. It runs off St.-Honoré?'

'That's right.'

'Busy at lunchtime.'

'Yes, a commercial neighborhood, but quiet in the evening.'

'Home around six-thirty.'

'Yes. A pipe, a comfortable chair, a newspaper.'

'A pleasant life.'

'It is. The family is completely intimidated — they wait on him hand and foot.'

Serra shook his head. Handed the photograph back to Weiss and took the schedule from Ivanic.

'When do you want it done?' Ivanic asked.

'Up to you,' Weiss said. 'But as soon as possible. The Wehrmacht is just outside Moscow. They are burning the villages around Mogilev, taking the men away for slave labor. The local officials are simply shot. The way we make them pay for that is *partizan* action, behind the lines, which means anywhere from Mogilev to Brittany.'

'This *Hauptmann* Luecks,' Ivanic said, 'is he anyone special?'

'No,' Weiss said. 'And that's the point we want to make. He's a German, that's all, and that's enough.'

* * *

They killed him the following Thursday. At four in the afternoon they met in a greenhouse in the Jardin des Plantes, where the weapons were buried beneath the gravel. 7.65 pistols, fine automatics from J. P. Sauer und Sohn in the town of Suhl, normally issued only to Luftwaffe officers. They rode bicycles with crowds of homebound workers in a light rain across the Seine, then along the avenues to St.-Honoré. On the rue St.-Roch they waited until almost seven, when *Hauptmann* Luecks was dropped off by a Wehrmacht staff car, shoulders hunched as he hurried through the rain toward his doorway, carrying a paper-wrapped *pâtisserie* by its pink ribbon.

They followed him into the lobby. He didn't like it — two men in caps with their jacket collars up. He turned to glare at them and they took the automatic pistols out and fired three or four times each. The shots were thunderous in the small space, echoing off the marble walls. Luecks was knocked backward. He tumbled to the lobby floor and tried to roll toward the door. The two men shot him again and he lay still, a cloud of blue smoke hanging in the air, the echoes ringing away to silence.

They heard the whine of a motor and looked up, saw the elevator cables moving in the small cage. The car stopped in the lobby. A well-dressed woman stared out at them, at the German officer on the floor. She reached out and pressed a button, the elevator went back up.

PARIS. 2 OCTOBER.

It continued to rain. Jean Casson sat in the parlor of a small apartment in Neuilly, reading a newspaper — COWARDLY TERRORIST ATTACK IN THE RUE ST.-ROCH — for the second time. On the eastern front, retreating Russian divisions had been forced to blow up the Dnieper dam, the pride of Soviet engineering in the 1930s. Casson reread the movie section, the sports, the obituaries.

'Stay here and wait,' the detective had told him. He slept on a narrow bed in a spare room, took silent meals with Monsieur and Madame Kerner, an Alsatian couple in their sixties. He had been saved, for what or why he did not know. The people who had found him hadn't yet let him in on their plans but he had no doubt they would get around to it. Meanwhile, there was bread to eat, and soup, and long, silent evenings.

He was afraid of Kerner, a huge man with a tread that made the old floor creak. Kerner was his jailer — a courteous one it was true but a jailer nonetheless. A retired army officer. On the tables in the parlor there were photographs of Kerner in uniform — with brother officers, solemn faces staring into the camera — taken in Damascus, in Tunis, in

Dakar. A colonial soldier, apparently, with campaign ribbons and medals on a framed black velvet cloth hung on the wall, and a tiny Croix de Guerre in the lapel of his blue suit. One of the pictures was inscribed: *The Brotherhood of the IX Commando*. Casson could see some sort of insignia on the uniforms, but he had no idea what it meant.

The suit was worn only on Sundays, when the Kerners took turns going to Mass — they would not leave him alone in the apartment. Even so, life had improved. From time to time he insisted on going out. He couldn't go by himself, Kerner had to come along, but at least he could spend a few hours away from the stuffy apartment and its ticking clocks. The detective had supplied him with better identity papers, the real thing, made by the préfecture. Perhaps made 'during lunch,' when the supervisors were not in the office, but the effect was the same. He remained Jean Louis Marin. He'd also been given some money and ration coupons, enough for cigarettes and a few small necessities.

One afternoon, special dispensation, he went to the movies, to the little Régence out by Auteuil. The second feature was his own *Night Run*. It was heaven to Casson to lose himself in the fragrant darkness of a movie theatre, even with Kerner sitting beside him. Three minutes in, Citrine, as *Dany*, a clerk in her parents' drapery shop. She is sitting in a crowded train compartment with *Valmas*, the small-time hood who, eighty minutes later, will die for love of her. Dany: in her new suit bought in Auxerre's best shop, hopeful, shy, burning.

They find each other immediately, as the train to Paris is leaving the platform. On Valmas's face, the smile of a predator — *If I want you, I can have you.* After a moment, Dany looks away. *Yes, I know.* They pass a small station north of the town. The camera cuts to the passenger next to Dany: a middle-aged lady with a gimlet eye, a mouth tight with disapproval, and a hat laden with artificial fruit.

Bernadine Chouette, Casson thought. Who had disapproved of every imaginable thing in twenty films. How good she was, a stage actress with years of character roles. She'd been horrified when the director, old Marchand, had produced the ghastly hat. 'Oh no, you can't be serious!' But he was — serious, and right. She had the pickle face and the vinegar stare, but the hat made it all work. Of course real life didn't play that way. Chouette, a cigar-smoking habitué of garter-belt parties at the Monocle Club, was famous

66

for exquisitely filthy songs, music-hall routines that caused tears of laughter to ruin mascara.

Toward the end of the movie, a scene in a hotel room — a hideout. For Dany and Valmas it's the last time and they know it. Citrine sits on the edge of the bed, her lovely breasts in a soft sweater. 'No one else,' she says, shaking her head, slow and resolute. 'Not ever again.' Casson bit his lip. She'd been eighteen when *Night Run* was shot. Later she became an actress, but not that day, not that day.

As good as it was to be in a movie theatre it was just as bad to come out, into the brutal daylight. 'Did you like it?' Casson asked.

'Well, that sort of thing . . . '

Casson nodded. He'd guessed that Kerner didn't know who he was, just a fugitive that had to be hidden. 'Would you like to walk? It's not so far.'

'No,' Kerner said. 'We must go home now.'

The rain had started again, it was a different city when it rained. They walked to the Métro. That day, Gestapo troops had begun to burn the synagogues of Paris; brown smoke drifted across the gray afternoon, sometimes visible above the rooftops.

PARIS. 20 OCTOBER.

Madame Kerner was knitting, her needles clicking as she worked. Casson stared out a window at the apartment across the way, whose curtains were always drawn. The boredom of being hidden gnawed at him, he was ready to escape. By now his life at the Hotel Victoria glowed in recollection — he'd been hungry but he'd been free.

The Kerners' telephone was on the wall in the kitchen. It rang, for the first time since Casson had been in the apartment. Madame Kerner looked up from her knitting. Kerner went to answer it. From the parlor, Casson could hear the conversation.

'Who is it?'

Kerner listened.

'Very well. What time?'

Again.

'Yes, sir,'

And again.

'Yes, sir,'

And, finally: 'At fifteen-thirty, you say. In Courbevoie.'

An hour later, Casson left. Madame helped him fold 'his things' — two books from a secondhand stall, some socks and underwear — into brown paper, which she tied for him with string. 'Adieu, monsieur,' she said. And

68

wished him good health.

Kerner led the way to the meeting. They took several Métros, waited on line at a Gestapo *Kontrol*, eventually reached Courbevoie, just across the Seine from Neuilly but a separate municipality. They walked to the Hotel de Ville, the town hall, a complicated maze of bureaux with long lines outside offices that handled taxes, licences, ration coupons, marriage certificates, stamps, and *attestations* for nearly everything — all the bureaucratic witchcraft of French existence. At the entry to the building, Kerner told him where he was to go, and then they said good-bye.

'Thank you for letting me stay with you,' Casson said.

'You're welcome.' Very formally, they shook hands. Casson entered the building and climbed a staircase to the second floor. The halls were crowded, people everywhere; some wandering lost, some grimly determined, some glancing from the address on an official letter up at the titles on office doors. *Is this it?*

Finally, Casson found the Department of Birth Registry, shuffled through the line, gave his name as Marin, and was directed to a small office at the end of the hall. He opened the door, and there at the desk, in a dark suit,

69

was a man he had known as Captain Degrave.

In May of 1940, when Casson was reactivated as a corporal in the *Section Cinématographique* of the Forty-fifth Division, Degrave had commanded the unit. They'd taken newsreel footage of the French defense of the fort at Sedan, then headed for the relative quiet of the Maginot line, only to find the roads made virtually impassable by refugees from the fighting in the north. On a fine May morning, in a field near Bouvellement, a Stuka dive-bomber had destroyed both their vehicles and their equipment, and Degrave had disbanded the unit, sending Casson south to Maçon to wait out the end of the war at an isolated army barracks.

Wherever he'd been since that day, and whatever he'd done, Degrave was as Casson remembered him: a heavy, dark face, thinning hair, perhaps a little old for the rank of captain, with something sorrowful and stubborn in his character. Degrave had always been distant, a man not given to idle conversation. Still, they had served together under fire, in a blockhouse defending the French side of the river Meuse, and they were glad to see each other.

'So,' Degrave said as they shook hands, 'we survived.'

'We did,' Casson said. 'Somehow. What about Meneval?' Meneval had been the unit cameraman. Every day he'd called his wife from phones in village cafés.

'He returned safely to Paris.' Degrave smiled. 'And to married life.'

'And then, you left the army?'

'I'm with the Office of Public Works, now, in Vichy. We're responsible for the maintenance of roads, bridges, that kind of thing.'

'In the *ZNO?*'

'Yes, but we have projects in the German-administered region as well.'

Such as hiding film producers in Neuilly apartments, Casson thought.

Degrave put a packet of Gitanes on the table. 'Please,' he said, 'help yourself.' Casson took one and lit it, so did Degrave. From the offices around them they could hear a steady murmur of conversation.

Degrave shook out the match. 'In fact, I remain what I always was, a captain in the army, and an intelligence officer.'

Casson thought that over, recalling what the unit had done. 'Was the work we did — an intelligence mission of some kind?'

'Yes and no. It wasn't clandestine, but in time of war there is a great need for documentation. It was a job I, well, the truth is they stuck me with it. You know France, you know bureaucracy, you know politics, so you will understand how I got sent off to make newsreels of forts on the Meuse. In the end it didn't matter, we lost the war. But life goes on, and some of us continue to serve.'

'With de Gaulle?'

Degrave's *no* was emphatic. 'The public works office is a cover organization. We have reassembled the former *Service des Renseignements*, the intelligence service — the operational arm of the *Deuxième Bureau*'

Degrave waited for a response, Casson nodded.

'As for de Gaulle, and the Gaullist resistance, of course we support their objectives. But they are based in London, they exist on British goodwill and British money. And they have close ties — maybe too close — with British intelligence, whereas our service acts solely in the interest of France. That may sound like a fine distinction, but it can make a difference, sometimes a crucial difference. Anyhow, the reason I'm telling you all this is that we want to offer you a job. Certainly difficult, probably dangerous. How would you feel about that?'

Casson shrugged. He had no idea how he felt. 'Is it something I can do?'

'We wouldn't ask if we didn't think so.'

'What is it?'

'Liaison. Not the traditional form, but close enough.'

'Liaison,' Casson said.

'You would work for me.'

Casson hesitated. 'I suspect you know I was involved with espionage. In the first year of the war. It was a disaster. One factory was burnt down, but British agents were arrested, and a friend of mine was killed.'

'Did the factory need to be burnt down?'

'It made war material for the Germans.'

'Then maybe it wasn't a disaster, maybe getting the job done simply cost more than you felt it should.'

Casson had never thought of it that way. 'Maybe,' he said.

'Tell me this, do you have a family? Are there people who depend on you?'

'No. I'm alone.'

'Well,' Degrave said. The word hung in the air, it meant *then what do you have to lose?* 'You can turn us down right away, or you can think it over. Personally, I'd appreciate your doing at least that.'

'All right.'

Degrave looked down. 'The sad truth is,' he said quietly, 'a country can't survive unless people fight for it.'

'I know.'

'You'll think it over, then. Take an hour. More, if you like.'

There was no point in waiting an hour. He took the job; he didn't have it in his heart to refuse.

* * *

Casson walked for a long time, his worldly goods in the brown-paper package under his arm. Degrave had given him a few hundred francs and the name of a hotel, and told him he would be contacted.

He crossed the Seine on the pont de Levallois. Barges moved slowly on the steel-colored water, swastika flags flapping in the autumn breeze. Leaning on the parapet, a few old men fished for barbel with bamboo poles. There was a market street at the foot of the bridge; long lines started at the doors and wound around the corners. Some of the windows had *Enterprise Juive* painted in white letters, two or three had been smashed, the shattered glass glittering on the floors of the empty shops. On the walls of the buildings, the Germans had posted proclamations: 'All acts of violence and sabotage will be punished with the utmost severity. Acts of sabotage are held to include any damage to crops or military installations, as well as the defacing of posters belonging to the occupying powers.' An old poster, Casson saw, dated June of 1940, the heavy print faded in the sun and rain. Newer versions promised death for a long list of violations and, Casson noted with regret, they had not been 'defaced' — no cartoons, no slogans.

There was a café across the street, he sat at the bar and ordered a glass of wine. *Je m'en fous*, he thought, fuck it. He didn't want to fight. He wanted to hide, that was the truth. Find a woman, crawl up into some garret, and wait for the war to end.

He drank the wine, it burned his throat going down. 'What is it?' he asked the man behind the bar.

'Sidi Larbi, fourteen percent. From Algeria. Care for another?'

'All right.'

Degrave had been a good officer, up on the Meuse. And when it was clear that the German tanks would cross the river, his friends on the general staff had pulled them out. He owed his life to Degrave.

He paid the bill and headed west, toward the 17th. It was almost dark. It had been gray all afternoon, the autumn *grisaille* settled down on the stone city. Now, just at dusk, the sun came out, lighting fires in the clouds on the horizon as it set.

PARIS. 26 OCTOBER.

The Hotel Benoit. It was a place, as it happened, that he'd visited more than once, though he'd never actually slept there. The hotel was a monument to the midday love affair. The proprietors were discreet, and had an ancient well-seasoned arrangement with the police, so identity cards were never too carefully scrutinized and generations of 'Duvals' and 'Durands' had found comforting anonymity at the Benoit. 'Society must have laws,' his lawyer friend Arnaud used to say, 'and society must have convenient means to evade them.'

Casson's room looked out over the street and a small park — the sound of dead leaves rattling in the wind put him to sleep at night. The secret life of the hotel sometimes reminded him too much of his past — couples with averted eyes, the scent of perfume in the air, and now and then, in the afternoon, a lover's cry.

Degrave left a message at the desk for him and on the night of the 26th they met in a nearby hotel.

'You're comfortable?' Degrave said.

Casson said he was.

Degrave took his jacket off and hung it on the back of the chair. Casson sat on the edge of the bed. 'What we are trying to do right now,' Degrave said, 'is get in touch with the various resistance groups and establish lines of communication with them. Eventually, we will all have to work together. It's now clear that Germany will not invade Great Britain, so Great Britain will have to find a way to invade occupied Europe. And they can't win without aggressive resistance and intelligence networks on the Continent.

'At this moment, the most active resistance group is the FTP, the *Francs-Tireurs et Partisans*, named for the guerrilla fighters in the Franco-Prussian war of 1870. The FTP is the clandestine action group of the French Communist Party. We want you to make contact with them, on behalf of the intelligence network we're operating in Vichy.'

Degrave paused, waiting for Casson to respond. 'How would I do that?' Casson said.

'You'll find a way. We'll help you, but in the end you will do it by yourself.'

That's madness, Casson thought. It would never happen. 'You want me to pretend to join them?' he said.

'No, that won't work. They're organized in cells, units completely separated from each other, to make penetration agents virtually useless. You will have to approach them as

Jean Casson, a former film producer, acting on behalf of the network in Vichy. Honesty is the only way in.'

Casson nodded — that much at least made sense. 'Why me?' he said.

'It must be somebody neutral, apolitical, not a socialist, not a conservative. Somebody who has not fought in the political wars. You have certainly had contact with party members in the film industry — incidental, without problems. They will know who you are, they will know you haven't worked against them.'

That was true. His screenwriter, Louis Fischfang, had been a Marxist — in fact a Stalinist. He wasn't the only one. There was Fougère, from the electricians' union; the actor René Morgan, who'd fought in Spain; many others. He'd never cared about their politics as long as they didn't shut his sets down.

'The fact is, Casson, everybody likes you.'

From Casson, a very hesitant nod. First of all it wasn't true, there were plenty of people who hated him. Second of all, a certain professional affability wasn't, he thought, the key to being trusted by gangs of red assassins. But then, Degrave wasn't exactly wrong either. People did like him — often enough because, when it came to money or social

78

status, to sex lives or politics, he truly did not care.

'The more you think about it,' Degrave said, 'the more you'll see what we see.' He paused a moment. 'It's also true that you will come bearing gifts. What those might be I can't say, but we know the party, we've had agents among them from time to time, and we know how they operate. They will demand concrete evidence of good faith — they couldn't care less about words. Does all this make sense?'

'Yes.'

'We've been fighting the party since 1917, there is no question that their aim is to rule this country. All during the 1930s they established networks in France, particularly in the armament industry. There was the Lydia Stahl case, the Cremet case, operations of all kinds. Some of them made the newspapers, some simply died a quiet death, and some we never uncovered. They tried to steal our codes, they agitated on the docks and in the defense industries, they spied on the scientists.

'The party was declared illegal — driven underground — in '38. They survived, they *prospered* — for them, secrecy is like water in the desert. And in 1940, when France was invaded and the Hitler-Stalin Pact was still in effect, they urged the workers not to fight their German comrades. After the surrender, the Germans allowed the party to publish *Humanité*, which labeled de Gaulle a tool of British imperialism. Then, when Russia was invaded last June, a somersault.'

'That I do remember.'

'Shameless. But, up to that point, there was virtually no French resistance to German occupation. Oh, you'd see things now and then. In the window of a bookstore on the rue de Rivoli, there was a china figurine of a spaniel lifting its hind leg — it just happened to be adjacent to a copy of *Mein Kampf*. There'd been a few student demonstrations, one of them, in the Bois de Boulogne, was bloody, but not by intention. We saw a few leaflets — 'Frenchmen, you are not the stronger side. Have the wisdom to await the moment' — but that was about it. The French people had adopted *attentisme*, the strategy of waiting. That was tantamount, as far as we could see, to collaboration.'

'I saw it firsthand,' Casson said.

'In Passy?'

'Yes. Most people were afraid to do anything.'

'Not the communists. Last June, when Russia was invaded, it was as though somebody had kicked a hornets' nest.

Suddenly, German officers were being shot down — it wasn't hard, they walked around the town as though they owned it. In October, the German commandant of Nantes was assassinated. In reprisal, forty-eight hostages were killed. Other attacks followed, the Germans retaliated. They guillotined Jean Catelas, a member of the party's central committee, they executed communist lawyers and Polish Jews — forty for one, fifty for one. The FTP never blinked. According to the old Bolshevik maxim, reprisal killing simply brings in new recruits, so it wasn't hurting them.'

'Is that true?'

'It is. But for some, a little too cold-blooded. The policy of the Gaullist resistance is to assassinate French traitors, but they don't attack German nationals. The people in Moscow, who run the French Communist Party, no doubt find that a rather dainty distinction, but then their war is much worse than anything that goes on over here. We've heard, for instance, that the Germans around Smolensk were having hunting parties, like English county foxhunts, with beaters flushing Jews and peasants from the woods and soldiers shooting them down.

'The Russians retaliated. An SS *Obergruppenführer* heard a rumor about buried gold at

81

the Polyakovo state farm. He led a unit to the farm and they started to rip the buildings apart, looking for it. The manager begged them to stop, explained that without shelter the peasants would die of cold when winter arrived. Please, he said, give me twenty-four hours to produce the gold. The SS officer agreed, and left a detachment of four men there to ensure the manager didn't make a run for the forest. The next day, the SS unit returned. All the buildings had been burned down, only the office was left standing. Inside, on a desk, was a large leather box with the word *Gelb*, gold, written on it in white paint. When they opened the box, they found the heads of the four soldiers they'd left on guard.'

Degrave paused, waited for Casson to respond.

'And this is just the beginning,' he said.

'That's right, and it may go on for twenty years. The FTP leadership is certainly under intense pressure from Moscow — do *something*, anything — which is why we feel they can be approached.'

★ ★ ★

He went for a walk after the meeting, to clear his head in the night air, and thought about

82

what Degrave *hadn't* said. The war between the secret services and the French communists went back a long way — maybe all the way to 1789. The working class and the aristocracy had been at it for at least that long. Casson remembered a time when he was at university, at the *École Normale Supérieure*. Some of the conservative *normaliens*, wearing white gloves, had taken over the running of the building to break a strike by the maintenance workers. Degrave, and no doubt his colleagues, came from that class, which had always provided officers for military service. Not so much rich as old, very old, a landed aristocracy that took its names from the villages it had named in the Middle Ages. What, Casson wondered, were they doing with somebody like him? He wasn't leftist, but he wasn't one of them. He wasn't a Jew, but he'd worked in a Jewish profession. He was, when all was said and done, a Parisian. And not a Parisian from the *deux-cent familles*.

He stopped at a café, stood at the bar, and ordered a beer — it would do for dinner. He'd told Degrave the story of his escape from the Gestapo office. 'Don't worry about it,' Degrave said. 'Their list of wanted suspects runs into the thousands. We think you'll be safe if you stay out of trouble

—most of the people arrested these days are betrayed. Jealous neighbors, jilted mistresses, that kind of thing.'

No *danger there*, Casson thought.

More than likely, the communists would kill him. These people didn't spend time brooding about your motives. If they sensed a threat, they shot you. They were idealogues, at war with anyone who stood in their way. One of Casson's university friends used to say, with a flicker of contempt, 'They believe everything they can prove, and they can prove everything they believe.' True. But they'd fought in Spain, and they died for what they believed in.

$$\star \quad \star \quad \star$$

He left the café, headed away from the hotel. He was restless, wanted to avoid the small, silent room as long as he could. Suddenly, the streets were familiar, somehow he had worked his way back to his old neighborhood, the Passy district of the 16th. He crossed the rue de l'Assomption, where his wife, Marie-Claire, lived with her boyfriend, Bruno, the owner of an automobile dealership. Casson stared up at the blackout curtains. Were they home? You could usually tell if there was a light on. No, he thought not. They were out, probably at a dinner party. He moved on. Coming toward him, a Luftwaffe officer with a Frenchwoman on his arm. A handsome man, hawk-nosed, with proud bearing, the brim of his hat shadowing his eyes. 'Oh but no,' the woman said, 'that can't possibly be true.' Then she laughed — apparently it was true.

The rue Chardin. His old building, his apartment on the fifth floor with a small balcony. Through the glass doors he had looked out at the top third of the Eiffel Tower. From the telltale glow at the edge of the curtains he was pretty sure somebody was home.

A silhouette moved toward him through the darkness. A woman, bent over slightly, walking quickly. 'Madame Fitou!' It was out before he could stop it — his old concierge.

She stopped, peered at him, then clapped a hand over her heart and breathed, 'Monsieur Casson?'

He crossed the street. Madame Fitou, in a long black coat with a black kerchief tied under her chin, clearly dressed for night raiding. A string bag of potatoes suggested a visit to the black-market grocer, or maybe one of her countless sisters, all of whom lived in the country and grew vegetables. As he approached she said, 'Can it be you?'

'*Bon soir*, madame,' he said.

'I knew you would return,' she said.

'As you see.'

'Oh, monsieur.'

'Everything going well, madame? With you and your family?'

'I cannot complain, monsieur, and, if I did . . . '

'Not so easy, these days.'

'No, we must — Monsieur Casson, you are here for the shirts!'

'Shirts?'

'I told . . . well, it was a year ago, but I thought, well certainly Monsieur Casson will hear of it.'

'Madame?'

She came closer. 'When the German came, Colonel Schaff — Schuff — well, something.' She snorted with contempt — these foreigners and their bizarre names! 'However you say it, he had his driver throw your things out in the street. I was able to save, well monsieur, it was raining that day, but I did manage to save some shirts, two of them, good ones. I kept them for you. In a box.'

'Madame Fitou, thank you.'

'But a moment!' she said, very excited, disappearing into the building. Casson stepped back against the wall. He could hear keys in locks, doors opening, then closing.

Overhead, a flight of aircraft — no air-raid sirens had sounded so they must be German, he thought. Heading west, to bomb Coventry or the Liverpool docks. The bombers droned away for what seemed like a long time, then Madame Fitou reappeared, very excited still and breathing hard. 'Yes,' she said in triumph. 'Here they are.'

He took the package, wrapped in a sheet of newspaper, and thanked her again. 'Madame Fitou, you must not tell anybody you've seen me. It would be very dangerous if you did. For both of us. Do you understand?'

'Ahh' — she said, her expression conspiratorial — 'of course.' *A secret mission.* 'You may depend on me, monsieur. Not a word.'

He wished her good evening, then hurried off into the night, damning himself for a fool. What was the *matter* with him? A few blocks away, in the shadows, he peeled back the newspaper. His dress shirt, for a tuxedo — he used to wear it with mother-of-pearl studs and cufflinks that came to him when his father died. Well, it didn't matter, he could sell it, there was a used-clothing market on the rue des Francs-Bourgeois. And then, a soft gray shirt he'd worn with sweaters on weekends. It smelled of the cologne he used to wear.

EVREUX. 27 OCTOBER

Six-thirty in the morning, the night shift at Manufacture d'Armes d'Evreux rode through the factory gates on their bicycles, heading home to the workers' districts at the edge of the city. Weiss moved along with them, pedaling slowly, his briefcase under one arm. Down a cobbled street — mostly dirt now — past a few ancient buildings and into a small square with a church and a café. He chained his bicycle to the fence in front of the church and went into the café. It was crowded, wet dogs asleep under the tables, a smoky fire in the fireplace, two women, their makeup much too bright, served chicory infusions to the men at the bar.

Weiss looked around the room and spotted Renan in the corner, playing chess. A hard head with a fringe of gray hair, a worn face, maybe handsome long ago. He rested his chin on folded hands and concentrated on the board. When he saw Weiss, he spoke quietly to his opponent, who rose and left the table. Weiss sat down and studied the board for a moment. 'So, Maurice,' he said, 'it looks like I've just about got you.'

'Don't be so sure,' Renan said. He had a deep voice, hoarse, his words fast and clipped.

'How's life treating you?' Weiss said, moving a rook.

Renan glanced up at him, almost smiling. He'd obviously made a poor move. 'It goes along.'

'And work?'

Renan raised his eyebrows, not much of a gesture but from him it meant a lot. 'The boches have their noses everywhere. It's pretty bad just now.'

'We need some things.'

Renan nodded. Took a pawn with his knight.

'Still making the MAS 38?' *Pistolet Mitrailleur MAS Modèle* 38 — a 7.65 caliber submachine gun.

'Yes. The word's around that we're going to be retooled, for German weapons but they're still in production.'

'We need some.'

'How many?'

'All we can get.'

Renan looked doubtful. 'Not so easy, these days. They've got informants. And there are German guards, field-police types, at the factory gates. Sometimes they make us turn out our pockets. And they control the trucks and railroad cars as they leave.'

'Can you try?'

'Of course.'

Renan took out a pipe and a tin of tobacco, packed the bowl with his index finger, and lit up. He'd been a militant for thirty years. Back in the labor wars of the late thirties, the armament workers at Renault, who built tanks, and at Farman, where they made airplanes, had sabotaged the weapons. Loose nuts and bolts were left in gearboxes and transmissions, iron filings and emery dust in the crankcases. When the tank crews tried to fight in 1940, they discovered saw marks on the oil and gasoline ducts, which made them break open after a few days' use. At Farman they had snipped brass wires in the engine, allowing aviation gas to drip on hot exhaust pipes. Some of the French fighter planes went down in flames before they ever saw a Messerschmitt.

When Renan had been asked to do the same sort of thing at Evreux, he had followed orders. In fact, he had never said no — not to Weiss, not to the Comintern operative who had preceded him.

'How soon?' Weiss said.

Renan thought it over. 'Maybe on the weekend. We have one German, he used to be an ironworker in Essen. We set him up with a girlfriend in town, which is how we talk to him, and we keep him in a good mood with brandy, whatever we can lay our hands on.

But then, you understand, we're talking about one or two pieces, if he'll agree to look the other way. Some things he can fix with his pals at the gate, tools and so forth, but not this.'

Weiss nodded grimly. It was the same story at Saint-Etienne and the Schneider works — France's equivalent of Krupp.

'Want us to try it?' Renan said.

'Yes. Do the best you can.'

They sat for a while. Weiss stared at the board. The rook really had been the wrong move. 'Well,' he said. 'Time to be going.'

'Have somebody stop by the first part of next week.'

'Here?'

Renan nodded.

'Thanks for the help,' Weiss said.

'Don't mention it.'

Outside, Weiss unlocked his bicycle and pedaled off toward the railroad station. *Want us to try it?* Quietly, in his own way, Renan had told him it wouldn't work. Of course he would make the attempt, and take the consequences, he simply wanted Weiss to know that the attempt was going to fail.

But Weiss had no choice. Moscow Center was pressing him harder than it ever had: he *must* acquire battlefield weapons, he *must* be prepared to arm *partizan* units, he *must* attack German targets in occupied France. He worked with the senior operations officers of *Service* B — the FTP's intelligence section — which made him roughly the equivalent of a colonel in the army, and he had been ordered to send troops into combat.

What he had, in Paris, were assassination teams, like Ivanic and Serra, perhaps twenty operatives at any given moment. Then there were the longtime militants, like Renan, and the volunteers, almost all of them young and inexperienced.

The Center did not care. They'd let him know that wounded soldiers had been let out of military hospitals to serve on the defensive line that ran through the suburbs of Moscow. In Paris, they wanted action, bloody and decisive, and right now. The cost was immaterial.

PARIS. 2 NOVEMBER.

Isidor Szapera climbed the dark stairs quickly, his fingers brushing along the banister. Up ahead, rats scurried away from the approaching footsteps. *Time to go, mes enfants, the Chief Rat himself has arrived.* Big talk — the building scared him, it always had. The wind sighed in the empty halls and woke up old cooking smells. Sometimes it opened doors, or slammed them shut. The building, on a small street in the back of the 11th Arrondissement, had been vacant since one corner of the roof had collapsed in 1938, when the tenants were thrown out, the doors padlocked, the windows painted with white Xs.

Now it served as the secret base of the Perezov unit, named for a heroic Bolshevik machine-gunner in the civil war that followed the revolution. Unit Commander Szapera opened the door to a room on the third floor, made sure the blanket was securely nailed over the window, and lit a candle in a saucer on a wooden chair. He didn't own a watch, but he could hear the eight-o'-clock bells from Nôtre Dame de Perpétuel Secours. Ten minutes later, the Line 9 Métro rumbled beneath the building. His meeting was set for 8:20, he was early.

He'd been born in Kishinev — sometimes Rumania, sometimes the Ukraine or the USSR, but for Jews pretty much the same thing. His family got out in 1932, by bribing a Turkish sea captain in Odessa. They reached Poland that summer, when he was ten, then made their way to Paris in the fall of 1933, where his father found work as a salesman for a costume jewelry manufacturer. Isidor went to school in the 11th, essentially a ghetto. He managed to learn French, by force of willpower and repetition. It was hard, but not as hard as the *cheder* in Kishinev, where he'd sat for hours on a wooden bench, chanting passages of Torah to commit them to memory.

That old stuff, he thought. It kept the Jews down; weak and powerless. In the struggle of the working classes, you didn't pray, you fought back. *Did Rabbi Eleazer mean this? Or did he mean that?* Meanwhile they kicked the door down and took you away.

It wasn't a theory. They'd escaped from the cossacks in Kishinev and the anti-Semitic gangs in Lublin, but the Germans came for them in Paris. In the fall of 1940 his father sensed what was coming, tried to get a letter out to the relatives in Brooklyn — by now named Shapiro — then made arrangements for the three children to stay with a French Jewish family in Bobigny, on the outskirts of the city. A year later, August 1941, they heard a rumor: the police were planning to detain Jews of foreign nationality. Home from school with a cold and fever, Isidor was sent off to Bobigny. The rest of the family wasn't so lucky. The police had come through the 11th on a *rafle*, a roundup. When Isidor came home, the apartment was silent. They were gone.

At that point, the Kornilov unit had been in operation for six months. Commander Szapera, just turned nineteen; his cousin Leon — two years younger — his classmate Kohn, and his girlfriend, Eva Perlemère. Eva was not a refugee like the others. She came from a good family — her father was a theatrical agent — with money, a family that had been in Paris for generations. But, since the August *rafle*, she had been a dedicated member of the unit.

In the fall of 1941, Isidor Szapera left school. He got a job unloading trucks at Les Halles, stayed in contact with party militants, broke a few windows, left a few leaflets in the Métro, organized spontaneous labor actions.

Not enough, not nearly. By then, it wasn't only the Germans who wanted race war. He had come to hate them *physically*, to hate their faces, the way they walked, or laughed. They had stolen his family. His poor father, not a strong man, much better at love than anger, would try to protect his wife and children, would *protest* — Szapera knew this — and would, trembling and indignant, be casually knocked aside. Commander Szapera refused to mourn, tears of sorrow and tears of

95

rage were just tears as far as he was concerned, and he had more important things to do.

* * *

Footsteps on the stairs, light but certain. Weiss. Szapera stepped into the hall, called out softly, 'I'm up here.'

Weiss came toward him, his briefcase beneath his arm.

'I hope you put the door back,' Szapera said.

'I did, yes.'

After scouting the building for several days, Szapera and his friends had gone to work on the door in the back courtyard, carefully prying the metal flange free so the screws could be reseated in the wooden frame and the padlock stayed in place.

Weiss sat on a blanket on the floor and they made small talk for a time. Did Szapera need food? Another blanket? It was almost paternal, but Weiss couldn't stop himself. Szapera was like the kids he'd grown up with. Much too pale, with curly hair and soft eyes — everything was a joke, nothing could hurt them. A long time ago, Weiss thought, long before he had become 'Weiss' — his seventeenth name.

96

'The car,' Weiss said. 'Can you depend on it?'

'Don't worry. It's a good one. A Talbot.'

'How many doors?'

'Four.'

'Where is it?'

'In a village. Bonneval, near Chartres. The Perlemères have a little house there, for vacations. When the Germans came, they hid the car in a barn.'

'Forgive my asking — you know how to drive?'

'No. Eva does. Her father used to let her drive around the village.'

'How will you get it there?'

'We'll come at dawn, just after curfew. We found a garage nobody uses, in Saint-Denis. We can get there from the village on back roads, then we're eight minutes from Route 17, near Aubervilliers.'

'Eight minutes?'

'Yes.'

'How do you know?'

'We timed other cars. German cars.'

'All right. Eight minutes.'

'What about the guns?'

Weiss unbuckled the straps of his brief-case, opened the flap, and took out three revolvers and a small box. The guns were used, sixshot models with medium-length barrels. Szapera took one and examined it. The handgrip was scarred and scratched, the front sight filed flat, so it wouldn't snag a pocket; the chambers were empty. Below the cylinder, the name of the manufacturer was stamped into the metal, then a word in a language he didn't know that probably meant *company*.

'There's a fourth,' Weiss said. 'But it can't be picked up until tomorrow. Be here tomorrow night, same time, I'll have somebody bring it around. As for ammunition, you have thirty rounds in the box.'

Szapera nodded. 'Good,' he said. 'There won't be time for more.'

Weiss had wanted to arm the group with a submachine gun, but they would have to do the best they could with the pistols. The man he'd sent up to Evreux on Monday had returned empty-handed. 'According to our friends,' he'd told Weiss, 'Renan and a comrade called Bernard attempted to steal six crates of MAS 38's from a loading dock. Somebody knew about it because the Germans were waiting for them. Bernard is in jail. Renan tried to run away and they shot him.'

★   ★   ★

Eva came up the stairs at ten. She brought him a delicious sandwich, liverwurst with mustard between thick slices of freshly made white bread, and a jar of cold tea spiked with sugar. 'Very good,' he said.

She smiled. 'Somebody has to feed you.'

'Oh, I get what I need.'

She lifted an eyebrow, knew it wasn't true. She had lank brown hair, a narrow, watchful face, and wore thick glasses. He'd never seen her with makeup. 'But then she takes her clothes off,' he'd once told Leon, 'and you faint.'

'You fainted?'

'I should've.'

'What did she look like?'

'Hey, don't pry.'

He finished the sandwich, it was too late now for her to make it back home before curfew. They talked a little, but they couldn't wait. She blew out the candle, stood, and undressed. A *goddess*, he thought. Hips swelling from a narrow waist, full breasts, long sweeps of sallow skin. She was careful with her clothing, folded everything into a neat pile, then lay down beside him. They kissed for a while, then he rolled on top of her.

He shuddered to feel her skin next to his. 'Hold me,' she said. 'We don't have to hurry.'

'No, we don't.' She excited him too much, he thought. She would encourage him to slow down and enjoy it, rest her warm hands below his shoulder blades, a gentling touch that made it happen even faster.

'Oh, my glasses,' she said. She took them off, squinted up at him through the darkness. 'Put them where they won't get broken.'

He reached out, set the glasses down by the wall, just off the edge of the blanket.

'Mm,' she said.

'I love you, Eva,' he said.

'Don't move,' she whispered. 'Just stay in me.'

SAINT-DENIS. 4 NOVEMBER

A cold morning, the sky at dawn blue and black, trails of fiery cloud on the east horizon. The garage in Saint-Denis smelled like hay. After several tries, the engine turned over and Eva started to maneuver out of the narrow entry. Backing up was not something she did well — in fact, she'd only done it once before. Szapera's cousin Leon stood to one side of the car, waving his arms. Szapera, turned halfway around in the passenger seat, called out directions. 'Now to the left. More, he says. No, stop. *Stop!*'

They had less time than they'd thought. Kohn had been late. 'A problem at home,' he said sheepishly. Szapera wondered what that meant.

'Everybody be quiet,' Eva said. 'Let me do this by myself.' The car crawled backward. Szapera looked out the rear window. She was off to one side, but made it with inches to spare.

The courier from Weiss had shown up the night before, a young man in a seaman's jacket. He'd handed over a fourth weapon, an automatic pistol manufactured in Spain. 'Good luck, comrade,' he'd said to Szapera. 'Here is something extra from Weiss. Remember, no closer than thirty feet.'

A hand grenade. Szapera held it tight in his left hand. In his belt was the revolver. He'd given Leon the automatic — none of them was exactly sure how it worked, and Leon, just turned sixteen, with glasses much thicker than Eva's, probably couldn't hit anything anyhow.

Eva had negotiated the garage by backing straight out, blocking traffic in both lanes. Ignoring the furious honking, she made several moves until at last she got the car headed north. She should probably drive with a cushion, Szapera thought, she could barely see over the steering wheel.

'Can you manage?' he said.

'Don't make me nervous.' She shifted from first to third. The car rattled and jerked, then ran smoothly.

Just outside the town of Aubervilliers, Eva pulled off the road and waited. Kohn was holding a pocket watch. '7:22,' he said. Szapera had a school friend — a redhead who looked more Irish than Jewish — who worked as a clerk at one of the offices of the Banque de France in Paris. Twice a week, an armored car left the bank with bundles of occupation money, which it took to a Wehrmacht office at an army barracks near Aubervilliers. Szapera had ridden his bicycle out there, observed the armored car going through the gates, and established the time of delivery. He went out again a week later to make sure he had it right. Stalin had robbed banks in Baku to finance underground work, Szapera meant to follow his example. He had proposed the idea to Weiss, who resisted at first, then, in early October, changed his mind.

They waited. Kohn kept looking at his watch. It was quiet in the car, even the crazy Leon shut up for a change. Szapera felt it would be better if they talked, but his mind was blank. He was breathing hard, the hand grenade clutched in his fist.

7:31. 7:34. 'They're late,' Kohn said.

Just then the armored car rumbled past. A van, steel plates bordered by double lines of bolt heads. A very old van, Szapera guessed, box-shaped, tall and unwieldy, like one of those oddlooking machines in newsreels of the 1914 war.

'Let's go,' Szapera said.

Eva pulled out into traffic, the truck driver she'd cut off thrust his arm out the window and shook his fist.

'You go to hell,' Leon sputtered.

Eva's face was white. There were two cars between the Talbot and the armored van. A long minute ticked by. Heavy woods on both sides, then the road narrowed for a tiny village. 'Now,' Szapera said.

Eva waited — for a car coming toward them in the other lane, followed by two women riding bicycles — then swung out to pass. She oversteered; a wall loomed up in front of them, Leon and Kohn shouted warnings. She managed to get straightened out, then pushed the gas pedal to the floor. The Talbot roared with power, sped past the intervening cars, ran alongside the van. Szapera looked up, the driver turned to see who was next to him. For a moment, they started at each other.

'Cut him off,' Szapera said.

Eva hesitated — *the car* — then stepped on

103

the gas and threw the wheel over to the right. But the van driver saw it coming and accelerated, so they didn't cut in front of the van, they hit it. Just behind the driver's door, a loud bang of metal on metal then, surprisingly, the two vehicles, tires shrieking, spun around together and slammed into the front of a building.

Side by side, the Talbot and the van faced out into the road. Szapera looked down at his lap, he was covered with broken glass. Carefully he reached over and tried his door. Jammed. Next to him, Eva was holding her head. He had to get out, the plan was to run to the passenger side of the van, threaten the guard with a pistol while Kohn kept the driver at bay, and force them to open the door. In the newspapers, armored car robberies were described in just this way. But the rest of the plan would have to be changed, he realized. They wouldn't be driving off with the money. Through a hole in the front window he could see steam pouring from beneath the Talbot's hood.

He turned around, the door on Leon's side was open. He climbed over the seat, and stumbled into the road. A bicycle lay on its side, a sack had split, spilling onions. A few feet away, Leon was pointing his automatic at the van and pulling the trigger.

In the front seat of the van the Wehrmacht driver looked dazed. Szapera drew the revolver from his belt, pointed it at the driver, and shouted for him to open the door. The man didn't move. Szapera pulled the trigger, nothing happened. He released the safety and fired again, this time the glass in front of the driver's face turned to frost and Szapera couldn't see anything. He suddenly remembered the hand grenade, realized he didn't have it.

The escort car that had been trailing the armored van finally managed to wind its way through the stalled traffic and skidded to a stop about fifty feet away. A Wehrmacht sergeant rolled down the passenger window, rested a machine pistol on the door frame, aimed carefully, then fired a long burst. A bullet went through Kohn and hit Szapera in the lower back, knocking him on his face. From there, he saw Eva stagger out of the car, revolver in hand. A second burst, the gun flew away, Eva fell in the road.

Szapera started to crawl toward the van — he would kill the guard, start the motor, and ram the escort. Then he saw Leon, running at the escort car with the hand grenade. Szapera heard shots, Leon almost fell, but regained his balance. There was blood on his neck and he clapped his free hand over it as he ran, staying low, in a kind of comic crouch. The dirt in front of him sprayed up as the gun fired. He jerked backward once, then sprinted to the car and jumped through the open window. An instant later, a yellow flash, the doors buckled out and black smoke poured from both sides of the car. A Wehrmacht officer appeared, walking slowly, like a man hypnotized. Five, six steps. He stopped, sat down carefully in the road, and toppled over.

Szapera managed to get to his feet. His back was wet. He reached around, saw blood on his hand. He went to Eva, who was lying facedown, and carefully rolled her over. Her eyes were wide open and she was dead. He stared at her, could not look away.

The sound of approaching sirens startled him. He looked around for Kohn, but he had disappeared. He started running. A man in a suit jumped out of the back of the van and started chasing him. Szapera shot at him, he turned around and ran the other way.

Away from the road. He saw an alley, followed it to the end, and emerged on a village street. To his left, a sign: BOUCHERIE CHEVALINE, and a gold horse's head. Szapera lurched into the shop. He was out of breath, chest heaving. The butcher ran out from behind the counter with a long, thin knife in his hand. He was a big man and bright red, Szapera could see that he was trembling. 'What do you want?' He was shouting, clearly terrified. He had heard the crash and the gunfire, now the sirens were closing in.

'Help me,' Szapera said. He fell sideways against the counter, then slid to the floor.

The butcher cursed, threw the knife on the cutting block, wiped his hand on his spattered apron. He grabbed Szapera under the arms and dragged him toward the door.

A woman at the cashier desk cried out, 'Put him in the back!'

'No,' the butcher yelled. 'Not in the shop.'

'Then upstairs.'

'Ach,' the butcher said, infuriated. He took Szapera around the waist and heaved him onto his shoulder. Outside, a woman screamed, somebody ran past. They turned into a doorway, went up a staircase. The stairs seemed endless; four flights, five. The butcher wheezed as he tried to breathe, the rasping louder and louder as he climbed. At last they entered an attic — darkness, furniture, dust, and cobwebs. The butcher was gasping. He stopped, pressed a hand to his heart. '*Salaud*,' he growled. 'You'll kill me with this prank.'

He looked around, found an old armoire, set Szapera down inside it, then closed the doors. 'Now be *quiet*,' he hissed. Szapera

107

heard him leave, the whole room shook as he ran off. A door slammed. Then it was silent, and very dark. Szapera shut his eyes. He saw a spinning circle of golden dots, then nothing.

AUTUMN
RAINS

What has become of the adventures of the heart?
Killed by the dark adventures of existence.

ERICH MARIA REMARQUE

PARIS. 4 NOVEMBER.

At dawn, a few snowflakes drifted past the window of the Hotel Benoit. In the park across the street, piles of wet leaves had mounded up against the trunks of the chestnut trees. Casson stared out at the gray sky, no point in going to bed now. On the table by the bed a Remarque novel, a battered copy he'd bought at a *bouqiniste*'s stall by the river. He had been reading for most of the night — late summer in Paris, war on the way, a doomed love affair.

He got dressed, hating the clothes he put on every day. *Life without money*, he thought, shuddering at the cold, damp shirt against his skin. Out in the street it was busy, a sharp wind moving people along. He trotted down the Métro steps, waited on the platform, and worked his way into a crowded car. Silent, nobody talked, just the rumble

111

echoing off the tiled walls.

He got off in a nondescript district in the 15th. Just outside the exit, an arrest in progress. The Gestapo at work, he suspected. The men in suits, standing to one side, were Germans. They watched as French policemen led a line of men and women out of an apartment house, a long chain encircled their waists and they wore handcuffs. The Gestapo men were silent; speculative, watchful. It wasn't quite so easy as it used to be, being German in Paris.

He found the building and pressed the outside buzzer but the concierge didn't come. He had to wait for somebody to leave, then held the door, went inside, walked up three flights, and rang a doorbell.

'Casson! My God, of all the world.'

'Hello, Charne,' he said. They shook hands, then embraced. Charne was fat as an old bear, with long white hair that hung down the sides of his face like wings, and, as always, a cigarette with an inch of ash between his yellowed fingers. 'Come in, come in,' he said.

They sat in the kitchen, by a little coal-burning stove. Charne had worked for him on three pictures. He was one of the best makeup people in Paris, steady and sure. 'Are you doing anything?' Casson asked.

Charne shrugged. 'A little. Now and then.

Just to stay alive, you know.'

'You look well.'

'You also. I don't hear your name, lately, I thought, maybe . . . '

'I'm — well, I don't walk past police stations.'

From Charne, a laugh that ended in a cough. 'Who does?'

'Actually,' Casson said, 'it's a little worse than that.'

Charne nodded, he understood.

'I need, I need to be out in the city. I need a disguise.'

'Ah-ha, *la barbe!*' The beard. Charne made a face and winked, the comic conspirator.

Casson laughed. 'I know, but it's serious.'

'Forgive me, Casson, but the idea of you in a wig, well.' He smiled at the idea. 'That's not the way, believe me. From time to time I used to have, what would you say, a private client. Once, even, a bank robber. A Belgian, or so he said. And what I said to him I'll say to you: it's done with small touches, as many as you can manage.'

Casson nodded.

'Come to the window.'

Charne studied his face in the light, turned it sideways, then back. 'All right, then,' he said. 'Grow a mustache, just a plain one will do. No muttonchops, no goatee. Some hair

113

under the nose, to the edges of your lips, and if it comes in gray, so much the better. You can add a touch of color if it doesn't. Go to the *pharmacie*, they'll have something you can use. Then, let your hair grow, change the part, put it over on the other side. Wear a dark shirt, with a dark tie — you'd be surprised what that does, it changes your place in life, and that changes the way you look.'

He went into another room, rummaged around in bureau drawers, brought back a pair of eyeglasses with dark frames, and put them on Casson. 'There. Just grow a little mustache and you'll look like your poor cousin from Lyons.'

Casson stared at himself in the bathroom mirror. He brushed his hair back the other way. Now, he thought, he was beginning to look like somebody who looked like Jean Casson. Charne came over and stood in the doorway.

'Well?'

'I think it works.'

'Of course, we can do more. I had a look around back there — you can be Madame de Pompadour by dinnertime, if you like.'

'Powdered wig?'

Charne raised his hands — *of course*. 'Even a beauty mark on your boob.'

'I've always wanted that.'

'We'll rent you a little dog.'

'Don't tempt me,' Casson said.

'There is one thing you had better be prepared for.'

'What's that?'

'You'll run into somebody, barely an acquaintance, it never fails. 'Hello, Casson. You look like you've lost weight.' But, even so, you're better off keeping it simple. Stuff your cheeks with cotton wadding and it'll wind up in the soup.'

Back in the kitchen, Charne poured two little glasses of Calvados, precious stuff. 'For old times,' he said. 'I liked working on your pictures, Casson. You knew what was what.'

'*Santé*,' Casson said.

'*Santé*.'

Casson drank the Calvados and was silent for a moment. 'Do you ever hear anything of Citrine?' he said.

Charne thought a moment. 'Somebody mentioned her,' he said. 'But I don't remember who it was.'

'I just wondered,' Casson said.

They talked for a while, old times, studios and directors, how it was before the war. Finally Casson stood to go. 'Thank you for the eyeglasses,' he said.

'Oh, don't mention it. Maybe sometime

115

we'll work on a picture.'

'Sometime,' Casson said.

*   *   *

It rained the first week in November. The streets were dark and he felt safe, invisible, head down like all the world, moving quickly, just one more shadow in the twilight. He found Fougère, from the electricians' union, at a small office out in Sarcelles, in the Red Belt to the north and east of the city. But there was nothing for him there. They talked for a few minutes, Casson probed for an opening that he was never offered. Fougère had no reason to trust him and they both knew it. 'It seems,' Casson said, 'that only the FTP is fighting the Germans.'

'Yes, it does seem that way,' Fougère said. 'But you know how they are.'

He retreated, asking Fougère not to mention that he'd been by. That much he thought he'd won, but nothing else. The party had always been secretive — Lenin and Dzherzhinsky and the Cheka and all the rest of it — communists didn't chatter, not even in France.

Next he looked for Louis Fischfang, his former screenwriter. They'd said good-bye in

116

the spring of '41, when Fischfang disappeared into the underground, taking up full-time work for the party. Casson had wished him well, and given him money. He tried the various contacts he remembered — the owner of a newsstand, a furrier in the 13th, but nobody had seen him. One apartment he'd used had a new tenant. A woman he'd lived with had 'gone away,' according to the neighbors.

A few days later, he had another meeting with Degrave. He said he'd managed to make a few contacts, but had nothing in particular to report. Degrave was understanding, it was early in the game. After ten minutes, another man joined them. Degrave's superior, he guessed, though like Degrave he was in civilian clothing. He was introduced as 'Michel,' obviously an alias. Casson thought of him as *de Something*. Nobility. He was older than Degrave, white and soft, with small, sharp eyes sparkling with the de Somethings' ancient amusement at the play of human weakness, and pleasure in what it brought them. *Power and privilege*, Casson thought, but that sounded too much like a tract. 'What you are doing is important, monsieur,' the man said to him. He had a high, gentle voice, every word beautifully formed.

Coming out of the Métro that night, Casson was approached by an older woman. '*Pardon*, monsieur, I believe you dropped this.' She handed him a slip of paper:

Citizens of Paris! On 4 November, three militants of the FTP were martyred on behalf of the French people. Eva Perlemère, Leon Szapera, and Natan Kohn died as heroes in action against the Wehrmacht on Route 17 outside Aubervilliers. Follow their example! For Hitler, not a grain of wheat, not a foot of railroad track or an inch of telephone cable, not one hour of peace. *Vive la France!*

Casson had seen this reported on the front page of *Paris-Soir*. TERRORIST ATTACK THWARTED ON ROUTE 17! They were Jews and communists, the story said, 'social criminals,' and they didn't care if they brought down heavy reprisals on the French people in their 'blind pursuit of a Bolshevik France.' They were inspired, it turned out, 'not by patriotic motives, but by slavish obedience to Article 25 of the Communist Party program drawn up at the Sixth Congress in Moscow in 1928.'

* ★ ★

Where are you? Casson thought. Who do I know who knows where you are? He sat in his room and made lists of names. Radicals from his days at the Sorbonne. Friends from his early twenties in the Latin Quarter. People in the film business — directors, agents, actors, accountants, lawyers, producers, and more. Eventually, he wrote down the name *Alexander Kovar.*

Kovar was a writer. Anything you could write, plays, novels, newspaper articles, and pamphlets, Kovar had written, going back fifteen years at least. In 1936, Casson had come across one of his novels, *The House on Calle Alcalà,* based on the outbreak of fighting between monarchists and anarchists in Madrid in 1931, fighting set off when two aristocrats beat a taxi driver to death in front of a monarchist club on the *Calle* Alcalà — beat him for calling out '*Viva la República!'*

Casson had liked the story — almost unconsciously blanking out the political posturing and the straw men — in the way that film producers like certain novels. He had persuaded himself he might buy it, at least take an option if he could get it for a good price. There was rioting, plotting,

119

passionate conspiracy in the back rooms of cafés and, by the time the book was published and Casson got interested, the novel had proved to be prophetic — it was 1936 and Spain was truly on fire. In fact, and Casson was honest with himself, he was more than anything curious about the writer, who had a knowing hand with action scenes. In the end, however, lunch and a meeting and life went on.

But he'd liked Kovar. And he knew how to find him. If he was alive, if the communists or the fascists or the Germans or the street girls hadn't already done for him, because they'd certainly all tried it. If he was alive, Casson thought, and not locked up in some dungeon.

He took a train ride to Melun, a little way south of Paris. Found the shoe-repair shop, left a message, for 'Anton,' that he was an old friend and could be found by calling at the Hotel Benoit and asking for 'Marin.' The following night, a young woman came to his room. 'I'm a friend of Anton,' she said. 'Who are you?'

'I used to be a film producer, called Casson.'

She glowered at him. 'Oh. And now?'

'A fugitive.'

'For a fugitive,' she said, looking around the hotel room, 'you don't do too badly.'

'*Quand même*,' he said. Even so.

As she left, Casson was reminded of a rather casual remark Degrave had made in one of their discussions. 'When you're looking for somebody, and you find yourself in contact with people you've never met, you're getting close.'

The next morning he found a message waiting for him at the desk: Gare du Nord, 5:15 P.M., Track 16. He waited there for fifteen minutes, took a few steps toward the exit, then the young woman from the day before appeared at his side and said, 'Please come with me.'

He followed her through the rain to a run-down office building a few blocks behind the station on the rue Pétrelle. She turned, came back to him and said, 'On the third floor, turn left. It's at the end of the hall.'

The building was ice-cold and dark. And silent — when he left the staircase at the third floor, his footsteps echoed down the corridor. On the door at the end of the hall, the former tenant's name, the ghost of lettering scraped off the pebbled glass.

Casson knocked, then entered. Kovar was sitting in a swivel chair behind a desk piled with account ledgers. On the pull-out shelf was an old Remington typewriter.

'Nice to see you again,' Casson said.

Kovar inclined his head and smiled to acknowledge the greeting. He indicated a chair, Casson sat down. 'A surprise,' Kovar said. There was faint irony in his voice but, as Casson remembered it, that was true of everything he said. 'Sorry I can't offer you anything. This is somebody else's office by day, I only use it at night.' His chair creaked as he leaned forward. 'You can't really be a fugitive, can you?' The idea seemed to amuse him.

'I escaped from the rue des Saussaies. Last June.' The address was that of the Gestapo administrative headquarters. 'Then I was staying up in place Clichy, here and there, until a week ago.'

Kovar nodded — it might be true. 'And now?'

'I've been asked to make contact with the FTP.'

'Is that all?'

'Yes.'

Kovar smiled. Casson could just manage to see him in the dark office. He hadn't changed, had been fifty years old all his life. A shaggy, tobacco-stained mustache on the face of a mole, receding hairline, slumped shoulders. His body small, meager, almost weightless — a rag doll to be punched and kicked and thrown against the wall, which

122

pretty exactly described what had been done to it. Gray shirt, green tie, a shabby jacket. Years earlier, Fischfang had told him Kovar's story: his father a French citizen of Russian birth, his mother, born in Bratislava, died when he was twelve. He'd been in and out of prison in France, for political crimes, had broken with Stalin, then with Trotsky. The NKVD had tried to assassinate him after he'd been thrown out of the party. He'd essentially raised himself, educated himself, trained himself to write, got himself into trouble, found misfortune wherever he went, and somehow survived it all. 'He's worse than a Marxist,' Fischfang had said in 1936, 'he's an idealist.'

Kovar sighed. 'You weren't such a bad sort,' he said. 'A romantic, maybe. But now you've gone and — I mean, who asked you to find the FTP?'

'Army officers. A resistance group.'

'They know you're talking to me?'

'No.'

'But you believe what they tell you.'

Casson thought about that for a moment. 'When the occupation began, I tried to do nothing. It worked for a time, then it didn't. So I decided to do whatever I could, and very quickly came to understand that you can never be sure. Either you put your life in the

123

hands of people you don't entirely trust, or you hide in a corner.'

'Yes — but army officers?'

'Why not?'

'I don't know. For one thing, they probably hold the FTP responsible, the entire Left for that matter, for what happened here in 1940. What do they want with them now?'

'To talk. A marriage of convenience, perhaps. We're in trouble, Kovar, that much I know. My friends, the crowd I knew before the war, either do nothing or collaborate. They've adapted. It's reported in the newspapers that one of the city's most prominent hostesses gives dinner parties for German officers. At each place, for table decoration, are crossed French and German flags. Her toast to the commandant of Paris, the paper said, was dedicated to 'the most charming of our conquerors.' Well, it's not news that some of us are whores in this country. But it's just possible that some of us aren't.'

'You'll pay for that, you know,' Kovar said, rather gently. 'If they find out you feel that way.'

'Then I'll pay.' He paused, then said, 'Can you help? Will you?'

Kovar thought it over. 'I understand what you're doing, looking for party combat units.

What your army officers see is action — blood spilled for honor, and that they understand better than anything in the world. Problem is, I don't think I'm the one to help you. These people, the FTP, are Stalinists, Casson, and they don't like me. They don't like anarchists — they were killing them in the fall of '17, in Moscow and Saint Petersburg. They murdered the POUM leadership in Spain — NKVD operatives did that — and I'm no different. I grew up with a copy of Verhaeren in my pocket. 'Drunk with the world, and with ourselves, we bring hearts of new men to the old universe.' By all odds I shouldn't even be alive, I've been living on borrowed time since 1927. I'm sure you know, Casson, I *tried* being a communist, I managed for ten years but in the end it didn't work. They saw, finally, that they couldn't tell me what to do, and that was the end of that.'

'You have friends,' Casson said.

A long pause, and a reluctant nod of the head. 'Maybe,' he said. 'I have to think about it.'

★ ★ ★

'*Petit conard!*' You little jerk. A woman's voice, furious, held, barely, just below a

125

full-blooded scream, thundered through Casson's wall.

'No, wait, now look, we never said . . . '
The whine of the falsely accused.

'I hate you.'

'Now look . . . ' He lowered his voice as he told her where to look.

Casson had fallen asleep, face down on Remarque. He looked at his watch, 2:20 in the afternoon.

The middle of the day, offices closed for lunch, a busy time at *le* Benoit.

★ ★ ★

Degrave took him to dinner, brought along his mistress, Laurette, and her friend, Hélène. Laurette blonde and soft, Hélène the prettier one, dark, with a lot of mascara, glossy black hair cut stylishly — expensively — short, wearing *bijoux fantaisie*, gold-painted wooden bracelets, that clacked as she ate. Fortyish, Casson thought. She was tense at first, then talkative and bright. Casson liked her. While Degrave and Laurette were busy with each other, he told her how he'd once been hounded by lawyers when his production company had misplaced four hundred false beards meant for a musical version of Samson and Delilah. She hooted, covered her mouth, then put a hand on his arm and said, 'Forgive me, I haven't done that for a long time.'

Generous of Degrave to take them out, Casson thought. A black-market restaurant, one the Germans hadn't yet discovered. Roast chicken: months since Casson had tasted anything like that. He wanted to tear it apart and eat it with his fingers, maybe rolling around with it under the table. And a '27 Meursault. From beneath the table, excited growling and snarling, then silence, then a hand appears, holding an empty glass.

'*Je vous remercie*,' Casson said, the nicest way to say thank you. Degrave shrugged and smiled. 'Why not,' he said.

When the chicken bones were taken away, the owner came to the table. '*Mes enfants*,' she said.

They looked up expectantly.

'I can make an egg custard for you.'

'Yes, of course,' Degrave said.

'Twenty minutes.'

'All right.'

'Are you going back tonight?' Hélène said to Degrave.

'I'm staying over,' he said. 'If I can get a train reservation for Friday.'

'He can,' Laurette said. She had moved her

127

chair so she could be close to him. 'If he likes.'

Degrave's smile was tart. 'I can do anything.' He rested a hand on Laurette's shoulder and kissed her on the forehead.

'*Salaud*,' she said.

★ ★ ★

Degrave and Laurette went off in a bicycle taxi, Casson and Hélène stood in the drizzle. 'Can I take you home?' Casson said.

She hesitated.

'See you to the door, then.'

'Could we go to your room?'

Tiens. 'Of course.'

The hotel was not far from the restaurant, so they walked. She lived, she explained, in a maid's room in an apartment owned by an old woman, a family friend. 'I am an Alsatian Jew,' she said, 'from Strasbourg. Ten years ago I moved to Paris and rented a small apartment. Then, a few weeks after the Germans came, the landlord told me I had to find someplace else — his sister wanted the apartment. I don't think he has a sister, but at least he was polite about it. I went to see my mother's old friend, a widow for many years. She was lonely, she said, would I come and stay with her?

'For a few months, everything went well. This woman — who is not Jewish, by the way — had been a teacher in a *lycée*. We talked about books and music, we were good company for each other. But then, she changed. She was ill in the winter of '41, and she became obsessed with the Germans. She made it clear that she'd like me to leave. The problem is, when they said Jews had to register, I didn't — something told me not to. Now I can't get a change of residence permit from the préfecture — if she throws me out I have nowhere to go. So, I stay. I'm very quiet. I don't cause trouble. She *has* made a point of telling me not to bring strangers there. She's afraid of being robbed, or murdered, I don't know exactly what.'

'Why not move to a hotel?'

'Can't afford it. I work in a travel agency, a good one, on the Champs-Elysées. The offices are splendid, but the pay is low.'

'Can your family help?'

'I don't think so. The family's been in Strasbourg since the Middle Ages, but when my parents heard the stories of the refugees coming from Germany, they became frightened. The Germans have always claimed that Alsace rightfully belongs to them. My parents feared, after Chamberlain gave away the Sudetenland in '38, that France might use it to buy off Hitler. So they sold everything and went to live in Amsterdam. My brother and his family had emigrated just after the first war — he went into business with his inlaws in Montreal. My mother pleaded with me to come to Holland with them, but I wouldn't. I liked the life in Paris, I was seeing someone, and nothing was going to happen to France and its glorious army.'

★ ★ ★

It had been a long time, Casson thought, back at the Benoit. For her too, apparently — trembling as he undid her bra and her breasts tumbled out. He almost fell asleep afterward, warm in a way he barely remembered. He propped himself up on one elbow and smoothed the damp hair back off her forehead.

'It's funny,' she said, 'how things happen. Laurette asked me to come along. I said no, she insisted. She's been kind to me, more than kind, so finally I had to come. I'm going to hate it, I thought. But then . . . ' Idly, she ran a fingernail up and down the inside of his thigh. 'See?' she said. 'I'm flirting with you.'

'Mm.'

'Is your name really Jean?'

'I'm called Jean-Claude.'

'A film producer.'

'Yes, before the war. But I shouldn't talk about the past.'

'It doesn't matter. Laurette told me all this has to be kept quiet.' She laid her head on his chest, heavy and warm. 'Poor Laurette,' she said. 'Degrave's wife is rich. And mean as a snake. Laurette used to dream of marriage, but it's not to be.'

Casson put a hand on her hip, smooth down there. 'I shouldn't talk about these things,' she said. 'But it all seems like nothing now, with the world the way it is. I never imagined what it would all come to. Never imagined.'

His fingers traced idly along the curve, up and back. 'Yes,' she said, 'I like that.'

* * *

They stopped Weiss at a *Kontrol*, the early evening of 15 November, in the Saint-Michel Métro station. Pulled him out of line and made him open his briefcase. 'What's all this?' the German sergeant said, holding a sheaf of blank paper. 'For *leaflets*, maybe, huh?'

Weiss studied the hands; thick fingers, with cracked nails and callus. 'I'm a printing salesman,' he explained. 'See, it's the same

131

name and address on each piece of paper, but the lettering is different. Personal stationery. Maybe, ah, maybe you'd like to have something like this for yourself?'

'Me?' the sergeant said. This was something that had never occurred to him. 'Well, I don't know. I mean — what could I have? I stay at a barracks.' He paged through the sheets. 'But my wife, in Germany, she would be thrilled to have such a thing.'

Weiss took a pen from his pocket. 'Here, just write down your name and address, and I'll get it made up for you.'

'French stationery?'

'Yes.'

The sergeant began writing, slow but determined, carving the letters onto the paper, then handed it over to Weiss. 'Jürgenstrasse,' Weiss said.

'Yes. And it must look exactly that way. Can you print the German alphabet?'

'Oh yes. We have all the German fonts.'

'Well.' He was very pleased. 'Could I have it by the twentieth, to send to her?'

'Of course. I'll see to it.'

'It's her birthday.'

'You may count on it, sir.'

'It must be quite costly, this kind of thing.'

'With my compliments.'

'Ah, all right then.'

'If you write down your name and address in Paris, I'll have it sent over in a day or two.'

'Yes, of course.' He started writing. 'Meanwhile, maybe I'd better have a look at your work permit.'

Weiss thumbed through the papers in his wallet, took out his work permit, and showed it to the sergeant.

'Good,' the sergeant said. Then, in a stern voice, '*Alles in Ordnung.*' He gave Weiss a friendly wink and a smile, then whispered 'She will be so happy.'

PARIS. 16 NOVEMBER.

He had a second meeting with Kovar, this time in response to a note slipped under his door at the Benoit. Late at night he thought he heard something, then decided he didn't and went back to sleep. They met in the same office, in the early evening. The weather had turned cold, he could see his breath when he talked. This time the shade was up and the moon, in the upper corner of the tall window, cast silver shadows on the walls.

'I found a way to talk to some friends,' Kovar said.

'Good.'

'Old friends. We were in the streets

133

together, marching, fighting, and we were in the jails together. One doesn't toss that away so easily. They follow the line, of course, they are good communists. But then, they are also Frenchmen, some of them anyhow, and for the French, having one's own opinion is a kind of religion.'

Casson smiled.

'There's one in particular — he made no promises, simply said he'd see what he could do. I hope you understand that he's putting himself in danger. The Paris *apparat* is under intense pressure right now, because the Germans are about to take Moscow, they're close enough to see the last stop on the tram line.'

'Will Stalin fight in the city?'

'To the end. Then he'll burn it to the ground. But, so what? The reality is, all they have now is the weather. The *rasputitsa*, the autumn rains. The earth turns to mud — some days they have to maneuver their tanks with shovels and logs. And, soon enough, it will snow. Not German snow. Russian snow.'

'General Winter.'

Kovar shrugged. 'So-called. But the signs are all bad. The Moscow factories have been moved to the Urals, and the NKVD has packed up and left town. Sometime last week, wireless transmissions broken off in midsentence. What does that say to you?'

'Nothing good.'

Kovar thought for a moment. 'Of course, Russian wars always seem to go like this. Chaos and defeat and slaughter. Followed by the execution of those who tried to sound the warning. It's just the way they are. But then something happens. In Napoleon's campaign it was winter, and some kind of tick that killed thousands. In 1917 it was revolution. The Russian land defends itself — that's the mystics' version.'

'I've read it can be sixty below zero in December.'

'And colder. The Wehrmacht will have to heat their machinegun barrels over a fire before they can use them.' Kovar smiled. 'Only the Russians could get themselves into a position, in 1941, where sabers and horses really matter.'

'How do you know all this?' Casson said.

'Oh, it's talk,' Kovar said. 'But it's good talk.'

Casson was cold; he got up, walked around, rubbed his hands together. 'Your friend,' he said. 'When do you think he might try?'

'Who knows? He's a survivor, he'll wait for the right moment. Of course, he might move

135

a little faster if he knew a little more.'

'I don't think it's all laid out. Just French army officers, a center of resistance. I don't know what they intend to do — spy for the British? Blow up power stations? It could be anything.'

He walked to the window and stared out. 'We're just attorneys, Kovar. We represent two principals who may need to cooperate but cannot be seen to do so. A few years ago I worked with a Swiss lawyer. This man had a particular specialty, back-to-back negotiations. Two parties negotiate entirely through a third party so that they don't ever know who they're talking to. We may, eventually, come to something a lot like that — the parties will be known, the individuals invisible.'

Casson could see that this made sense to Kovar. 'On the other hand, it may just be a matter of setting up a single meeting, then gracefully leaving the stage.'

Kovar shook his head slowly. 'Somehow I doubt it will be that easy.'

Casson laughed. 'No, it never is.'

They were silent for a time, then Casson said, 'How do you make a living these days?'

'Oh, I survive. Always under false ID, always in some lost corner of the world. For a time I had the perfect job, at Samaritaine, the big department store. Every night, after hours, they wax the floors. First it's the cleaners, then the waxers and polishers. The wax is rubbed in with cloths and left to dry for a half hour or so. The best way to polish it is with felt slippers — shuffling along from one end of the room to the other. I'm sure somebody used to do it at your house.'

'Yes,' Casson said. 'Once a week.'

'What they do at Samaritaine is hire people to wear the felt slippers, a dozen or so. The usual crowd who work the night in Paris, each one a little more cracked than the next, 'the princess,' 'the Albanian,' I suppose I was 'the novelist.' The boss wasn't a bad guy, lost an arm in the 1914 war, he'd play music on a Victrola, usually waltzes, but you could do any step you liked as long as you stayed in contact with the floor. It's hypnotic, of course. The wood is dull to start with, then glows as you polish. We'd work our way from floor to floor, skating around the towels and the blankets and the brooms. On the sixth, we'd each put on a lady's hat from the display trees — a little joke — the violins sawing away on *The Vienna Woods*. Well, I used to think, Cocteau really ought to see this. Truth is, I liked it, it *suited* me.

'But eight months for somebody in my position was too long, I had to quit. For the moment, I'm writing the occasional

137

newspaper feature, under an alias, of course. It gets me a few francs, mostly from old friends I've known for years, mostly the socialists, a very tolerant crowd. Articles on soccer, on sound health, tips for cooking turnips. And then, I've always got a novel going.'

'Will you stay in France?'

'Maybe. For one thing, it's not so easy to get out, now. And you have to find a country that will take you. I can't go near Spain. Switzerland is out. Hard to say, maybe Mexico. For the moment, I'm here. If I vanish, it'll mean somebody's police finally stumbled over me and that was that. What about you?'

'I take it a day at a time,' Casson said. 'Count myself lucky to have a roof over my head and something to eat. Beyond that, God only knows.'

This is the BBC, broadcasting from London. Here is the news in French. The Comité Français de Libération National announced today in London that, after a trial *in absentia* and review by the Judicial Section, *Hauptsturmführer* Karl Kriegler, an SS official at the Santé prison in Paris, has been condemned to death. He was sentenced for the torture and murder of prisoners-of-war under confinement at the Santé, specific instances are cited in the indictment. The sentence is to be carried out at the discretion of the CFLN, at any time after the official declaration of the verdict, by any means necessary, or at the end of the war. Other personnel at French prisons are reminded that all wars eventually do come to an end, records are being kept, and they will be held to account for their actions. In other news . . .

Damn their eyes.
In a cellar on the outskirts of Paris, Weiss had to acknowledge that he had nothing like the powerful BBC at his disposal, and de Gaulle's people were using it to full effect. Not that he disagreed with the strategy — the sentence *in absentia* might have a sobering effect on the *Hauptsturmführer*, as it had in other cases. It was just that he had an executive's view of the world, and as an executive he was stung when competitors had resources he didn't. He could turn out endless editions of the underground *Humanité*, his best writers storming and threatening, but it didn't begin to add up to the power of the BBC.
This in a week when things were not going

139

well. He had been reprimanded by Moscow Center for the Aubervilliers raid — *dear comrade.* They might have moved their wireless operation back to the Urals, but they'd only been out of contact for two days and then — he suspected he was now receiving from a relay station in Sweden — then they'd let him have it. Operational rules specified a second automobile, to provide a getaway after an attack. How could he not have known that the Germans would use a chase car? Why wasn't it spotted during surveillance?

A *second* car? From where? How?

They'd obviously seen the French police report, and he hadn't sent it to them. Somebody after his job, maybe. He leaned on the table he used as a desk and closed his eyes. *Just ten minutes.* The BBC droned on — a *lycée* class in Belfort had come to school wearing Cross of Lorraine armbands, the Gaullist symbol. He could do that, out in Montreuil or Boulogne, and tell the world in leaflets, but it would never have the impact of a BBC broadcast. Above his head, the floorboards creaked as people cooked dinner and the aromas drifted down into the cellar; *museau* — jellied beef muzzle — and cabbage.

A knock at the door. 'Comrade Weiss?'

'Yes?'

'Dinner?'

'Maybe later.'

'Comrade Somet is waiting to see you.'

'All right. Five minutes.'

What was this, he wondered. Narcisse Somet had been in party work for twenty years. A journalist, cheeks and nose colored by the broken blood vessels of the longtime drinker, eyeglasses with tinted lenses, gray hair cut *en brosse*. He had always worked for trade weeklies, especially those that covered the mining and metals industries. Secretly, he wrote for *Humanité*, at one time contributing to its most popular feature — *L'Huma* consistently picked more winners at the Paris racetracks than any other newspaper.

Weiss went to the door and called upstairs, Somet shuffled in a moment later.

They shook hands. Somet settled himself in a chair, coughed a few times into his fist. They made small talk for a while, then Somet said, 'I've been contacted by Alexander Kovar.'

★ ★ ★

Casson took his nightly meal at a small café on the place Maillart. The plane trees on the square were bare now, and the branches

141

dripped, but it was at least something to look at. He ate at a table by the front window, a newspaper folded beside his plate. He'd run out of ration coupons for meat or fish, which left him with the only nonrationed dish on the menu, soup. Thin and yellowish, a few lentils, some onion, and a small piece of carrot. Served lukewarm, with a slice of coarse gray bread. The trick was to think about lentils as he used to know them, in a salad with mustard sauce and lean bacon. His father used to say, 'You can't eat dreams!' But, in a way, you could.

He turned to the entertainment section of the newspaper; reviews, ads, and a few brief news stories. Such as — FILM STAR WEDS IN SOUTH. In Villefranche, to be precise, the actress Citrine (Danielle Aubin) had married the director René Guillot (*The Shoemaker's Wedding, Blackbeard the Pirate*). The newly-weds to honeymoon on Cap Ferrat, then, early next year, to work on Guillot's new project, *Hotel de la Mer*. With a photo of the happy couple.

He felt, at that moment, not very much. A flash of sorrow, an iron band around his throat, a small voice saying *what did you expect?* He paid for dinner, clamped the paper beneath his arm, and headed back to

142

the hotel. *Just hope you aren't in for a night of Wagnerian orgasms from the room next door.* See? A joke. He wasn't going to let this hurt him, he had too many other things to worry about.

It did occur to him to go back up to the little bistro on place Clichy, where he might find the girl who called herself Julie. But that was asking for trouble and he knew it. So he went home, turned the light out, crawled under the thin blanket on the bed in the unheated room, and lay there.

It doesn't matter, he told himself, you fall in love more than once in life. You're lucky to have had what you did. *Cold.* He was already wearing underwear and socks, trousers, and shirt, only one more step he could take. A week earlier, in the Ternes Métro station, he'd managed to buy an overcoat. This one in about the same condition as the one he'd pawned. Shivering, he got out of bed, took the coat down from a peg behind the door, put it on, pulled it tight around himself, and crawled back under the blanket. *Not much better.* Outside, the wind moaned around the corner of the building, it rained in sheets, then abated.

The first time he kissed her he'd thought *she'll never let me do this.* But she did, and kissed him back, passionate, almost a little crazy. That confused him. She seemed desperate, as though she felt somebody like him could never fall for someone like her. What was she then, nineteen? On location for *Night Run*, down in Auxerre, in a room in the inevitable stucco hotel by the railroad station.

He undressed her, she helped, both of them desperate to get it done. Then it was his turn, and they'd stood there, staring at each other.

Married. It was the intimacy of it that stung him — how could she? With René Guillot? A crocodile with a winter tan and fine white hair. Famously arrogant, selfish, successful. Who no doubt courted her when he was given the director's job for the movie that Casson had thought up and Fischfang had written — given the director's job at the insistence of one Jean Casson.

Thanks for the movie, I'll just take the woman you love too, as long as I'm at it. He didn't blame Guillot, a force of nature, an *homme de la gauche* who swam cleverly through Parisian life and took whatever he wanted. He blamed Citrine. Bitch! *Connasse!*

Cold, the window rattled in the driving rain. Cold outside, cold inside. Casson rolled out of bed, tore off his overcoat, put on his jacket and shoes. The curfew was in force, he couldn't actually go anywhere. He went down to the lobby, a gloomy nest of velveteen love seats and occasional chairs, now lit by a single ten-watt bulb in an iron floor lamp that appeared to have been built as a gallows for mice.

Another lost soul had preceded him, a tall man in a blue over-coat, who looked up from his magazine and stood when Casson entered the room. He had the face of a hound; sunken eyes, a drooping mustache. 'Da Souza,' he said, handing Casson a card, 'fine linens.'

On the card was the name of a large company and an address in Lisbon. After a moment da Souza said, 'How are you tonight?'

'I've been better.'

'Not too bad, I hope.'

Casson shrugged. 'It's nothing. An *histoire de coeur*.'

'Oh that.'

Casson nodded.

'What did she do, go off with someone else?'

'Well, yes, that's what she did.'

Da Souza shook his head, *yes, that's what they did*, then went back to reading. After a few minutes he yawned, tossed the magazine

145

aside, and stood up. 'I'd offer to buy you a drink, but the curfew . . . '

'Some other time.'

Da Souza nodded, then gave Casson a gloomy smile. 'Still,' he said. He meant it had all happened before and would happen again. 'You might as well keep the card.'

PARIS. 20 NOVEMBER.

Casson returned from lunch a little after three. The woman at the desk said, 'Monsieur, a friend of yours came by. He's going to wait for you at the Ternes Métro.'

He went back out, taking the rue Poncelet, head down against the sharp wind. The rain had stopped, wet leaves were plastered to the sidewalk. Halfway between the hotel and the Métro station, a van pulled up to the curb, both doors opened.

'Yes?'

'You are Marin?'

'Yes.'

'You're to come along with us.'

There was no question as to who they were, or where they came from. Heavily built, with battered faces, one had a white scar cutting through both lips. They wore oil-grimed coveralls, and the van was marked as a Métro maintenance vehicle.

'In the back.'

He did what he was told. There were wooden racks bolted to the walls of the van, holding heavy pipe wrenches and a variety of shovels and prybars. The truck smelled of lubricating grease and burnt cinders.

'Lie down,' the driver told him. An old blanket was thrown over him as he lay on his side on the metal plate of the floor. The van started and drove smoothly away. The second man stayed in the back with him, sitting propped against the door.

They drove around for a long time, Casson could hear trucks and cars, and the occasional ringing of bicycle bells. Near his head was a small hole through which he could see the pavement, sometimes stone, sometimes asphalt. When they crossed the Seine, he looked down at the river through the strutwork of a small bridge. The van made several turns after that, on what sounded like narrow lanes. The men didn't talk. Casson tried to concentrate, to keep himself calm. He'd thought this meeting might be in a little bar somewhere, or in the office of a union local, but apparently it wasn't going to work like that.

By the time they rolled to a stop the daylight was just about gone. The engine was turned off and someone took the blanket away and said, 'You can sit up now.'

He was sore where his ribs had banged against the floor. The man now kneeling next to him reached in his pocket and brought out a black cloth. 'Just stay on your knees a moment.'

The man twirled the cloth around until it lapped itself into a blindfold, which he placed across Casson's eyes and tied firmly at the back of his neck.

'Can you see?'

'No.'

'You're sure?'

'Nothing.'

If they didn't want him to see where he was being taken, he didn't want to know where he was. They took his elbow, talked him out of the van, then guided him along a street. The walk seemed to go on forever, but it was probably no more than ten minutes before he was taken into a building — a garage, he thought, with hammers pounding on metal and the smell of tires. He was led out the back and into another building. A door was closed, then barred. He was seated in what felt like an old swivel chair.

'Just stay quiet. Somebody will come for you.'

He sat there, scared. He knew that from

where he was now he could disappear off the face of the earth. A few minutes crawled by. The door opened and shut, a chair leg scraped on cement, and a woman's voice, heavily accented, said, 'All right, you can take that thing off him.'

He was in a small workshop, from what he could see, with a blanket over the window. It was almost completely dark. Ten feet away from him, a woman sat at a table near a lamp with a very bright bulb. Its position made it hard for him to see her clearly, or anything beyond her, although he sensed that there were people in the darkness.

The woman was perhaps in her fifties, with gray hair pulled back and pinned up, a dark suit, and, beneath the table, lace-up shoes with low heels. A university professor or a doctor, he would have thought, seeing her on the street. 'Very well,' she said, taking a few sheets of paper and squaring them up in front of her. She unscrewed a cap from a pen, making sure it worked on one corner of the paper. 'You're called Marin, these days — correct? And you stay at the Hotel Benoit?'

Probably the accent was Russian, but he wasn't completely sure. 'Yes, that's right.'

'In fact you are Jean Casson, formerly a film producer.'

'Yes.'

'Born in Paris? Of French nationality?'

'Yes.'

'Your military service?'

'In the first war, I served as a corporal with an air reconnaissance squadron, changing film canisters on Spad aircraft and sometimes supervising the development of the negatives. In May 1940, I was reactivated and returned to service as a member of the *Section Cinématographique* of the Third Regiment, Forty-fifth Division. I saw action on the Meuse River, near Sedan, and was discharged from the unit later that month, when its cameras and equipment were destroyed in a bombing raid.'

'Then you eventually returned to Paris.'

'That's right.'

'By the way, are you aware that you were followed, as you set off for this meeting?'

'Followed? No, I don't think so.'

'It isn't important, and we took care of it, but we wondered if you knew.'

'No, I didn't.'

'Now, monsieur, why have you been looking for us?'

'To offer you the opportunity to meet with members of a resistance group.'

'Why would we want to do that?'

'To discuss matters of mutual concern.'

'Such as?'

'I have no idea.'

She stared down, read a note she'd written. 'Are you sympathetic to the objectives and programs of the Communist Party?'

'Sympathetic? Well, I'm certainly aware that there are poor people, and that they suffer. On the other hand, I don't believe in the revolution of the working masses, or the dictatorship of the proletariat.' He paused, then said, 'Or, in fact, the dictatorship of anybody.'

She didn't smile, but it crossed his mind that a young and long-ago version of her might have. 'You are naïve, monsieur,' she said quietly.

Casson shrugged.

'Why do you live as a fugitive?'

'Last May, I was taken in for questioning by the Gestapo, held for a few hours in a cell in the basement of the old Ministry of the Interior on the rue des Saussaies, then brought up to the top floor for questioning. I was led down a hall to use the WC and left alone. I saw that the window wasn't barred. I crawled out on the roof, and escaped.'

'Why were you taken in for questioning?'

'I lied on a form and they caught me.' That was, technically speaking, true. But it was also the story he'd been told to follow, and he followed it.

'What lie was that?'

'That I had not returned to military service in 1940 — working with a film unit would have been seen as an intelligence function.'

She read through the papers for a moment, looking over what she'd written. In the shadows behind her, somebody lit a pipe, he could see the rise and fall of the yellow flame held above the bowl.

'The people who sent you here,' she said. 'Who are they?'

'Army officers.'

'Members of the intelligence service? The former *Service des Renseignements?*'

'Yes. I believe so.'

'What do they want, information?'

'I don't know what they want.'

'Then what do you believe their objectives are?'

'To resist the German occupation.'

'Are they in Vichy?'

'Yes.'

'Officers of the present service?'

'Yes.'

'And why did they choose you as their representative?'

'Because I'm neutral.'

'What does that mean?'

'Unaffiliated. With no aims of my own.'

'And what do you bring, Monsieur

Casson, to this negotiation? What do you offer us, as an incentive for discussions, or doing business together, or whatever it might turn out to be?'

'No specific offer — but they are waiting to hear from you, and they will do whatever they can.'

'Monsieur Casson, are you a spy?'

'No, I'm not.'

'We shoot spies. Certainly you know that.'

Casson nodded.

'We're going to send you back now. You can report this conversation to your army officers. And tell them that if they wish to pursue any kind of dialogue, the first step will be to provide evidence of good faith. What we want is this: weapons. Guns, Monsieur Casson. Do you think they will accept that condition?'

'I can't say. But, why not?'

'What we want are automatic weapons, short-range, rapid-fire machine guns. Six hundred. With a thousand rounds of ammunition for each weapon. The terms of delivery will be spelled out when we receive your signal that the negotiation will go ahead. Do you understand?'

* * *

153

The trip back to Paris took forty-five minutes. It was dark when he was let out, and for a moment he had no idea where he was, somewhere in the streets of eastern Paris. He eventually found a Métro, and rode back to the place des Ternes. He wanted to walk, to think, but it was too cold, so he headed down the rue Poncelet toward the Benoit. Out on the boulevards, the street lamps had been painted blue, to make them less visible to aircraft, but in the narrow rue Poncelet it was almost completely dark.

Midway down the street, a man was sleeping in a doorway. This was not something Casson was accustomed to seeing, the police didn't allow it, certainly not in that arrondissement. Casson stopped and peered through the darkness. The man's back was to the street, his overcoat hiked up, the tails moving in the wind. His hat was halfway off, the brim caught between his head and his forearm. His other arm was flung out behind him.

He was dead, Casson knew that. *By the way, are you aware that you were followed? It isn't important, and we took care of it.*

Casson stood there, staring, holding his coat around him. Then he started walking, heading back to the hotel.

THE
LAWYER

CORBEIL-ESSONNES. 3 DECEMBER.

It was the safest house they had. Thirty kilometers from Paris, it stood invisible behind twelve-foot walls at the edge of the village, with a separate garage that could hide four cars. The property was nominally owned by a company in Stockholm.

4:50 A.M. On the first floor, Ivanic and three others lounged in the kitchen and read newspapers. Two more men stood watch outside. In a parlor on the second floor, a meeting had been in progress since the previous afternoon. Seated at a dining-room table were: Lila Brasova, political commissar to the FTP, who had questioned Casson in the machine shop; an NKVD officer called Juron, of Polish origin and French nationality; Weiss, as liaison officer with *Service B*; and, chairing the meeting, Colonel Vassily Antipin, a senior executive sent in by Moscow Center. 'By way of Berlin,' he'd said dryly.

Square-faced and solid, with neatly combed brown hair, Antipin was in his late thirties. He had enlisted in the GRU, military intelligence, at the age of twenty and had risen to power on the strength of clandestine operations in difficult countries, including recruitment in Bulgarian river villages in the mid-1930s.

Brasova asked him about Berlin.

'It smells of fire,' he said.

Stacked against the wall were some three hundred dossiers of French army officers who had worked in the SR. 'The problem is,' Weiss said early on, 'that the officer corps is dispersed. Some are prisoners of war in Germany, some have been deported to North Africa, some have fled to London. Some are dead, a few are in hiding. There may be twenty or thirty in Vichy. As we watch Casson we'll see at least one of them, but he will represent others, and they will be hidden.'

'And the ones who specialize in the French Communist Party?'

'By May of 1939 we'd identified ten officers. There's one left in Vichy, a lieutenant — much too junior to run an operation like this.'

'What's Casson like?'

Brasova shrugged. 'Intelligent, a good heart, some professional success, some failure. Would like to believe himself a cynic — *'Que l'humanité se débroulle sans moi,'*

158

the world will just have to muddle through without my help. In fact he isn't like that, quite the opposite.'

'And Kovar?'

'Impossible.'

They broke for dinner, went back to work at ten. Given the difficulty of moving Antipin through enemy lines, Moscow had put together a long agenda. Sometime after four, they returned to the discussion of the SR. Antipin leaned back and knotted his fingers behind his head. 'Are they simply trying to see over the wall, is that it? Trying to find out who's running the FTP — in particular, who's running *Service B*.'

'Of course that's what it is,' Juron said. He was the youngest there, bald at thirty-five, with thick glasses.

'It's more than that,' Weiss said. 'This is a struggle between de Gaulle's clandestine service and the old-line SR. In that conflict, a working relationship with the FTP is an asset, potentially of great value.'

'To the British,' Antipin said.

'Yes. Whoever wins gets British guns and British money and the aid of the British secret services. De Gaulle, based in London, is ahead in the race, so this could well be SR's attempt to catch up.'

'What's British power to us?' Juron said.

159

'We've been at war with them, more or less, since 1917.'

'What would you do, then?' Antipin asked.

'Take what they offer, find out everything we can, then cut the lines.' Antipin nodded. This was, Weiss realized, the Center's point of view. 'Comrade Brasova?' Antipin said.

'I would wait and see,' she said. 'They will use us, we will use them, the Germans will suffer.'

Outside, the darkness had begun to fade. The bell in the town church rang five. Weiss met Antipin's eyes. 'I'm going to step outside for some air,' he said.

He waited at the back door, Antipin showed up a moment later. They walked on a gravel pathway at the foot of the wall. 'The Center has decided that Juron should take care of this,' Weiss said. 'Is that it?'

'That's their preference, but the final decision is up to me.'

'You know what he'll do, don't you?'

'Liquidate.'

'Yes. Their answer to everything.'

'We are at war,' Antipin said.

'Can you give me a month?'

'What for?'

'To do what Moscow wants done here, I need help.'

Antipin thought it over. 'I'll give you a

160

month. But Casson and Kovar may have to be sacrificed — that's the trade-off. No matter how you put it, spies are spies, and, to the Center, this has all the earmarks of a classic penetration. After all, if the Germans allow some form of SR to exist in Vichy, what would it do? Fight the communists. How to do that? One way is to fake a resistance group, approach the party, and tell them you want to work with them.'

'Maybe,' Weiss said, 'but maybe not. I think Brasova is right, what's proposed is a temporary alliance, and I want to take the next step. For that, I'll need Casson and Kovar. Can you keep Juron away from them?'

'He stays in Paris, but I won't let him do anything right now. However, when the time comes, you will have to follow his orders. Agreed?'

Weiss agreed.

★   ★   ★

They stirred in their sleep, Casson and Hélène, gliding spoon-style through the December night in the battered old Benoit. She reached back, pulling him tighter against her, then sighed and, in a moment, fell asleep again, breathing slow and steady, dreaming

161

away, with a muted cry or mumble every now and then.

He had been just too lonely that afternoon, he could not bear it. So he'd found the travel agency she'd said she worked for and, at six in the evening, had waited for her to appear. She came out alone, walking quickly, head down. Carefully put together, he saw. The long black coat that half the women in the city wore, a lavender scarf to improve it, setting off her dark eyes, her dark hair. She was startled to see him. 'Did you just happen to be passing by?'

'No,' he said. 'I was waiting for you.'

They headed up the boulevard, paused for traffic at a side street. 'Perhaps,' he said, 'you'd like to come back to the hotel with me.' She didn't answer, just took his arm, her shoulder pressed against him as the cars and trucks rumbled past.

Back in his room, he watched her undress in the darkness. A little leaner than he might have preferred, but sinuous, with a narrow waist and supple hips. In bed, buried beneath the thin blanket and their overcoats, they waited to get warm. 'Do you miss Strasbourg?' he asked.

'Sometimes. I miss living in a home, just the small things that go on all day. And I miss the flowers.'

162

'In December?'

'Always. Vases everywhere, mostly red gladioli in December. My father was a florist. Actually, my father was *the* florist. *Les Trois Rosiers* — his great-grandfather started it, a long time ago.'

'What happened to it?'

'It went, everything went. I miss that too, working in the shop. We did weddings and funerals, banquets, anything important in the city. My uncle had greenhouses in Italy, in San Remo, a little way down the coast from Menton. It's all gone, now.'

'What made you leave?'

'By the time I was thirty, it was pretty clear I wasn't going to get married. Not a conventional marriage, anyhow — within the Jewish community in Alsace. I had my chances: a pharmacist, a teacher, but I wasn't in love. I had affairs, quiet as could be, but people find out. So, I did what all the unmarried girls in France do — or would if they could. I went to Paris.'

'And fell in love.'

'Yes, a real *folie*, but it didn't stop there. I was in love with the city, with everything. Of course for you, born here, it would be different.'

'No, the same.'

'Were you rich?'

163

Casson laughed. 'I never could figure that out. We lived among the rich, in Passy, but we never had any money. Somehow, we survived. When I left the Sorbonne I decided to go into the movie business so, once again, I was living without money, or at least living well beyond what I had. But I was young and I didn't especially care. I was happy to be alive, and I expected I'd get rich someday. And, like you I suspect, I was always in love. First one, then another. Eventually, I got married. She was from a wealthy family, but she didn't have anything either. We both thought that was funny. After we got engaged, she was summoned to a lunch with her grandparents and they gave her the bad news. She came to my apartment that afternoon, we told each other it didn't matter, made love, went out and ate at Fouquet.'

'But later, it didn't work out.'

'It was good for a few years, then we separated. With the way life went on in the sixteenth, maybe it was inevitable. We started seeing other people — everybody we knew did that so we did it too. Drifted apart, fought too often, decided we'd both be happier if we didn't live together.'

He reached over to the night table, lit a cigarette and shared it with her. 'Looking back now, of course, those days seem like paradise. Even the bad times.'

She nodded. 'Yes, for me too. Now I'll be happy if I can hang on to what I have.'

'The job?'

'Yes. It isn't so bad, it makes the day pass. What's extraordinary is that there is an entire class of people who don't seem to be affected by the war. Some of them French, a few Americans, Argentines, Syrians. They book staterooms; mostly to resorts, in sunny countries. They know about the submarines, but they don't seem to care.'

'Have you thought about getting out yourself?'

'Yes.' She paused. 'Laurette came to me one day, after the registration of Jews last October, and said that Degrave would help me get out. I could go to Algiers.'

'And you didn't go?'

Slowly, she shook her head. 'I thought about it for days, but I was afraid. What could I do? How would I survive? Also, I felt I was abandoning my parents. I'd been able to talk to them once, the day after the invasion. They actually had visas to go to Canada, my brother managed to get them, and space on a steamship — on May tenth. But Rotterdam was being bombed, the city was in a panic, and the dock area was mobbed. They could see the steamship, but they couldn't get on it.

I tried again, two days later, but by then the telephone lines had been cut. Still, I felt that if I stayed in Paris, somehow they would contact me, but they never did.'

'Hélène, what if I asked Degrave again, would you go?'

'Yes,' she said quietly. 'Now I would.'

★   ★   ★

Casson woke for a moment — had he heard voices in the hall? No, it was silent. God he was cold, the window was white with frost flowers. He pulled Hélène tighter against him. *Crazy to take off all our clothes* — to make love like aristocrats. Sirens in the distance, south of them somewhere. It didn't mean anything. He drifted back toward sleep.

Suddenly, a door opened, another slammed, somebody called out 'Odette!' in a shouted stage whisper, and footsteps pounded down the hall.

Hélène sat bolt upright, a hand pressed against her heart. 'What time is it?'

Casson rolled out of bed, put on pants and shirt, opened the door a crack, and peered down the corridor. At the end of the hall, the woman who worked nights at the desk was talking to a heavy woman in a nightdress, her hair gathered up into blond tufts and tied with ribbons. When Casson appeared they turned and glared at him for a moment, then went back to whispering.

'Madame, *s'il vous plaît*, what's going on?'

'The Japanese, monsieur.'

'The Japanese? Here?'

'No — not here! Over there somewhere. They have sunk the American navy.'

They all stared at one another for a moment, the clerk in a smock and two sweaters, the blond woman barefoot, toenails painted pink, Casson in his shirt and pants, hair still rumpled with sleep.

'It is the end, monsieur,' the blond woman said dramatically. Her eyes were shining with tears.

'What is it?' Hélène called softly.

Casson went back to the room, got undressed, and burrowed under the covers.

'The Japanese have attacked America,' he said. 'Defeated their navy.'

'Oh no.'

'It's for the best. Now they will come into the war.'

'How will they get here?'

'They will build another navy.'

'A long time, then.'

He had no idea. 'A year,' he said, in order to say something. She held on to him, he could tell she was crying. 'It's too long,' she said.

How long, Casson wondered, would it really take? The Americans would have to land somewhere in Europe. He had no idea what it would take to do that — a million men? Hundreds of ships? What he did know, as a film producer, was what it took to assemble a fifty-guest wedding party. So, the Americans weren't coming anytime soon.

They lay awake in the darkness. Casson imagined he could almost sense the news as it made its way through the hotel. He had experienced a surge of hope, now he felt it drain away. In the morning, he would have to be Jean Marin again, and for many mornings after that.

'I can't sleep,' she said. 'What time is it?'

'Two-thirty.'

She moved closer, rested her head on his shoulder. He whispered to her, she laughed. Suddenly, a drunk started singing in the hall, somebody opened a door and yelled at him to shut up.

★ ★ ★

Weiss got off the Métro a stop short of his destination, then walked around for a time, making sure he hadn't been followed. Soon he'd have to get somebody to watch his back. Now that they'd started to kill Germans, the security noose around Paris was being drawn tight. A new permit needed here, a new rule there, a form in the mail that directed you, in ten days, to call at an office you'd never heard of. It was the same technique the Germans had used against the Jews in the 1930s. But, he thought, not the worst thing that could happen, at least it would drive the sheep his way.

He turned down a tiny passage, stepped over a dead cat — they weren't eating them yet, but they would — and out onto the fashionable rue Guynemer that bordered the Jardins du Luxembourg. Home and office to one Dr. Vadine, a dentist of genteel Bolshevik sympathies who had, from time to time, assisted Comintern operatives. I hope he's still in business, Weiss thought. And doing well.

Money. He needed money.

Before the war, moving secret funds from Moscow to Paris was easy, using couriers or borrowed bank accounts or phantom companies. In fact, the party had been notorious for its money. On a trip to London during the spy panics of the 1930s, he'd seen tabloid headlines plastered all over the kiosks — HE BETRAYED HIS COUNTRY FOR RED GOLD.

Weiss smiled at the recollection. He supposed that calling money *gold* made it more sinister.

He entered the dentist's building and climbed the stairs. The receptionist, an attractive woman in her forties, said, 'Do you have an appointment, monsieur?'

He waited a moment in silence. The woman was Vadine's long-time mistress, she'd last seen Weiss in 1939. 'No,' he said, 'I don't.' Again he waited. She was pretending she didn't know him.

'Doctor is very busy today, monsieur.'

'Tell him it's Monsieur Berg.' Weiss paused a moment. 'I'm an old friend. He'll remember me.'

They stared at each other, she lowered her eyes. 'Very well,' she said.

He stood by the desk and waited. Why did he have to spend time on these errands? He needed help, somebody smart who could take orders and get things done. A door opened at the end of the hallway, he heard the whine of a drill, then an urgent, whispered conversation. Vadine came toward him, wiping his hands on a towel. The receptionist was right behind him.

'What do you want?' Vadine said. He was a thin, nervous man, perpetually irritated, and now he was frightened.

'Your help,' Weiss said.

'Can't we talk about this later?'

Weiss shook his head slowly. 'It won't wait. We're having difficulty moving funds into the Occupied Zone.'

'Oh,' Vadine said, 'money.' He was clearly relieved. Apparently he'd feared they would ask him for more than that.

'Yes. Five thousand francs would help.'

Vadine nodded. 'All right,' he said. 'I'll get it for you. Is there some way we can do this . . .'

'Without meeting?'

'Yes.'

'Of course.'

The receptionist said, 'It would be better if you didn't come here.'

Weiss agreed, told Vadine that a young woman would contact him in a few days, and left immediately. They didn't want him there, he didn't want to be there.

Outside, he headed back toward the Métro. His next call was on the other side of the city — a socially prominent woman whose father owned a coal mine. He had two other donors in mind — add Brasova's contributors and some money from the unions, and they could survive for another month.

* ★ *

3:30 P.M. Casson and Degrave sat at the bar of a café on the place Blanche. Dry snow floated past the window and covered the outdoor tables.

Degrave had spent three days in Vichy. 'I couldn't wait to get out of there,' he said. 'It's like a comic opera. It says it's a government, it says it's France, but it's all a fraud. Everybody in uniform — sashes, medals, gold braid — you expect them to sing and dance.' He ran a hand over his face. 'Have a cognac with me.'

'All right.'

Degrave ordered the cognac. 'We had meetings that went on for hours. I told them everything about your contact with the FTP, and the demand for guns, but nobody wanted to make a decision.'

The barman set two cognacs in front of them and Degrave paid.

'Is it over?'

'I can go ahead, if I want to, but there won't be a lot of support. My friends will help us, when they can. We'll have to do most of it ourselves.'

'They don't like the idea?'

'They don't like the risk. The problem is, we need the alliance, it will allow us to do things we can't do ourselves. But there are difficulties. For example, we don't have the

172

guns. We've been disarmed, which is what happens to defeated nations, and the Germans, using the Armistice Control Commission, are making sure it stays that way.'

'But you — of course you know arms merchants.'

'Out of business. For the moment, anyhow. Put out of business by national industries running twenty-four hours a day. We'll have to work with the black market.'

'You mean criminals, smugglers.'

'Yes. If we can find somebody, we'll be allowed to spend whatever it costs. That much I did get. But I want to make sure you understand that this is well beyond what we originally asked you to do. So, if you're going to say no, say it now.'

Casson hesitated, but he couldn't say no. 'You'll have to help me get started.'

'The inspector who found you up in Clichy is an old friend. He'll know somebody — there isn't much he doesn't know.'

'How would I find him?'

'He's at the main préfecture. On Thursday mornings he supervises the office that accepts denunciations.'

Casson nodded.

'This will work,' Degrave said. 'It won't be easy, but it needs to be done. The principle is right, believe me it is, I just couldn't get the people in Vichy to see it that way.'

'Why not?'

'I don't know — tradition, living in the past. French military officers don't like secret committees, they believe in chain of command. They don't like communists, and they don't believe in *partizan* operations — assassination, dynamite, luring the enemy into reprisals against civilians. They think of that as terrorism, that it turns the population against the resistance.'

'Are they wrong?'

'They could be right.' His tone was almost sarcastic. 'Wait a few months and see what the Germans do here — then let me know what you think.'

They had another cognac. Degrave went to the back of the café and made a phone call. When he returned, Casson said, 'I want to ask you about Hélène.'

'You're seeing her?'

'Yes. Now and then.'

'She's been a real friend to Laurette.'

'She mentioned that you offered to help her leave the country.'

'I did. She wanted to go, then decided against it.'

'She's changed her mind.'

'I don't blame her,' Degrave said. 'It's a

174

little more complicated now, but we can probably do it. I'm in Paris for the next three weeks, then I go down to Vichy. Unfortunately, there's a limit to how many people we can move. She may have to wait until February, or March. Tell her I'm working on it. Meanwhile, she should be careful — respect the curfew, avoid the black market.'

★ ★ ★

The préfecture, on Thursday morning, was a living hell. Mobs of people; some of them scared, all of them uncomfortable. Who knew what buried sins might suddenly spring to life in a place like this?

Daily life in Paris had always churned up business for the *flics*, but the Occupation, with its curfew, black market, and hundreds of petty rules and regulations, had provoked a tidal surge of activity at police headquarters. A madhouse, Casson thought. Permits and papers to be applied for, changed, renewed. Summonses answered, fines paid. And all of it required standing on line — one of the few Anglo-Saxon perversions that Parisians truly disliked.

Casson had to present his identity card three times; first at the courtyard entry, then in an office, then again in another office, where the information was laboriously copied down in a huge, frightening ledger. Each time his heart pounded, but the false identity held. He also had to show his work permit — Marin was a claims investigator for a large insurance company, a job that allowed him to travel, and explained his presence in any town or neighborhood.

Worst of all, for Casson, was that his progress through the tight-lipped crowds in the maze of corridors turned up two acquaintances from his former life. In one case, a woman who had worked in the office of a film distributor. Their eyes met, Casson turned sharply and walked away. Then he came face to face with a distant social connection of his former wife, a man who called out 'Jean Casson!' in a great, rumbling voice. Casson simply said *'Pardon?'*and glared at the man, who apologized and retreated into the crowd.

Room 15 was off by itself on the second floor, in a cul-de-sac isolated by some ancient renovation. Casson was given a brass disc with a number on it and told to wait. There were two other people on the wooden benches and only later did Casson realize that he never saw their faces. He sat there for almost an hour, staring into space, the monotony broken only by the delivery of the mail, a large canvas sack so heavy it had to be dragged across the floor before being left by the secretary's desk.

The inspector was just as Casson remembered him. A heavy old man with thick white hair, a battered face, and pale blue eyes. 'Monsieur Casson,' he said, jovial as before, apparently quite pleased to see him. 'I am sorry you had to wait in that shithouse out there, but we must pretend that all is as usual.'

Casson said he understood.

'*Dégueulasse!*' Sickening. 'The boss makes me do this once a week because he knows I hate it. A national illness, this business. We get them all, jilted lovers, angry wives, the *petits commerçants* trying to wreck the competition. And the rather ordinary people who get up one morning and look at their neighbor and say to themselves, see how they live! What right do they have to such good fortune?'

'Sad,' Casson said.

'Yes, I suppose that's the word.' He paused a moment. 'But nothing new. Back when I was young I worked in the countryside, a small town in the Sarthe. We used to get letters from a man whose apple tree had a branch that grew over a neighbor's fence.

When the apples fell on the ground, the neighbor ate them.'

'The scoundrel.'

'It's funny, yet it's not funny. This man brooded over his lost apples, and the idea that someone else might profit from his labor drove him to the edge of madness. Well, in those days it didn't matter. We'd read his letters, put them in a file — he accused the neighbor of everything he could think of — and forget about them. But now, with the Occupation, and the Gestapo . . . ' He looked grim and shook his head in sorrow. 'Well, to hell with the things you can't change, right?'

Casson nodded. 'Our mutual friend suggested I come to see you.'

'How can I help?'

'We need to buy — '

The inspector smiled. 'I've heard it all,' he said.

'Guns.'

'Meaning?'

'Submachine guns, a few hundred.'

The inspector scowled. 'Morphine, not a problem. White slaves, maybe. But that — ' He let it hang.

'It's important,' Casson said.

'It may not be possible.'

'We have to try.'

The inspector stared at him. Finally he

sighed. 'I hope you know what you're doing.' He took a fountain pen from his pocket and deliberately unscrewed the cap. He hesitated a moment, wrote a few words on a slip of paper, blew the ink dry, and handed it to Casson. Then he stood abruptly and walked to the window.

'We have dinner with our daughter out in Thiais tonight, and I worry about the roads. Snow, it said in the paper. Meanwhile, you can memorize that.'

Casson worked at it, it wasn't very hard. 'Vasilis,' he said. 'Greek?'

Staring out the window, the inspector shrugged. 'Greek, Turkish, Bulgarian. Just keep asking till you hear one you like.'

The inspector returned to his desk, took the piece of paper from Casson, leaned forward, and said, 'Some personal advice. You should keep in mind that these people in Vichy have to walk a certain line. What they are doing with you is all well and good. I don't know that it matters, but it might. However, the rest of the time, they are part of the government. Which means doing what Pétain and Laval and their friends think they ought to be doing — working against the enemies of France. That's a big category, a lot fits in it. If the war ended tomorrow, and Britain won, they'd say, 'Look what we did, we were on the right side.' On the other hand, if the war ends tomorrow and Germany wins, God forbid, they could say the same thing.'

'All right,' Casson said after a moment. 'I understand.'

'I hope you do. Maybe you don't like it, but that's the way life is. Not that we're any better. When the Germans took over, the préfecture went back to work, just like it always had. The files were all in place, and if a call came and somebody said, 'Send over Pierre's dossier' in a German accent, there went Pierre. *Comprends?*'

'Yes.'

'Still a patriot?'

'Trying,' Casson said.

The inspector smiled.

★ ★ ★

SS-*Unterscharführer* — Corporal — Otto Albers strolled up and down the rue St.-Denis, where two or three women were posed in each doorway. From the way he looked them over, casual and thoughtful at once, it was clear that he considered himself a connoisseur, a man who knew precisely what he wanted and would insist on having it. To the women in the doorways there wasn't much new in that. They smiled or sneered, opened their coats to give him a glimpse of the merchandise, made kisses in the air, or just looked haughty — *I have not always been as you see me today.* This last was not easy, wearing red panties or nothing at all under a bulky coat, but a proven technique with German customers. 'Hey, Fritz, got a big wiener?' one of them called to Albers. But that was an act of spontaneous resistance, she'd already given up on him.

In fact, whores were not really what Albers wanted — there were dangers here, one had to be careful of one's health — but he had been driven to it. Before the war, life in this area had always gone his way, he'd never had to pay for it. In what the Americans called the Roaring Twenties, he'd done his roaring in the nightclubs of Berlin, where sad days — a war lost, inflation, ruin — led to wild nights. What those girls wouldn't do! Nothing he'd ever been able to think up. His complicated suggestions had always been met with greedy enthusiasm. *Ach ja!* How fine to encounter such an ingenious gentleman.

In the thirties, his luck held. Joining the Nazi Party in 1933, he'd made good use of the blond maidens whose patriotic duty it was to fuck his brains out. Usually in a forest, on a carpet of pine needles, but he'd learned to live with that. The fantasies were pretty much the same, only the girls had given up slinking in favor of frolicking, the prescribed form for Aryan womanhood. Sullen ennui gave way to lusty giggles and they saved a bundle on the eye shadow.

But Paris was a different proposition. Stationed at Gestapo headquarters, essentially a military clerk, he discovered that Frenchwomen were not quite as he'd imagined. Many of them wouldn't have anything to do with Germans, which was understandable, but some would. Unfortunately, the best of those went to the officers, and what remained for the enlisted men was not to Albers's taste. Very materialistic, he thought. They didn't want exotic adventures, they wanted little gifts.

For a long time, he tried. A chubby redhead, who worked in a shop; an overworked housewife, her husband off somewhere; but they turned him down. For one thing, there were language difficulties. He wasn't sure how the French talked about such things, to be subtle or artful was out of the question. 'What,' they said, freezing up, 'do you want?' Forced to say words from a dictionary, he came off as a boor or a pervert, or both.

But none of this mattered on the rue St.-Denis. You paid for your pleasures and the

182

women were quick to figure out what you wanted and what you would pay to get it.

A gray, bleak afternoon, Albers walked with hands in pockets, past frowzy blondes and swarthy Corsicans, past a fat girl stuffed into a child's jumper, past a *dominatrice* wearing a broad leather belt and a fearsome scowl. Past housemaids and Marie Antoinettes and femmes fatales with cigarette holders. Oh the trashy circus of it, he thought, yearning for the giggling pine maidens in their dirndls.

But wait, wait one minute, what have we here? Brown hair snipped off in a pageboy, tatty old coat, submissive little smile, spectacles, and holding no less than a Bible in both hands. Both mittens. A mouse! Why not? It was, Albers thought, at least a beginning.

EVREUX. 14 DECEMBER.

They drove north in the late afternoon, slowly. With snow and ice on the roads, the old Renault skidded now and then. Bare trees, empty fields. Weiss did not like the countryside in the winter.

He was a doctor that day, which allowed him, under Occupation rules, to drive the car. A pediatrician, working in the factory districts. Surprising, the number of doctors and nurses in the party — a year or two working with the poor and they joined up. But, of course, nothing guaranteed anything; the doctor who wrote under the name Céline had worked with the poor, and now shrieked against the Jews on the radio.

Outside the town of Mantes he had to apply the brakes and slid to a stop behind a Wehrmacht truck. Troops with rifles between their knees sat on facing benches.

'Look at them,' Ivanic said.

'Better not,' Weiss said. 'They don't like to be looked at.'

Slow truck, Weiss thought, maybe he should pass. But there was possibly a motorcycle in front, or a staff car, and they might stop him. His papers were good. A doctor's black bag was on the seat in the back, and Ivanic would be explained as a patient. *This man has tuberculosis, please don't get too close to him. Sir.*

Weiss looked at the men in the truck. A sergeant sat on the end of the bench, his white face vacant, almost hypnotized. Weiss pulled out to pass, the Renault coughed and sputtered. Slowly, he overtook the truck. Then he saw a car speeding toward him. Now this, he thought. The other driver saw he was stuck in the passing lane and slowed to a crawl, but the driver of the truck never touched his brakes. Weiss finally pulled back in — behind another Wehrmacht truck. Apparently he was in the middle of a convoy.

'Where are they going, do you think?' Ivanic said.

'One of the ports, Caen or Antwerp. Off to Russia, maybe.'

'That must be it,' Ivanic said. Then, softly, to the men looking out the opening in the canvas cover, 'Good-bye.'

The Russians were fighting back now, finally. It took forever to get anything organized in that place, Weiss thought. With them, chaos was fine art. He'd been there twice — more than enough. Ordered to Moscow in 1934 and again in '37, he'd somehow survived both purges. He'd made a point of staying away from the cliques, the *khvosts*, and luck had handed him one or two of the right bosses. Also, he kept his mouth shut, kept his opinions to himself. In Paris, before the war, he'd met Willi Muenzenberg, who ran magazines and cultural events for the Comintern. A law unto himself, Muenzenberg — Moscow could say what it wanted, he was a citizen of the world. 'We should get together sometime,' he told Weiss. 'And talk things over.' It never happened, Weiss made sure it never happened. In the days after the Germans reached Paris, amid the general disorder, Muenzenberg was beaten up and hanged from a tree.

He passed the second truck, and a third, the road was empty after that. Weiss accelerated. The Renault backfired, ran like a greyhound for half a mile, then settled back to three cylinders, valves tapping like a drum solo, the smell of gasoline so strong they had to open the windows.

'What's going on with Casson and Kovar?' Weiss said.

'Kovar's not so easy. We had him, then we lost him. We've gone back to Somet but, according to him, Kovar materialized out of the night, then disappeared. We'll find him, of course. Only a matter of time.'

'What about the other one, Casson?'

Ivanic shrugged. 'Say when.'

★ ★ ★

They came to a village, shut down for winter, squat little granite houses and a Norman church. 'What's this?' Weiss asked.

'Bonnières.'

'Hm.'

'Not far now.'

'No.'

'Looks like the road goes left, over the bridge.'

He drove straight ahead. The street narrowed to a lane, a young girl leading a cow on a rope moved over to let them by. '*Merde*,' Weiss said. The lane ended at a meadow. Weiss started to back up to turn around. Reverse gear whined and the wheels spun in the icy mud. He swore.

'Hold on, I'll give us a push.'

'In a minute.' Weiss pressed the clutch pedal to the floor, let it up very, very slowly until he felt the wheels start to turn. The car moved backward. He stopped, shifted into first gear, got halfway round, backed up, then drove down the lane. The little girl still had the cow over to one side — she lived in Bonnières, she knew they'd be back.

Weiss turned right at the bridge, a sign on the other side said EVREUX 34.

* * *

It took some time to find Brico's street. The workers' district ran on forever, high walls, barely enough room for the car. Weiss could see redbrick chimney stacks in the distance, smoke barely moving in the frozen air. Finally, rue de Verdun. The Germans would eventually change the name, but they probably weren't in a hurry to come in here. Weiss looked at his watch. It was a few minutes after five. Unless the shift worked overtime, the workers would be heading home. Brico was a party member. He'd helped to distribute *Le Métallo*, a version of *Humanité* for metal workers, edited by Narcisse Somet. Too bad, Weiss thought, but that didn't change anything, that only made it worse.

Weiss parked the car, then settled down to watch the rearview mirror. The street was deserted, only an orange-and-white cat lying curled up on Brico's windowsill. Brico's door opened, a lean woman in an apron banged a dust mop against the edge of the stone step, said something to the cat, then went back inside.

The first workers started to come off shift; a teenager racing his bicycle, two men riding side by side. The factory whistle sounded twice, and twice again.

'Any sign?' Ivanic said.

'No.'

Ivanic reached inside his jacket, took out an automatic pistol, and freed the magazine from the grip. He studied the top bullet and pressed it lightly with his finger to make sure the spring had tension before reassembling the gun, ramming the magazine home with the heel of his hand.

'Everything all right?'

Ivanic nodded.

'Don't go inside,' Weiss said.

'I won't.'

Weiss glanced in the mirror. A crowd of men were walking up the street. A moment later, Brico. Ivanic knew before Weiss had a chance to say anything, pulled the brim of his cap down low and got out of the car.

Weiss watched the two of them talking. He saw Ivanic nod his head toward the car. Brico said something, Ivanic agreed, and the two of them walked slowly toward him. Ivanic waited while Brico climbed into the back seat, then got in next to him. As the car moved off, the two of them talked, about production schedules, cell meetings, leaflets. Brico seemed to know a lot about what went on in the factory. He was short and muscular, with big hands, and very sure of himself.

'They put the shift back up to twelve hours,' he said. 'After all the shit we went through in '38.'

Weiss turned down a back road at the edge of the town and parked by a field. Brico said, 'What's all this?'

Weiss spoke for the first time. 'When Renan was shot, the Germans knew what was going on. You turned him in.'

'That's a lie,' Brico said.

'No,' Weiss said. 'We know.'

189

'I have a family,' Brico said.

'So did Renan.'

Ivanic took the gun from inside his jacket. Brico swallowed. 'It had to be like that,' he said. 'You people sit down there in Paris — ' He didn't finish. It was quiet in the car.

'Out,' Ivanic said.

Weiss watched as Brico, head down, walked away from the car. Ivanic took him into the field and shot him.

★ ★ ★

The lawyer's office was in the lawyers' district, on the rue Château-d'Eau. This was not the neighborhood for grand offices, Casson thought, his old lawyer friends wouldn't be caught dead here. This was where the notaries worked, and the *huissiers* — bailiffs — who collected bad debts by breaking down the door and taking everything except, by law, a bed, a chair, and a cooking pot. The lawyers on these streets made out wills, then helped the heirs sue each other, these lawyers presided over property disputes that carried over from one generation to the next. And these lawyers defended criminals, like the merchant Vasilis.

Casson climbed the staircase, passing a variety of *avocats* and *notaires*, a marriage broker and an astrologer, before he found the office — a cramped room on the top floor. 'Georges Soutane,' the lawyer said, as they shook hands. Sharp, Casson thought. Beginning to thicken in his late thirties but still boyish, with sharp eyes, and essentially fearless. His desk was piled high with papers — separated only by a green ribbon tied around each file. After a few pleasantries, he got down to business. 'Captain Vasilis is in prison,' he said.

That much Casson knew, the inspector had told him.

'In Holland,' he added.

'For a long time?'

'A couple of months to go,' the lawyer said. 'It's an occupational hazard.'

'What's he in jail for?'

'Herring. A boat working out of Rotterdam, without licenses.'

'We have something a little different in mind.'

'Of course. But what matters here is money. If you're prepared to pay, we're ready to consider almost anything.'

'We're prepared to pay.'

'What, in general terms if you like, are we talking about?'

Casson paused. 'I would prefer to discuss it with Captain Vasilis.'

191

'Well, I'll have to take you up there, so you can expect to pay for my time along with everything else. What's the scale of the purchase?'

'Significant. A million francs at least, likely a good deal more.'

Now the lawyer was interested. He looked Casson over. One of those individuals, Casson thought, with no family or social connections to ease his way in the world, but smart, very smart — only his mind between him and the poorhouse. 'There's question of currency,' he said. 'It's something we'll have to talk about.'

'You have a preference?'

'We'll take Swiss francs, gold, diamonds, American dollars. If this is going to involve French francs, it will require some negotiation. I won't say we'll refuse, but the figure is going to be higher — we'll have to discount the rate heavily in our favor. To be blunt with you, monsieur, French currency simply isn't worth anything.'

'Yes, we know that.'

'And you will have to pay a very substantial portion of the money before we can proceed.'

'We know that too,' Casson said.

The lawyer nodded — *so far, so good.* 'We will consider anything of value,' he said.

'Paintings, for example. Substantial properties in the countryside. A business, or even a hotel.'

'Money would be best,' Casson said.

'For us as well.' The lawyer opened a drawer and took out a small calender with circled dates. 'This coming Thursday — is that too soon for you?'

'Not at all.'

'Thursday is visiting day. Other arrangements are possible, but this is the simplest way. You'll have to tell the prison authorities you're a lawyer, or a relative.'

'What kind of prison is it?'

'The administration is Dutch, not German. It's a prison for tax evaders, people like that. Captain Vasilis has a room in the hospital.'

'Not too bad, then.'

'No. This is the sort of thing that can happen in peacetime just as easily as in war. One other thing I'll need to ask you. I trust your identity papers will permit you to cross borders — without, ah, special attention?'

'It won't be a problem.'

'Good. Officially, you'll be my associate. The prison administration is quite understanding.' He took a railway timetable from the drawer. 'There's a local that leaves from the Gare du Nord Thursday morning at 9:08. The local is the French train — the Germans

193

like to get places in a hurry so they take the express. If the track hasn't been blown up, we'll be in Amsterdam by early evening, and we can see Captain Vasilis the following morning.'

Casson stood to go. 'I'll see you on Thursday, then.'

'Yes. One last thing — of course we assume that you're coming to see us in good faith. I should mention, however, that Captain Vasilis has friends, loyal friends, everywhere. As long as you're legitimate, pay what we agree, take delivery, and that's the last we hear about it, there would be no reason for you to meet them.'

'That's understood,' Casson said. 'And equally true for us.'

★ ★ ★

7:30 A.M., Hélène Schreiber walked through the morning darkness and went into the travel agency. Her friend Natalie was already at her desk and they chatted for a while. Office buildings had at least some heat, apartments were cold in the daytime — better to come to work early and stay as long as possible.

Hélène was filing carbon copies when somebody said good morning. She looked up

194

to see Madame Oris, the supervising agent. They smiled as they said hello, had liked each other since the first day they'd met. 'Can you come and see me, Hélène? Around eleven?'

Hélène agreed. Madame Oris returned to the glass-topped cubicle that went with her position. She was a tall woman, thin and worried and courtly, who had worked for the agency for thirty years, a dedicated soul who had made a career of cleaning up other people's messes. When she'd first met Hélène she'd recognized a kindred spirit — one didn't cut corners, one rose to emergencies. Now nearing seventy, Madame Oris had let it be known that she was going to retire.

Natalie leaned over and said, 'Today is the day.'

'I think so,' Hélène said. The job was hers if she wanted it.

'What are you going to do?'

Hélène shook her head, as if she didn't know.

Natalie's whisper was fierce. 'You can't give in to that *garce*!' Bitch.

Hélène had an enemy in the office, a young woman named Victorine; pretty and cold, with a bright manner, and very ambitious. She wasn't shy about going after what she wanted. 'I'm sure you've heard that Madame

Oris is leaving,' she'd said. 'There's a chance I can have her job.'

Only if Hélène turned it down. Back in May, when Madame Oris first mentioned retirement, most of the people in the office had let Hélène know they were glad she'd be taking over. But Victorine had a different view. 'What a terrible day,' she'd said one evening as they were leaving the office. 'A couple from Warsaw, they wouldn't take no for an answer.' Hélène was politely sympathetic, but Victorine's voice sharpened as she continued. 'Isn't it odd,' she'd said, 'how *certain people* feel they should have whatever they want? They just grab it, not a thought for the rest of the world. What would you call such people?'

You, Hélène thought, *would call them Jews*.

How had she found out? Hélène didn't know, but the statement was aimed directly at her, a threat, and it had to be taken seriously. Because a German decree in April had forbidden Jews to work in companies where there was contact with the public. Would Victorine turn her in? To the owner of the agency? To the Gestapo? Or was it a bluff?

In the next few weeks, a number of things went inexplicably wrong. For example, Madame Kippel's lost steamship ticket

— Hélène's fault? Or stolen from her desk? Or, mysteriously, Monsieur Babeau in the wrong Spanish hotel; a sputtering, static-filled phone call summoning up the lower depths of Madrid, bandits and highwaymen and no flush-chain on the porcelain squatter.

'No highwayman would ever put up with *that*,' Natalie said later. But it wasn't exactly funny. If Victorine had sabotaged Hélène's clients, she was easily capable of denunciation.

You have until eleven, Hélène told herself. But she'd already made a decision. 'I don't want to give in to anybody,' she explained to Natalie. 'On the other hand, what I really want is peace.'

Natalie looked glum. If Victorine got the job she'd make Natalie's life miserable, because Natalie was Hélène's friend. 'But,' she said, 'what about the money?'

She'd thought about it. The raise wasn't much, but it might be enough for her to bribe her way into a new apartment — even without a residence permit. Tempting, but Victorine could kill any chance of a paycheck. 'The money's not bad,' she said. 'But money isn't everything.'

Natalie was about to answer, then abruptly said, '*Attention!*'

Victorine was coming down the aisle, back

straight, chin held high, a stack of dossiers in her hands.

'*Bonjour,* Hélène,' she said.

'*Bonjour,* Victorine.'

'Did I see Madame Oris stop by?'

'You did.'

'Oh Hélène, this is going to be such an important day for you. I hope you do the right thing.'

Behind her back, Natalie made a Victorine face — a beaming mock smile.

'I'm sure I will,' Hélène said. She could hear the defeat in her voice.

Victorine swept off, her skirt swinging. 'See you later,' she sang.

Natalie shook her head in disbelief. 'Hélène, can I ask you a question?'

'Of course.'

'Does she *have* something on you?'

'No.'

'It's in her voice,' Natalie said. 'We're friends, Hélène. If you need help, you should tell me.'

'I know.' The urge to confide was strong, but she fought it off. 'Really, I know.'

Natalie waited a moment longer, then went back to work. Hélène stared at a pile of confirmations that had come in by teleprinter the night before. Herr and Frau Von Schaus, arriving 20 December for one week at the

Plaza-Athénée. Madame Dupont, by first-class compartment to Rome.

Her phone rang, the office intercom. 'Yes?'

'Hélène, there's a couple waiting in the *réception.*'

'I'll be right there.'

'You're going to give up, aren't you,' Natalie said.

Hélène nodded.

⋆ ⋆ ⋆

She saw Casson that night — waited for him in the park across from the Benoit. He came over and sat next to her on the bench, sensed right away that something was wrong. 'What is it?' he said. She told him everything. He sighed at the end, a fatalist, a realist — he didn't want her to know what went on inside him. 'Well,' he said, 'of course you had to give her what she wanted.'

'I know. It just made me sick to do it.'

'Now that she's got the job, will she shut up?'

'I think so. The triumph should be enough for her, that, and rubbing my nose in it.'

Casson sat back against the bench and put his hands in his pockets. 'The war will end, Hélène. And, when it does, a lot of scores will be settled.'

'Yes, that's what I keep telling myself. Oh, if you could just see her. She has the shape of a hen.'

'How did she find out?'

Hélène shook her head. 'Guessed, maybe. Do I look Jewish?'

He didn't think so. She had dark, glossy hair, deep eyes, strong features, a face that was, at times, seductive for no reason he could think of. Like half the women in Paris, he thought. 'Not to me,' he said.

She stood and took his hand; despite the cold her skin was hot and damp. 'Let's walk,' she said.

They walked through the park. The bare branches of the chestnut trees were stark against the sky. At the entrance there was a bust of Verlaine.

'I've talked to Degrave,' he said. 'He told me he might be able to get you out in February, or maybe March. Until then, the important thing is to survive. Whatever you have to do.'

'You must survive, you must survive.' She stared down at the ground for a time. 'I'll tell you something I discovered, JeanClaude. You can be scared for only so long, then a day comes when you don't care anymore.'

★　★　★

Belgium in December. Through the cloudy window of a slow train. Like a pastoral drawing from the nineteenth century, he thought. Black and white and a hundred shades of gray; cows by a stream in a field, cows by a stream in a field, cows . . . A lone elm in the mist, a farmer in rubber boots, his dog by his side.

Casson dozed off, then woke up suddenly and made sure the paper-wrapped parcel was still on the seat next to him. Expensive, almost *very* expensive. What seemed like a mindless errand had sent him deep into the heart of his old neighborhood, where every passing stranger threatened to turn into somebody he knew.

The train rattled along, stopping at every village. He shared the first-class compartment — the German border guards tended to go easy on first-class passengers — with a Belgian couple and two French businessmen. The lawyer was riding in another car, a safety precaution. The Belgian couple started eating in Cambrai and never quite stopped. Slow and determined, unsmiling, they opened a wicker basket and worked their way from radishes to salted beef tongue, to some kind of white, waxy cheese, then to small, dried-out winter apples, demolishing a loaf of bread in the process. They didn't talk, or look out the window. Just chewed, from Valenciennes to Mons. Casson pretended not to notice. It made him hungry, but he was used to that. When the couple got off the train, one of the businessmen, in an aside to his friend, said something about *vaches*, cows. But it was just bravado, Casson realized, they were hungry too.

* * *

The guards at Esschen, on the Dutch-Belgian border, were looking for somebody. They made all the passengers get out and stand by the train. *The package.* He made a fast decision, fumbled with his coat until everyone had left the compartment, then slid it under the seat across from his.

On the platform, the border guards were angry, Casson was shoved with a rifle. 'You. Get over there.' It hurt more than it should have. There was an old Frenchman next to him, a dignified little man in a white goatee, who stood at attention, shoulders back, waiting for the Germans to let them go.

Casson could hear the guards searching the railroad car. Stomping down the aisles, slamming doors. He heard glass breaking, somebody laughed. An hour later, when they got back on, his package was where he'd left it. The train crawled north. Night fell. Casson could see the evening star. The old man, now sitting across from him, fell sound asleep, mouth wide open, breath whistling through his nose.

★ ★ ★

The prison was in Zunderdorp, across the Nordzee Canal from the main part of Amsterdam. They walked through silent streets for a long time, showed their papers to various guards, and finally to a prison official in a gray suit. They climbed an iron staircase to the top floor and were led past a tier of cells to a small, private room in the hospital.

Captain Vasilis rose from a hospital bed, embraced his lawyer, and shook Casson's hand. He wore a robe over silk pajamas and good leather slippers. He had red-rimmed eyes set in heavy pouches, two days' growth of gray beard on a face that ended in three chins, a voice like a rake drawn through gravel.

'Forgive us a minute,' he said to Casson. The accent was so heavy it took Casson a moment to realize the man had spoken French. The three of them sat at a small table. Vasilis and the lawyer leaned close to each other and spoke in low voices.

Casson could hear what they were saying, but it didn't matter. 'Did he go over there?' Vasilis asked.

'Not yet. His friend wasn't ready.'

'When will it happen?'

'A week, maybe. The new figure is a little higher.'

'We don't care.'

'No.'

'You can say something?'

'It won't help.'

'Let it go, then.'

Eventually, Vasilis turned to him and said, 'Sorry, business.'

'I understand,' Casson said. He handed over the package.

Vasilis tore the paper off and cradled the melon in both hands. 'Thank you,' he said. 'Thank you.' He smelled the soft end, then pressed it expertly with his thumbs. 'Very nice,' he said. He took a pair of glasses from the breast pocket of his bathrobe, looked at Casson for a moment, then put them away. 'What are you?'

'I'm in the insurance business.'

'*Ouay?*' He drew the *oui* out to form the slang *oh yeah?* Then nodded in a way that meant *and if my grandmother had wheels she would've been a cart.*

'Yes, that's what I do.'

204

'D'accord.' If that's the way you want it, fine. He turned to the lawyer and said, 'What time?'

'Almost noon.'

'Hey!' the captain shouted. 'Van Eyck!'

The door opened, a guard peered into the room.

'Bring trays!'

'Yes, Captain,' the guard said, closing the door politely behind him.

Vasilis met Casson's eyes and shook his head sorrowfully — you can barely imagine what this is costing me.

'Sir,' he said to Casson, 'what you want?'

'Submachine guns. Six hundred of them. And ammunition.'

'Guns?' Vasilis sucked in his breath like a man who just burned his fingers. The expense!

'Yes,' Casson said. 'We know.'

'Very difficult.'

Casson nodded, sympathetic.

'What for?'

Casson didn't answer immediately — wasn't it obvious? — but Vasilis waited. Finally he said, 'Freedom.'

Vasilis sighed, the sound of a doomed man. Now he had to involve himself in difficulties. He turned to the lawyer. 'You tell him what cost?'

'No.'

'I can get MAS 38 for you. French gun. You know problem?'

'No.'

'Cartridge is 7.65. You still want it?'

'We're buying a thousand rounds per gun.'

'Yes, but after that, *pfft.*'

'That's our problem.'

'A hundred and fifty American dollars for each. Ninety thousand dollars. Three million six hundred thousand in French francs — premium sixty percent if you want to pay that way. Four hundred fifty thousand Swiss. We prefer.'

'What about ammunition?'

'Six hundred thousand rounds — a box of two hundred is three American, so nine thousand dollars, forty-five thousand Swiss. Still good?'

'Yes.'

'For guns, all paid before we ship.'

'All?'

'Yes. You want figs, or shoes, it's different.'

'All right. Agreed.'

'You sell to somebody?'

'No.'

'Four hundred ninety-five thousand Swiss. It's made?'

'Yes. When can it be done?'

'These guns are in Syria. In the armories of

the French Occupation force. We bring them in caïque — fishing boat. Two tons, a little more. You know Mediterranean?'

'Well — '

'It eat ships. And sailors. So then, we give back half.'

'All right.'

'Any chance you pay gold?'

'No.'

'Will discount.'

'It will have to be Swiss francs.'

'All right. We deliver to Marseilles, the lawyer will give you a few days' notice. It will be at warehouse, maybe on dock. We'll let you know.'

'Money to the lawyer?'

'Yes. When you bring?'

'A few days.'

'We start then.' He made a spitting noise toward his hand, thrust it out and Casson shook it. 'Done,' Vasilis said.

★   ★   ★

Isidor Szapera didn't really recover from being shot during the attempted robbery at Aubervilliers. He couldn't run — he dragged a foot when he walked — and he had almost no strength at all in one hand. At night, his back ached where he'd been wounded and it was hard to sleep. They'd taken him to a home for retired railroad workers out in Saint-Denis, where a doctor had removed some of the bullet, but not all of it. When he could walk again, the party had offered to hide him with a family in the south, but he'd turned them down, 'I can do something,' he'd said.

They trained him to operate a wireless telegraph — they suffered constant losses in radio operators, were always recruiting for that position. He worked hard hours, late into the night. He missed Eva Perlemère, and was angry at himself for having lost her. She haunted his dreams, sometimes he saw her undressing, sometimes he saw her face, eyes closed, as they were making love. The dreams woke him up.

Another loss, he thought, the Germans would have to pay for. He practiced on the dummy telegraph key until his hand throbbed. By late December he was ready to go to work and they stationed him in the attic of a house in Montrouge, just outside Paris.

He was assigned a liaison girl, Sylvie. Skinny and somber, eighteen, a pharmacy student at the Sorbonne. Her job was to maintain a clandestine apartment and telephone, to accept and relay messages, to deliver wireless transmissions as they came in from Russia, to take the answers back to the W/T operator for encryption and transmission. Liaison girls tended to last a few months, not much longer.

Szapera liked Sylvie because she was all business. *La Vierge*, they called her when she wasn't around, the virgin. Some of the FTP men had tried to seduce her, but she wasn't interested. That was fine with Szapera. When Germany was in flames it would be time enough for such things to begin again.

By late December, after the Japanese attack on the USA, the wireless traffic between the Center in Kuibyshev and the Paris stations had gone wild. Everything had changed. *Comrade*, went one message to an FTP commander, *this is no longer a twenty-year war, this is now a two-year war, and we must act accordingly.* Order-of-battle information about the Wehrmacht went east — this unit in Normandy, that divisional insignia seen on a train — along with production norms from French arms factories, diplomatic gossip, intelligence gathered from photographed papers and stolen maps, a vast river of coded signals.

In return, the Kuibyshev Center kept demanding more. They sent orders, instructions, requests for clarification, questionnaires for spies, directions of all kinds: *you will find out, you will watch, you will photograph, you will obtain.* The radio operators could transmit safely for fifteen minutes, but the Center kept them at it for hours.

German signal detection units worked around the clock. Vans with rotating antennas cruised the streets, listening for transmissions, working up and down the scale of the wireless frequencies. The radio operators were assigned lookouts at both ends of the street, to watch for trucks. The Germans knew it, and started to use men carrying suitcases with receiving sets packed inside.

It snowed on the night of 30 December. Just after midnight, a long message came in from the Center. Reception was difficult — somewhere between Kuibyshev and Paris there was an electrical storm, the airwaves crackled and hissed, the Russian operator's dots and dashes disappeared into sudden bursts of static. *Please repeat.* Szapera turned the volume on the receiver up to ten, the end of the dial, played with the tuning device — trying to find clear air on the edge of the frequency, then pressed his hands against the headphones.

At 1:20 the transmission ended. A signal indicated further transmission in fifteen minutes, change of frequency to 3.8 megacycles. Szapera rubbed his eyes, started to decode the previous message. For M20, Comrade Brasova, eight questions for the agent codenamed GAZELLE.

The phone rang. Once Sylvie looked up from her textbook, Szapera stopped writing. 'Signal,' she said.

'Have a look,' Szapera said.

She went to the window, edged the blackout curtain aside. The wet snow melted as it hit the pavement. The building across from her was dark and silent. She raised the window an inch and listened. Slowly, a car drove down the street, turned the corner, and disappeared into the night.

'A car,' she said.

'What kind?'

'Some old kind of car, I don't know which model.'

'Anything else?'

'No.'

Probably a false alarm. Szapera went back to work — after all, he was only in danger when he was transmitting. Final assignment for Brasova's agent: *Have her record the serial number stamped in the margin of the document.* The next section of the transmission was for J42. Weiss, he thought, Item one: At the Lille railway freight office on the rue Cheval . . .

Again, the telephone.

211

'Something's going on,' Szapera said.

'Yes.'

Szapera looked at the small coal stove in the corner, the edges of the firebox door glowed bright orange. He could start burning papers if he felt it was necessary. There was a revolver on the table beside the wireless.

'Who are the lookouts tonight?' he asked.

'There is only one, Fernand. The other is in the hospital.'

'Fernand.' Szapera didn't know him.

'He works in the Citroën plant.'

Szapera thought for a moment, and came up with a compromise. 'Take the messages now,' he said. 'Decryptions and the rest of it, everything that came in tonight.'

'What about you?'

'I'm going to stay for the 1:35 transmission.'

'He signaled twice,' Sylvie said.

'Here. Take it,' Szapera said. He handed her several sheets of paper, cheap stuff with brown flecks in it, covered with tiny numbers and block letters.

Sylvie put on her wool muffler, then her coat. She'd be safe enough in the streets, Szapera thought. The curfew had been moved back for Christmas and New Year, a reward from the Germans for a compliant population.

212

Sylvie stood by the door, her face taut and unsmiling as always. 'I think you should go,' she said.

'No. I'll be all right.'

'The rules are that you should leave.'

'I will. Fifteen minutes, plus whatever time they take to send.' *Goddamn her*, he thought, *she won't go.* She stared at him, her hand on the doorknob. 'I'll make some tea for us,' she said. 'In my room. After we drop off the papers.'

What was this? She felt nothing for him, not that way anyhow. A ruse, he thought. He wanted to mock her, but he didn't have it in his heart to do that, not anymore.

'Wait for me then,' he said. 'At the rue Lenoir apartment, then we'll have tea together.'

For a long moment she stood there, not wanting to leave without him. Finally she said, 'All right, then,' and closed the door behind her.

He heard her walk lightly down the stairs, heard the street door open and shut, then listened at the window as her footsteps receded up the street. Good. Whatever the phone signal meant, the night's transmissions were safe. It wasn't the first time there had been a false alarm. He paced around the room. Now, his decoding work gone, he had nothing to do, not even anything to read. Ah, Sylvie's biology text, left on the chair. He picked it up, thumbed through it. Look at this, he thought, she's written her name on the title page.

Smiling grimly to himself, he tore the page out, took a rag from a nail beside the stove, opened the door and threw it in. *Now she'll be mad at me for damaging her book.* But, really, she should have known better.

He walked over to the table, sat in the office chair and leaned back, putting his feet up. Only a few minutes until the last transmission of the night — his work would be complete, then he could relax. He flipped through the book, stopping now and then to look at the illustrations. A long time since he'd studied this kind of stuff. *The Sea Horse, fish of the genus Hippocampus (See Fig. 18 — Hippocampus hudsonius), belonging to the pipefish family, with prehensile tail and elongated snout, the head at a right angle to the body. While the habitat of the Sea Horse is known to include —*

He went back to the window. Checked his watch. 1:29. Quiet out, dead in this neighborhood. Footsteps? Yes, somebody coming home. No, two people. In a hurry. The street door flew open, the knob banging hard against the wall. People, several of them, pounding up the staircase. What?

His heart fluttered, but he was already moving toward the table. He grabbed the sheaf of encryption tables and shoved them in the stove, threw the rag in after them, and kicked the door closed. *Let them try to grab it barehanded.*

Next, the revolver. He swept it off the table as the footsteps came around the corner of the staircase and down the hall. Could there be some perfectly good explanation? No. Could he get to the roof? No, too late. He pulled back the hammer of the revolver until it cocked. He wasn't going alone, that was certain. And they weren't going to have him alive. A fist pounded on the door, a voice shouted in German.

He fired the first shot, was deafened by the sound. A ragged hole, chest-high, appeared in the door. From the landing, an indignant yelp. Streams of German, hysterical shouting. There was a whole crowd out there. He reminded himself to kneel down, fired a second time, and a third.

The return fusillade blew the door apart, two machine pistols firing on full automatic. Szapera was knocked backward, under the table. He worked himself around to shoot again, knees slipping in blood on the floorboards. He aimed the revolver, the room

215

echoed with the shot, his ears rang. Again they fired through the door. Szapera was amazed, not that a bullet had gone through his heart, had killed him, but that he could still be conscious for the instant it took to know such a thing.

MAS
MODÉLE 38

10 JANUARY, 1942.

Casson boarded the night train to Marseilles at 8:25, at the Gare de Lyons, but they didn't get under way until 10:40 — sabotage on the track at Bourg-la-Reine, according to the conductor.

The train slowed to a crawl and switched over to the northbound track. Casson rested his forehead against the cold window, saw twisted rails that glowed for an instant in the moonlight and a crowd of railwaymen warming their hands at a fire in an iron barrel. A few minutes later they were out in the countryside; patches of snow on the hills, the rivers under the railway bridges frozen to sheets of gray ice.

Just after four in the morning they passed Moulins, on the river Allier. It had become a border town, where the Occupied Zone met the area ruled by Vichy, a few kilometers down the river. By then only one passenger, perhaps a commercial traveler, remained in the compartment. Casson had waded over a branch of the Allier a year earlier, guided by the son of a local aristocrat. April of 1941, Citrine waiting for him in a hotel in Lyons.

The German exit *Kontrol*, leaving what was now called Frankreich, was located at a small station on the northern edge of the city. It was typical, Casson thought. The Germans always seemed to choose isolated, anonymous areas for their operations — you didn't know where you were, there was nowhere to run, whatever happened there was invisible.

But, this time, not too bad. Degrave had made sure he had all the right papers. A few German noncoms boarded the train, tired at that time of night. They glanced at his identity card, peered at the underwear and socks in his valise, then stamped his passport. He was sweating by the time they left the compartment — sometimes they arrested people for no apparent reason.

The train rolled slowly into the main station in Moulins, where the French border police ordered everybody onto the platform and made them stand in line. From all the muttering and grumbling that went on it was clear to Casson that this wasn't the usual procedure.

The line, heading to a table manned by uniformed officers, barely moved. The passengers breathed plumes of steam and stamped their feet. When Casson reached the table, he handed over his identity card with his travel and work permits folded in the middle. The officer took a long, careful look, then said, 'This one out.' He was escorted to a room inside the station, where a civilian official sat at an old metal desk.

He sat down as directed, and handed over his papers. They were spread out, slowly examined, notes were made on a sheet of paper. Outside, he heard the hiss of steam, then the slow progress of the Marseilles train as it moved out of the station.

The official was young, savagely combed and brushed and shaved, wore steel-framed eyeglasses and hair freshly clipped to a perfect line across the back of the neck. He had a sulky mouth, set against the world — born angry and meant to stay that way. Perfect, Casson thought, for a *petit fonctionnaire*. On his desk was a framed photo of Pétain, white-haired and godly. *A portable icon*, Casson thought. *He takes it with him wherever he goes.*

'Monsieur Marin,' he began.

'Yes, sir.'

'Your papers describe you as a claims investigator.'

'Yes, that's right.'

'For the *Compagnie des Assurances Commerciales du Nord.*'

'Yes.'

'Your business in Marseilles?'

'A fire in a storage shed owned by a steamship company.'

'And what will you do, precisely?'

'I will obtain the reports of the police and fire inspectors, will interview the client's representative, visit the site of the event, then make a determination as to the extent of the damage, and write a report for the central office with my recommendations.'

'Where is that office?'

'22, rue de La Boétie. In the 8th Arrondissement.'

'And your supervisor?'

'Monsieur Labatier.'

'And your address?'

'I live at 8, rue Fortuny.'

As Casson talked, the official made notes with a scratchy pen he dipped in an inkwell. 'Please step outside, monsieur,' he said.

Casson did as he was told. The official, in plain view, picked up the telephone on his desk, dialed the operator, requested a number, and waited for the connection. Casson could not hear the conversation, but he guessed that a call to another region probably meant Paris, and almost certainly the préfecture — who else did business on the telephone at that time of the morning? The call went through almost immediately, and the official began reading off information.

He glanced up at Casson, back to the paper, then again.

Behind Casson, in the empty station, a flight of birds took off, he could hear the beating of their wings.

'You will return monsieur.'

He went back into the little room, closing the door behind him. The official picked up the telephone, and dialed two numbers. 'Lieutenant, please station somebody outside my door.' Next, he reread what he'd written, underlining notes he'd taken during his interrogation of Casson and others made during the telephone call. When he was satisfied he had everything he needed, he looked up at Casson, checked the identity card one last time, then tossed it aside.

'Fake,' he said. 'The documents don't check out with the Paris registry.'

Casson looked puzzled. 'How can that be?'

'You tell me.'

Casson shrugged, amused by his own confusion. 'Well . . . ' for a moment, no idea what to say. 'I don't know — the spelling of the name, maybe.'

'There's a possibility you and I can work this out right here, and you can go wherever you're going, but you have to tell me

223

everything. If you do, I might, *might*, be able to help you.'

Casson shook his head. 'A fault in the records? I don't have any idea what it could be.'

The official stared at him. Casson waited.

Thirty seconds, an eternity of silence. The official slid the permits inside the folded identity card and pushed it back across the desk. Casson hesitated, unsure of himself, what was going on? Finally he took the card and put it in the inside pocket of his jacket.

'You may go,' the official said, pure hatred in his eyes.

He rose and left the room.

There was, in fact, a soldier stationed by the door. Casson walked across the platform and stood staring at the empty track. Looking around, he saw that the ticket window was shuttered. A baggage porter trudged past, pushing a two-wheeled cart piled with trunks and suitcases.

'The next train for Marseilles?' Casson said.

The man stopped, lowered the cart, pressed his hand against the small of his back. 'Marseilles?'

'Yes.'

'At noon, monsieur. If it's on time.'

'Thank you,' Casson said. 'Cold this morning.'

'Yes. My wife says it will snow.'

The man thrust his weight against the baggage cart until it started moving. Casson sat on a bench and settled down to wait. Suddenly he was grateful for the whole pirate ship of characters his life had stirred up — lawyers, studio executives, actors' agents. *Forgive me, my friend*, he thought, *but I have been down that road too many times.*

★ ★ ★

January in Marseilles. Gray cloud scudding in from the sea and a cold rain that dripped from the eucalyptus trees. In the Old Port, oil tankers and fishing boats rose on the swell. Casson took a trolley that swayed and clattered along the Corniche, then he climbed an endless staircase to a nest of winding streets where he found Le Pension Welcome. The old ladies who ran the place fussed over him — a wretched day, so cold, so *triste*. They took him to his room, damp as a dungeon with a view of the sea. Citrine, in these places, would say, 'Ah, but cool in summer.' He took off his clothes, washed at the sink, rolled up in a blanket, was glad to be alive.

225

A day later, a message was delivered to the hotel. He took a taxi for a half-hour ride to the village of Cassis. They worked their way up a winding road into the hills above the town, to a villa called La Rosette — the driver had to get out and ask directions along the way.

Degrave met him at the door, wearing a blazer and flannels and looking very much the country squire. Madame Degrave was waiting for him in the hallway, calling to the maid to get him a *kir vin blanc*. Casson remembered what Hélène had said about her — 'mean as a snake,' according to Degrave's girlfriend — but what a snake. Casson was impressed and she knew it. Golden hair turning coppery as she crossed forty, swept around her ears just above the pearl earrings. A thin, twitchy little nose, and the smile they taught in the rich girls' academies. She gave him her hand when Degrave introduced them, dry and fragile and cooperative.

They'd had the villa for years, Degrave explained later, and when the Germans occupied the northern part of the country and the office moved to Vichy, they'd found it prudent to leave the house in the Chevreuse, just outside Paris, for the time being. When

Vasilis had specified delivery in Marseilles — well, one should profit from coincidence.

Casson agreed. Only, washing his hands in the bathroom, staring into the mirror — mustache, glasses, all the rest of it — he hated playing the shabby little man. Because, for the moment, he was back in the 16th. Not really the same crowd, of course, but an outsider wouldn't have known the difference.

A dinner party. Monsieur and Madame this, Monsieur and Madame the other. One was the local something, another a former diplomat, somebody else painted divinely. There was a macedoine of vegetables and mayonnaise to start, Bellet to drink — one bottle followed another. To clear his head, Casson excused himself and stepped outside. A small swimming pool, a hedge of evergreen shrubs dripping rain, and, beyond, the dark sea.

He wondered if she would show up. Not that he would do anything, Degrave was his friend. He was just curious. It wasn't hard to figure out what went on with Degrave and his wife. He had sinned and was not forgiven. What sin? Simply, he had failed to rise. He was not Colonel Degrave and he never would be. Too aloof, too independent for his own good and, in his way, an idealist. His rich wife was disappointed, she made that clear, whenever she felt like it, and Degrave had a girlfriend to make him feel better.

He could see the dining room through the window. Madame, a silhouette in candlelight, got up to do something and glanced out the window. Casson closed his eyes and took a deep breath. Down below somewhere, the sea broke on a rocky beach. He threw the cigarette away and went back inside.

As he sat down at the table, she smiled, omniscient and amused. The woman on his left leaned close to him. 'So, Monsieur Marin, what are they talking about, up in Paris?'

Degrave filled his glass from the new bottle. 'They're cold,' Casson said, 'and miserable, and tired of waiting for it all to go away.'

A plate appeared in front of him, a slice of veal roast and a square of meat jelly, two potatoes, and a mound of those pale little canned peas the French secretly adored.

From the former diplomat: 'Yes? And de Gaulle? What will he do about it?'

'Oh, that man!'

'Pompous ass.'

'How does it go — 'He has the character of a stubborn pig — but at least he *has* character.' '

'Well, I agree with the first part.'

'Who said that?'

'Reynaud. Before the *boches* got him.'

'Reynaud!'

'*Really.*'

'De Gaulle has his friends.'

'Yes, and what friends to have! Poets and professors, philosophers, the whole St.-Germain-des-Près crowd, gossiping in the cafés day and night. Resistance indeed! Resistentialists, somebody called them.'

'Oh Michel, that's funny!'

'It won't be so funny when the war ends and they end up running the country.'

'Well, better than the British.'

'My dear husband sees always the bright side.'

'Damn it, Yvonne . . .'

'Conchita, dear? Yoo-hoo! Would you bring Monsieur Marin a little more of the veal?'

★ ★ ★

When everybody had gone home, Casson and Degrave had a last glass of wine in the living room. 'By the way,' Degrave said quietly, 'I talked to some people about Hélène. They can get her out in March — she has to see a man called de la Barre. He lives in Paris, in the Seventh. You'll tell her when we get back to the city.'

Casson said he would.

'I just wish it could be sooner.'

'Only two months. She'll get through it,' Casson said.

14 JANUARY.

Tuesday morning, the mistral blowing hard, sea ruffled to whitecaps. Casson walked down to the little store that sold everything and bought a copy of *La Méditerranée*. The Wehrmacht had retaken Feodosiya, in the Crimea, submarines had torpedoed an oil tanker off the coast of North Carolina, the Japanese advanced toward Singapore. Fighting the wind, Casson managed to turn to the *Petits Annonces*. Widows to marry, a ladder for sale. And, down the column: To *sell — small apartment above garage. Inquire at Café des Marchands, rue de Rome*. Which meant, your guns have arrived.

★ ★ ★

Later that morning he went to the address the lawyer had given him, the second floor of a building in the Old Port. Inside a high-ceilinged room with fans and tall shutters was one of the Frères Caniti, chandlers, dealing in rope, tar, varnish, and brass fittings.

A strange face, from another century. A black line for a mouth, eyes so deep-set they hid in shadow, sharp cheekbones, a monk's fringe of dark hair. Like a medieval Pardoner in a Book of Hours, Casson thought. A face lit with saintly corruption. 'You're the one come for the shipment?'

'Yes.'

'They've had to go back out to sea. Off Cap Ferrat this morning.'

'Why is that?'

'There's a problem.'

'Our understanding was that there wouldn't be any problems.'

'Well, even so.'

'What's gone wrong?'

'The customs service. Our person there has gone away.'

'And?'

'The new person will need to be compensated.'

'How much?'

'Forty thousand francs.'

Once this starts, he thought, *it doesn't stop.* 'I'll have to see if it's possible.'

'That's up to you. But I wouldn't waste too much time just now.' He nodded at the shutters, which banged and rattled in the wind. 'They can't stay out there forever, not in this. If they have to come into port, and the customs isn't taken care of, the cargo goes over the side.'

'A few hours, then.'

'As you like, monsieur. We stand ready to assist you.'

★ ★ ★

Casson tried the telephones at the central post office, but there were too many detectives — dressed variously as sailors and businessmen — standing around the *cabinets*. He went to a smaller post office. Not perfect, but better.

The lawyer answered immediately.

'What the hell is going on?' Casson said.

'Take it easy, will you? Tell me what happened.'

'We're being held up for money. 'Oh yes, one last thing.' '

'That's impossible.'

'No, it just happened.'

'Who's involved?'

'Someone in the Old Port.'

'*Merde.*'

'Do something or it's finished. We'll send people to get the money back.'

'Let me try to take care of it.'

232

'Please understand — we don't have a lot of time.'

'How's it being put?'

'Somebody who used to help us isn't helping anymore. Now, a new person has to be taken care of.'

'Hmm. Help in, uh, getting things stamped?'

'Yes.'

'All right. Where can I reach you?'

'I'll call you. How late are you there, tonight?'

'Seven-thirty. Eight.'

'I'll call back then. Maybe a little earlier.'

'All right. Don't worry, I'll get it taken care of.'

'Let's hope so. I'll talk to you later.'

'Good-bye.'

* * *

The Paris workshop of Robes Juno was on the second floor of a firetrap factory on the rue de Turenne, in the garment district. Marcel Slevin sat on a stool at his worktable, while up and down the aisles, women worked away at clattering sewing machines.

At twenty, a cutter, an aristocrat of the trade. If he didn't get the pattern just right, nothing fit, the stores shipped the stuff back, end of season, end of Robes Juno. He took a used piece of yellow tracing paper from the wastebasket, tore off a corner. A little note to Comrade Weiss, he needed to see him.

Tough at twenty, he'd been on his own since he was sixteen and his father threw him out. No use for school, ran with the wrong crowd, gambled, drank, screwed — 'Out!' That was all right with him. From then on, he did what he liked and made sure he had the *fric* to pay for it. He got a job as a delivery boy at Robes Juno, worked hard, played hard, and joined the garment workers' local of the CGT, the communist labor union.

The family wasn't completely gone, he had an uncle he kept in touch with, his mother's brother, who saw life the same way he did. 'We're two of a kind, you and me,' he'd say. Slevin *père* was a Talmudic scholar, too holy and righteous to soil his hands making a living. Now and then he would buy and sell used office equipment, but mostly they lived on little bits of money that came their way, which Slevin's mother managed so ferociously that they never quite starved. The evening of the Big Fight, Slevin had spent his savings to buy a Zazou coat, long and narrow, *très gangster*, much in favor among the guys who hung around the Pam-Pam and the

Colisée. He wore it home from the store, they told him to take it back, he told them what he thought of them, and out he went.

Well, that was that. But he'd survived, had worked his way up to cutter, and Uncle Misch kept an eye on him. Smart, Uncle Misch. December of 1940, he'd found a way the family could get out of France, an old friend in South Africa was willing to help. But they couldn't go — his father's mother and aunt, in their eighties and frail, had to be taken care of, would never have survived the journey. So now they were all stuck.

His uncle always had a few francs. He played the markets, bought and sold goods 'that fell off a truck,' and eventually came to own five or six little buildings around the ragged southern edge of Paris. Most of his tenants were Arabs, or Russian refugees from 1917, but one of his apartments wasn't all that bad. Now he had a German renting it. 'He lives in the barracks, down near Orly airfield, but he wanted a place in Paris.' A bomber pilot, his uncle said, who used the place for relaxation when he wasn't busy setting London on fire. 'A very refined gentleman,' his uncle said, 'with a *Von* in front of his name. Goes out in a tuxedo.'

A bomber pilot. Slevin thought about that for a long time. Like thoroughbred horses, he figured. Hard to replace — you lost one of them, it mattered. Right about then, the guys in the union had put the word out — *it's time to deal with these assholes*. For a year and a half they'd swaggered around the city, had free run of the place, made themselves at home. That had to stop. The message was clear: *Uncle Joe needs you to break some heads.*

A kid named Isidor Szapera, somebody Slevin knew to say hello to from the old neighborhood, had gotten there ahead of him. He'd never thought much of Szapera, with his good grades in school and his rich, *zaftig* girlfriend. Mr. Perfect. But Slevin had to admit, coming across the name in the newspapers — *a hunted terrorist, thought to have been wounded* — he felt a sharp little stab of jealousy. So now, it was his turn. And he wasn't after clerks, or payroll trucks. *Bomber pilots.*

Now, for the note. *Mon cher Monsieur Weiss?* No. *Cher comrade*, then. No. Still too flowery. Just *Comrade* would do. That was straightforward, man-to-man. He went on to request a meeting, and suggested an answer could reach him at the factory. He slipped the note in an envelope, put his jacket on, and headed for the door.

On the way out he passed the new Polish

girl, a whirlwind at her sewing machine. 'Hey,' he said.

She looked up, startled. He was beetle-faced and small, his eyebrows grew together, and when he stood still he seemed to tremble with something held tight inside him, energy or anger.

'You like to go dancing?' he said.

Now she got it. 'Well, sometimes.'

'Want to go with me? Thursday?'

'I can't, Thursday.'

'How about Friday?'

'Well, all right.' She shook her hair back and smiled at him.

'I have to go out for a minute, when I come back we'll make a time and place to meet.'

Whistling, he headed down the factory floor and out into the office. 'Back in twenty minutes,' he called to the receptionist. The boss, drinking a cup of tea at his desk, looked up at him, but didn't say anything. Bosses were a dime a dozen, the way Slevin saw it, but good cutters were hard to find.

Hunched over, hands in pockets, he hurried down Turenne, then turned on Ste.-Anastase. The street was blocked by trucks picking up racks of coats and dresses — it might be winter everywhere else but it was spring on the rue Ste.-Anastase. Florals, green and red, big patterns. And big sizes. *For the big German bitches,* he thought. Just once before he died he'd like to —

'Hey, *mec.*'

Louis, a guy he knew from party meetings. They shook hands, talked for a minute. 'I've got to run,' Slevin said.

Louis punched him on the shoulder. 'Sunday night.'

'I'll be there.'

Two models came toward him, holding their arms around themselves to keep warm; wool hats pulled down over their ears. No modesty in these girls, he thought. They walked around in their slips all day while the buyers and the salesmen used them as mannequins. He gave them a look, but they pretended he didn't exist. *Snobs.*

He cut over to Thorigny, then went down Elzévir. A nice laundress owned a shop there, sweet if you got on her good side. It was closed now — any reason? Stupid war, you never knew what was what. Over to Francs-Bourgeois, a narrow street but a main thoroughfare. Sometimes a German patrol came through here. He walked another minute, then stopped at an open stall where they sold dried fruit and nuts and took bets on horse races. He looked over the bins and his mouth watered; figs and dates and almonds and raisins. 'Fifty grams of dried apricots,' he said. He hadn't meant to do this, but he couldn't resist.

He got the fruit and ate an apricot while waiting to pay. Fresh inside, soft, sharp, and delicious. He handed over the money, then the envelope. 'This is for Monsieur Gris.'

The boy nodded. He was about fifteen, kept his yarmulke on with a bobby pin. The envelope disappeared into the fold of his apron.

'Thanks,' Slevin said.

★ ★ ★

Tuesday night, Casson called the lawyer in Paris. 'It's been straightened out,' the lawyer said.

'You're sure?'

'Very sure. Go back tomorrow morning, everything is arranged.'

'All right.'

'I don't know what gets into people. Enough is never enough.'

★ ★ ★

Casson went back on Wednesday morning — it was as though nothing had happened. *We tried to cheat you, but you refused to be cheated, so now life goes on in the ordinary*

239

way. *Business is business, we know you'll understand.*

'We'll bring it in tonight. Around 1:30, but it could be later if the weather stays like this.'

'Delivered to the pier.'

'Yes, as specified. We'd like it moved before daylight.'

'Of course.'

A clerk knocked at the door and brought in demitasse cups of strong coffee, the real thing.

'I hope you'll take a coffee with me.'

Nervous, Casson thought. Maybe even scared. The lawyer had found a way to be very persuasive.

'I wonder,' Casson said, 'If we could buy some kind of merchandise, a normal Marseilles-Paris shipment, to cover up our crates?'

'What did you have in mind? Something in bulk, like jute? We ship it in burlap sacks.'

'No, we'll want boxes of some kind. What about salt cod?'

'It would work, but we don't have it. Closer to Easter we have it all the time.'

'What, then?'

'Sardines,' he said. 'Tins packed in crates.'

'All right, sardines. How many crates would we need?'

'*Tiens.*' He took a stub of pencil and a

240

scrap of paper from a drawer. 'Your shipment from Syria is packed six to a crate — a hundred crates, thirty-eight pounds each, with the accompanying merchandise taking eight crates. So, a hundred and eight crates total, approximately . . . say, two tons.'

He jotted down a few numbers. 'So then,' he said, 'if you stack ten high, let's see, eighty inches, say you go two by five, six by eleven feet. Put your eight additional boxes on their sides, about a foot. Then, to cover, you need a height of ten inches — sardine crates — times eight, then, also, you'll want a double row in the back, given the way they operate at road blocks. So then, multiply by eleven, ten up. I would say . . . it looks to me like two hundred crates will do it. Which I can let you have at my price — ninety-six tins to a case, two hundred cases — call it a hundred and twenty thousand francs. Of course the jute would be less expensive, I'll be happy to give you a price. But if you put the sardines on the black market in Paris, you'll make that back easily. They aren't bad, by the way. Packed in oil.'

'Olive oil?'

'Oil.'

Casson nodded. 'I can give you the money tonight.'

'You see, if you have the two hundred crates, and you have a double stack in the

241

rear of the truck, it won't be a problem if you have to tell somebody, a policeman, 'and while you're back there, make sure and take a couple of crates for your family.' '

'You'll have them delivered to the dock?'

'Our pleasure, monsieur.'

15 JANUARY.

The mistral sharpened after midnight and it started to rain in sudden gusts that drummed on the roof of the Pension Welcome and spattered the open shutters. Casson stared down at the waterfront; a set of slow-moving headlights, amber blurs in the raindrops on the window. He put out a cigarette, lit another, looked at his watch. Paced the room, went back to the window.

A knock at the door.

'Yes?'

'Monsieur, your taxi.'

One last look around the room. He put on a sweater, a wool jacket, a peaked cap.

* * *

The dock was hidden away on the north side of the waterfront, beyond a long row of warehouses at the Bassin National. Just about abandoned, he thought. Built in Napoleon's reign of quarried block, with an old customs shed about halfway out and a green warning light at the far end. The night sea was heavy and black, it rammed into the stone, broke across it, and ran back in small rivers. Even in the wind, Casson could smell dead fish and diesel oil.

The Pardoner was already there, wearing an oilcloth slicker, and Degrave showed up twenty minutes later. They stood inside the shack and smoked as rain blew sideways through the broken windows.

It was 2:40 before somebody spotted a bow light, dim in the mist and spray, bobbing up and down as it tried to work its way into shore. It took a half hour before the boat managed to dock, the old tires roped to its bow slamming against the stone as they tied up. The captain was very good, Casson realized, but it helped that the old hulk he commanded, two boom derricks angled up from amid-ships, had powerful engines hidden down below. He jumped easily onto the dock, younger than Casson expected, with a thin line of beard tracing his jaw and a Luger automatic worn in a shoulder holster over an old sweater. He shouted to the crew in a language Casson didn't know, and they ran extra lines from the boat to iron rings set in the stone. He shook his head and said something to the Pardoner, who smiled sympathetically and patted him on the shoulder. The crew, barefoot, began to unload the crates, stacking them in the shed. Degrave set one of the crates on the floor and prised up the lid with a crowbar. The Pardoner took a flashlight from beneath his slicker, switched it on, then peeled back a sheet of oiled paper. 'As ordered,' he said. The light revealed six submachine guns packed side by side, the black steel gleaming with Cosmoline.

It didn't take long to finish unloading. And if, at some point, a customs officer was supposed to have played a part in this, he never showed up. They had paid for that, of course, along with everything else. When the crates were counted, everyone shook hands. The captain jumped back on deck, the engines growled as the lines were cast off, the bow light moved out to sea, then vanished.

★ ★ ★

Just after four in the morning, the truck showed up. Degrave had bought it in Nice a week earlier. Old and solid, it seemed to Casson, with a square radiator grille and a canvas tarpaulin stretched over metal hoops.

Degrave paid the hired driver, who took his bicycle from the back and pedaled off into the rain.

Casson and Degrave loaded the truck by flashlight. A fifty-five-gallon drum of gasoline rode just behind the cab. Slowly, they packed the sardine crates around and on top of the guns. Not much camouflage, but better than nothing.

It was almost dawn by the time Degrave got the truck started. 'There is one thing I promised to do,' he said. 'Not much out of our way.' He jiggled the shift lever, then slowly let the clutch out. Right away it was clear that the weight of the load was not insignificant, not for this truck. They moved, but they could feel the engine strain. The truck had obviously lived a long, hard life — the speedometer frozen at thirty-eight, the other gauges long gone, leaving empty holes with a few wires hanging out. The engine sang, hauling the load up the hill from the dock. At the top they got out, unlatched the hood, and felt the radiator. Hot, but not boiling over. Degrave nodded with grim satisfaction.

'We'll get there,' he said.

★   ★   ★

Degrave's errand was in Cassis, an hour away. They pulled up in front of the villa and Degrave went inside. He came back almost immediately, his wife at his side. They said a few words, kissed, and held each other for a time. When they moved apart she rested her hands on his arms, spoke to him, then kissed him quickly. Degrave nodded, *he would*, and walked back to the truck. His wife waited at the doorway while Degrave started the engine. The wind was blowing hard and she held her hair back with one hand and watched them until they drove away from the house.

The truck rumbled down the hill, through Cassis, and north on Route 8.

Degrave was very quiet. 'You've been married, I think,' he said at last.

'Yes,' Casson said. 'For a few years, anyhow.'

'Then you understand.'

Casson said he did.

With morning, the rain fell back to a drizzle. The black surface of the road glistened in the winter light. They passed a road marker, thirty kilometers to Aix-en-Provence, PARIS — 772.

★   ★   ★

There was a checkpoint north of Marseilles, where a few trucks and cars were pulled over by the side of the road. Most of the fish and wine moving up to Paris went by train, so the sardines were supposedly headed for Avignon. A gendarme glanced at the permit and waved them through without looking in the back.

Degrave took the main roads, kept a steady speed of fifty kilometers an hour, and reached Salon by midmorning. Then he drove northeast through the countryside, into the foothills of the Vaucluse and across the river Durance, where he turned into a country lane. 'They hunt around here,' he said. 'Mostly rabbits and birds, ducks sometimes, but every farmer has a shotgun.'

He parked under a plane tree, tight-mouthed as he turned off the ignition — *maybe it starts again, maybe it doesn't* — then pulled a valise from beneath the seat. He unbuckled the straps and took out an automatic pistol. 'Ever use one of these?'

'No. I shot a rifle — for a morning — when I was in the air service in 1916. The only time I've been around pistols is making movies.'

'It's a Walther,' Degrave said. 'German officer's side arm.' The pistol had a bare snout, like a Luger, but the barrel was shorter. He broke the magazine free, handed it to Casson with a box of 9mm bullets, and showed him how to load it.

They climbed down the embankment of a stream. Degrave found a rock, smooth black basalt, and propped it up at the edge of the water. He paced off a distance down the stream and turned to Casson.

'All right, try to hit it.'

Casson pointed the gun, sighted down the barrel, and pulled the trigger. The gun bucked in his hand, the impact blew some dirt around a few inches from the rock.

He tried again, this time he hit the water.

'Once more.'

He held his breath, squeezed off the shot, same result.

'Let me try,' Degrave said. He took the gun from Casson, held it loosely at his side, brought it up level and, without coming to a full stop, pulled the trigger. A white chip appeared on the rock.

'Should I keep trying?'

Degrave handed the gun back. 'Just keep it with you,' he said.

★ ★ ★

They drove into the late afternoon, Casson behind the wheel for a time, following the edges of the Rhône valley into the hills of

Provence. There were two routes to Paris from the south: straight up to Lyons and Dijon, the ancient trade route; or west into the Massif Centrale, the Auvergne, then due north into the city. The mountain route had hairpin turns and steep grades, the valley route had police. Degrave's idea was to work just east of the Rhône, village to village, on back roads.

They stopped in Carpentras and bought bread and cheese and pears and a few bottles of mineral water, enough for three days. When the sun was low on the horizon, they parked the truck and sat on the running board. Degrave cut up some of the bread and cheese and spread it on a sheet of newspaper. 'We dine in style, *chez nous*,' he said. He carved a bad piece out of a pear, sliced a half off, and handed it to Casson.

'Not too bad,' Casson said. It was hard and burned by frost, but very sweet.

Degrave finished his share and wiped his hand on the newspaper. 'I hope this is all worth it,' he said.

'There's one thing I've been wondering about,' Casson said. 'We're giving them a thousand rounds for each of these guns but, according to Vasilis, the cartridge is hard to find. So, when they've used up the ammunition, that's that.'

'Maybe, maybe not. You never know what they're going to come up with — or they may have to come back to us for more. Fact is, we don't want them to go to war. A thousand rounds doesn't mean much in a military action — the *Modèle* 38 empties a thirty-two-round magazine in a few seconds. What you can use it for is assassination, attacks on convoys or banks. At that level of *résistance*, a submachine gun with a thousand rounds will raise hell.'

Degrave cut up another pear and handed a piece to Casson. 'The sad fact is, the FTP is the best fighting group in France. They're organized, disciplined, they have clandestine experience, and they control the unions. They're brave. And cold-blooded — reprisals don't concern them. We know what they can do, we've been enemies for twenty years.'

'And now, allies.'

Degrave smiled. '*Raison d'état*, as old as the world. I'll tell you something, Casson. People in my trade have to live with some hard truths. One of them is that sometimes you want men and women to fight for freedom, sometimes you don't.'

Degrave finished his pear, worked the porcelain cap free on one of the bottles, took a long drink, and handed it to Casson.

The water was cold, and tasted good

despite the bitter mineral.

'I'm going to sleep for a while,' Degrave said. 'Four hours, then wake me up. You have guard duty until then.'

Casson tucked the Walther in his belt, back where it couldn't be seen. Then he leaned against the door of the truck and watched the sun set.

16 JANUARY.

He woke up suddenly, cold and stiff, with no idea where he was or what he was doing — for a moment he thought he was on location, making a film. No, he was lying across the front seat of a truck, breathing gasoline vapor, the night beyond the windshield black and starless. He forced himself to a sitting position, cranked the window down. Degrave was standing by the front fender. 'Almost dawn,' he said.

Casson took a sip from the water bottle, spit it out, then drank. He lit a cigarette, and rubbed his eyes. 'My turn to drive,' he said.

The narrow dirt roads zigzagged north-west, northeast. Sometimes they had to drive south. The villages got darker and quieter as they neared the center of the country, people stared from doorways. There were no cars on

251

the road, sometimes a horse and cart, once a wagon loaded down with cut lavender.

At seven in the morning they stopped so Degrave could probe the gas tank with a stick. 'Not good,' he said, checking the level against a mark he'd made the day before. 'Let's go another hour, then fill up.'

Casson tried to save gas, pushed the clutch in going downhill, which worked until he tried to slow down. Third gear screamed as the pedal came up, and he had to double-clutch to ram the thing into second. Still too fast. A sudden curve, he fought the wheel, the back end started to swing. He hit the brake, the pedal went to the floor. Degrave swore. Casson tried again, pumping gently until he felt it grab. At last the road flattened out and Casson let the truck coast to a stop. His hands were shaking.

Degrave stared out his window, into the gorge at the bottom of the hill. 'Probably all kinds of old trucks down there,' he said. He turned to Casson. 'I'll drive, if you like.'

'Next village,' Casson said.

★　★　★

The next village was Beaufort-St.-Croix. An old woman in a shawl hobbled past the parked truck, a basket over her arm. She stared at them — who are you? *Don't stop here.*

Degrave drove to the other end of the village and pulled over. By the road was a wayfarer's shrine, a cross of woven willow twigs on a wooden box atop a post; inside, a carved saint, his white robes and red wounds faded by snow and sunlight.

Degrave unscrewed the cap on the gasoline drum, ran a rubber hose from the drum to the gas tank, sucked on the line, and eventually got it to flow — siphoning worked better in theory than in practice. He spat gasoline on the ground when he was done, then got behind the wheel and started up the mountain road. Carefully, he maneuvered the truck over a long patch of black ice, then stood on the brake as they sped down a steep grade. 'Another day of this and it's behind us,' he said.

Casson leaned over to get a better angle in the rearview mirror. On the way into Beaufort he'd seen a black Citroën appear and disappear as the road curved. It could certainly go faster than ten miles an hour, but didn't bother to pass.

'You still have the Citroën?' he said a few minutes later.

Degrave looked up at the mirror. 'Yes.'

'What's he want?'

'Maybe nothing.'

He accelerated, a minute went by, then he sped up a little more. 'Stays right there,' he said. 'Since Beaufort.'

'Earlier,' Casson said.

The road widened and Degrave let the truck roll to a stop. 'Get out for a minute,' he said.

Casson stood by the side of the road, unbuttoning his fly. As he stared down at the weeds, the Citroën went by, very slow and determined. When he got back in the truck Degrave said, 'About nineteen, the driver. There are three of them, they're wearing armbands.'

'Who are they?'

'I don't know.'

★ ★ ★

They waited twenty minutes, plenty of time for the Citroën to go on its way, to disappear.

Degrave threw his cigarette away and looked at his watch. 'Enough,' he said. 'If they are actually going somewhere, we'll never see them again.' He got behind the wheel, coaxed the engine to life, and raced it in neutral a few times.

'It sounds to me,' Casson said, 'like we have unwatered gasoline.'

'We do. You wouldn't believe what I had to pay in Nice to get it. Nowadays it's like buying wine, you have to know the vintage.'

Degrave turned the truck onto the road and moved off slowly. Almost immediately they began to climb, past sloping meadows used to graze livestock in the spring and summer. Five minutes passed, then ten more. Casson kept looking at his watch. The road crested a hill, then turned left. The truck slowed as they climbed a steep curve past stone barns on the mountainside.

'I like this better than the south,' Degrave said.

'So do I.'

'Ever make a movie here?'

'No.'

'Nobody bothers with it, the Dauphine.'

'What would you do — lovers on the run?'

'Why not?'

Casson shrugged. 'You ever know any lovers on the run?'

Degrave laughed. 'No, now that you mention it.'

'And, if they ran, they wouldn't run here.'

'They'd run to Paris.'

'That's right,' Casson said. 'And there goes the scenery.'

★ ★ ★

Fifteen minutes. Casson had another look in the mirror. Black and low, long hood, flat top on the passenger compartment, running boards swept gracefully into panels that curved over the front wheels. A Citroën 7C — you saw them everywhere.

'Still with us,' Casson said.

Degrave sighed. 'I know,' he said.

The Citroën followed them around another curve, then, when the road ran level, it sped up and drove alongside the truck. From the passenger seat window, an arm waved for them to pull over.

Degrave took his foot off the gas. 'All right,' he said, sounding tired. 'Let's get it over with.'

★ ★ ★

The truck rolled to a stop. On both sides of the road were hay fields cut down in autumn; up ahead, an old forest with large, bare oak trees. The Citroën pulled up a few feet away, blocking a sudden escape.

Nineteen was about right, Casson thought as the driver got out. The second might be a little older — tall and fat, wearing a ski sweater with a snowflake pattern. The third was younger, maybe the driver's younger brother. They all wore armbands, white

256

initials stitched on a blue field — MF, for *Milice Française.* The driver, clearly the leader, was working on a mustache and goatee, but he was fair-haired and it was going to take a long time. Village lothario, Casson thought. The others waited by the car while the leader approached the truck. He had his hand in the pocket of his jacket — more than a hand, a revolver, from the way he strutted. Perhaps something Papa brought home from the war.

'*Milice,*' Degrave said. One of Pétain's militia units — *La Jeunesse de Maréchal, La Jeunesse Patriote,* they had all sorts of names. Dedicated foes of France's enemies: Jews, Bolsheviks — outriders for the Tartar hordes from the east, just waiting to sweep across Europe.

The leader stood at the door of the truck and stared up at Degrave.

'Good morning,' Degrave said. He said it well, Casson thought. *You're a kid and I'm a grown man and there can only be courtesy between us.*

Casson saw the leader's chin rise. 'We're on patrol up here,' he said. 'We watched you in Beaufort.'

'Yes?'

'That's right. Saw you put gas in your truck.'

'And so?'

'We could use some ourselves.'

'Hey, look,' Degrave said, man-to-man. 'We're taking some stuff up to Paris — you understand what I mean? We don't mind donating some money to the cause, but gasoline is hard to get, and we have to go all the way up north.'

'What stuff?'

'Sardines, this trip. We won't miss a couple of cases.'

'I guess you won't.' He laughed. It meant he wanted money and the sardines and the gasoline too. All of it.

'Take a look in the back,' Degrave said. Then, to Casson, 'Show him what we have.'

The leader made a gesture with his head and said '*Allez*, Jacquot.' His pal in the ski sweater walked toward the back of the truck. Casson jumped down to the road and went around the other side. He started to untie the rope that held the tarpaulin together. Jacquot stood next to him, too close. 'Get a move on,' he said. 'We don't have all day.'

Casson pulled the tarpaulin open. 'See for yourself,' he said. Jacquot put a foot on the iron step, climbed onto the truck bed, and started to inspect the merchandise. The crates were stenciled *CONSERVERIE TEJADA — BEZIERS. Sardines en Boîtes.*

Suddenly the leader started talking — Casson couldn't hear the words but the tone was tough and impatient. Degrave's answer was soothing. From inside the truck, Jacquot called, 'You better get up here and help me unload this stuff.' He was standing in shadow, one hand resting on the stacked crates.

'I'll be right there.'

Casson never knew who shot first or why, but there were five or six reports from the front of the truck. Somebody shouted, a car door opened, somebody screamed 'Maurice!' When Casson saw Jacquot's hand move, he grabbed for the Walther, pulled it free of his belt, and forced the hammer back with his thumb. In front, a shot, then another, from a different gun. Jacquot's hand came out from under his sweater, Casson fired twice, then twice more. Jacquot grunted, there was a flash in the shadows. Casson ducked away and ran around to the front of the truck. On the road by the Citroën, somebody lay on top of a rifle.

Casson crouched down, edged around the hood until he could see the other side. He heard somebody cough. It sounded strange in the silence. He leaned out as far as he

259

dared, the gun ready in his hand. The leader was sitting with his back propped against the rear tire, breathing hard, one hand inside his shirt.

'Casson?' That was Degrave, his voice hoarse and thick. Casson stepped out from behind the hood. The leader stared at him, then turned away and closed his eyes. Casson could see his chest rise and fall as he tried to breathe.

Casson opened the door, there were two holes in the metal. Degrave was white. He swallowed once, then said, 'I need help, I think.' There was blood on his shirt. For a moment he stared out into the distance. 'We have to go,' he said. 'But first, make sure here.'

Casson went to the back of the truck. Jacquot lay curled up on his side, eyes wide open. Casson could smell sardines, and an oil stain had spread across the wood flooring. Casson tugged at the body, dragging it back until its weight toppled it over the edge and onto the road.

He walked over to the car. The man he'd thought was a younger brother still lay sprawled across the rifle, his blood a dark patch in the dirt. Casson returned to the truck. The leader seemed to be resting, almost asleep. He opened his eyes and saw

Casson standing beside him. 'I surrender,' he said, raised one hand, then let it fall.

Casson aimed carefully and shot him in the temple. The report echoed over the fields and faded away.

SERVICE B

Night settled on the mountain villages in the late afternoon. Sometimes a small café lit up a cobbled street, but the cold drifted in with the shadows and the people disappeared. Casson drove with his hands tight on the steering wheel, stopping often to peer at a map, trying to stay on the deserted roads that climbed the western slope of the Basses-Alpes.

He'd spent a long time outside Beaufort, doing what Degrave told him to do. He had managed to drag the bodies of the three *miliciens* into the Citroën, then drove it back toward the village to a place where the hillside fell sharply away from a curve in the road. He turned the engine off, set the gearshift in neutral, and pushed it over the edge.

It barely moved at first, the dense brush crackling under the wheels, then it sped up, bouncing over rocks and fallen trees, finally slewing sideways and rolling over, coming to rest upside down, its tires spinning slowly to a stop. It would be found, he knew, but not immediately, and all he needed was a few hours to be somewhere else when the alarm was sounded.

Degrave died sometime in the middle of the day. After he'd pushed the Citroën down the hill, Casson walked a long way back to the truck and moved him, very carefully, to the passenger side of the front seat. He was conscious for a moment — looked at Casson as though he didn't know him, mumbled something, then closed his eyes and leaned his head against the window.

Casson drove to the next village as fast as the truck would go He had intended to seek help from the local priest. It was the general rule, since 1940 — if nothing else can be done, find the church, and the *curé*. But by the time they reached a village, Degrave was gone.

★   ★   ★

Casson drove north. The road wound through a narrow valley by a stream, its banks lined with poplar trees. He stopped the truck. Here, he thought. Degrave would have told him to do it this way, to do what needed to be done. But there was no shovel in the truck. He couldn't leave Degrave to the dogs and the crows, so he rammed the shift back into gear, and drove on. At the end of the valley he found a road marker, ST.-SYLVAIN — 14.

The church was in the center of the village. Just inside the door he found a stand with tiers of burning votive lights. Casson took a fresh candle from the box, lit it, and fixed it with melted wax beside the others. Then he went to the vestry and knocked on the door. The priest answered, his dinner left on the table. He was young and bearded, his face weathered by life in the mountains.

Casson explained. A friend had died, he was in the truck outside the church. The priest looked Casson over carefully. 'I will have to ask you,' he said, 'if your friend died a natural death.'

Casson shook hid head. 'He was a soldier.'

Together they went to the truck and Degrave was carried on a blanket into the vestry and laid on the stone floor. 'Can we put a marker on the grave?' the priest said.

'Better not to,' Casson said.

The priest thought for a time. 'A small plaque,' he said. ' 'Mort pour la France.' Among the dead of the last war, it won't be noticed.'

★   ★   ★

He drove out of Saint-Sylvain into the darkness. No moon. A fine, light snow dusted

267

the windshield. After an hour, he couldn't go on. He pulled off the road, forced himself to eat a piece of bread, and drank some water.

He stared out the window; a meadow, the stubble white with frost. The engine ticked as the metal cooled. He was numb, too tired to think about anything. He put the Walther on the floor where he could reach it, pulled his coat tight around him, and fell asleep.

PARIS. 21 JANUARY

Alexander Kovar wandered through the crowded waiting room of the Gare du Nord. He'd been contacted by Narcisse Somet — a meeting at 6:20 in the evening, when the station was busiest. He searched the faces, finally spotted Somet coming toward him from the entrance. Tinted spectacles, bluish-red nose and cheeks; easy to find in a crowd, Kovar thought.

They had been friends since they were fifteen years old, in Montmartre in 1908. This was not the artists' quarter, it was the Montmartre where anarchists and thieves lived side by side, where street performers like Hercules and the Boneless Wonder were local heroes. Somet and Kovar had been drawn there by the preaching of the crippled anarchist who called himself Albert Libertad. Libertad was a legend, a passionate free spirit who loved fighting — using his crutches as weapons, the streets of Paris, and the poor. And, especially, women. He had died later that year, after a savage beating in a street brawl.

Together, Somet and Kovar had battled the police, lived on bread and green pears, written poetry, and made speeches on the boulevards. *Revolution is now, today, in your heart, in the streets.* By 1912 they had gone their separate ways, Kovar wandering among the mining villages of northern France, Somet to sea on tramp freighters. They'd met again in Berlin for a few days, during the back-alley brawls of the 1920s, then they'd had to run for their lives.

By 1936 they were both in Spain; Somet an administrative officer with the XIth International Brigade, Kovar the foreign correspondent for half a dozen Left newspapers in Paris and Brussels. But they'd had guns in their hands more than once — had fought side by side in the November defense of Madrid. Using his empty rifle as a club, Kovar had saved Somet's life when a Moorish legionnaire had aimed a pistol at him at point-blank range.

The loudspeaker in the waiting room announced the seven o'clock train for Reims. Somet and Kovar embraced warmly and sat on a bench to talk.

'Alexander,' Somet said. 'I think it may be time for you to disappear.'

'You don't mean to Melun.'

'No. Far away. They've had some kind of meeting — a colonel brought in from the Center, a commissar, Weiss — '

'The eternal Weiss.'

' — and a man called Juron. Do you know him? Bald, wears thick glasses, doesn't say much.'

'An NKVD thug. From the Foreign Directorate.'

'Yes. There'll be another meeting, probably, with the French included, head of the FTP, head of the intelligence unit, but that will be a meeting for telling, not a meeting for asking. This was the Soviet control group, the shadow *apparat*.'

'What was it about?'

'I don't know, my friend was downstairs. But a few days later this Juron questioned me — just how did I go about making contact with you. It came up in the middle of the discussion, but that's what he wanted.'

Kovar thought it over. 'Maybe I'd better run.'

'Do you need help? Money?'

'I can manage. My friends in Mexico are trying to get me a visa. Until then, I have to stay in France. How much time do I have?'

'Not much. I think once they get what they want from Casson's friends, they'll come looking for you.'

'They haven't found me yet.'

'They will. Is there some way I can reach you quickly? By telephone?'

'I've been using a friend's office in Paris, mostly at night.' Kovar gave him the number. Somet looked at his watch. 'Are you taking the train for Reims?' Kovar asked.

'Yes.'

'If I don't see you again, thanks for letting me know.'

Somet smiled — they would see each other again. 'Take care of yourself, Alexander,' he said.

When they shook hands, Somet passed him five hundred francs and walked away before he could say a word.

* * *

Casson woke suddenly. It was 3:30. He reached under the seat for the map and the

271

flashlight. Degrave had made him memorize a number in case of emergency — Lyons 43 12 — and a protocol, then told him that in the Unoccupied Zone the safest telephones were to be found in railroad stations.

Casson ran the beam back and forth across the map and chose the town of Voirons. He started a few minutes after four and was there by midday, having stopped to siphon another tank of gas from the barrel in the back of the truck. He turned into the main street and asked a man walking a bicycle for the railroad station. *'Tout droit,'* the man said, waving directly ahead of him. That meant go *straight*, or, sometimes, *I don't know.*

The railroad station was in the next street. He parked the truck, found the telephones, and dialed the number in Lyons.

A woman answered. 'Calvert,' she said.

'This is Monsieur Rivette, I'm calling from the office.'

'Where are you?'

'Voirons. The railroad station.'

'Is there an emergency?'

'Yes. We were stopped by *milice*. Outside a village called Beaufort. The captain was killed.'

'Are you injured?'

'No.'

'Are you being pursued?'

'No. The *milice* are dead.'

'And the rest?'

'I have it.'

'You are meant to go to Chalon. Can you get there by yourself?'

'Yes.'

'Do you know where to go?'

'No.'

'First of all, you're not to arrive at night. Truck traffic enters Chalon late in the afternoon, you have to be in the middle of it. On the Quai Gambetta that runs by the Saône, you'll find the warehouses of the *négociants* — all the wine merchants in the region are headquartered there. The one you want is called Coopérative de Beaune. Pull up in the yard, ask for Henri. Clear?'

'Yes.'

'You have maybe a four-to five-hour drive from where you are. But you must go around Lyons — try to stay well east of the river. Understood?'

'Yes.'

'Then, good luck.'

He left the station. The train from Paris had just arrived and he found himself in the middle of a crowd, people greeting friends, carrying baskets and suitcases, hurrying their children along. He stood by the truck and took a long look at the map. Route 75 ran

273

north from Voirons, passing well east of Lyons, to Bourg, then to Tournus, where it joined the major north-south road, Route 6, and continued on into Chalon. All he had to do was drive to the edge of town and pick up Route 75. No problem. He started the truck, drove out of the railroad station area, and turned north on the *grande rue*.

Suddenly, metal ground on metal, the truck leaped forward and his head banged against the windshield. He went to jam the gas pedal to the floor — *escape* — then held up. Instead he braked hard and the truck rocked to a stop. He was a little dazed, stumbled out onto the street. All around, people had stopped to watch the show. A few feet behind the truck, a delivery van with its front bashed in and one headlight shattered.

The driver of the van was already out. A man in a peaked cap and an apron, his face bright red. He spotted Casson and shouted 'Annnnhh' — the *there he is*! understood. A traditional sound, prelude to Homeric indignation. The crowd was not to be disappointed. The driver ran at Casson, shaking his fist. 'You brainless fucking idiot,' he yelled, staggering to a halt.

'Wait — '

'Do you see what you've done to me? Dolt! Donkey! Don't you look where you're going?'

He was so drunk he swayed back and forth as he was cursing.

'Calm down, monsieur,' Casson said. 'Please.'

'Calm down?'

From the corner of his eye, Casson could see the approaching *flic*, walking toward them with that look on his face.

'Ah,' the driver said, glad to see the authorities.

'Shut up a second,' Casson said under his breath. 'We can work this out between ourselves. Or maybe you just can't live another minute without a visit to the police station?'

The man stared at him. *What?* He was so drunk, so much in the wrong, that he would defend himself like a lion. Casson, acutely aware of the Walther in his belt and the guns in the truck, took a wad of hundred-franc notes from his pocket and pressed it into the man's hand and, using his other hand, curled the man's fingers around it. Dumbfounded, the driver peered at the money; none of the catastrophes in his chaotic life had ever turned out this well.

The *flic* arrived. 'It's all settled,' Casson told him.

'You agree?' he asked the driver.

The driver blinked nervously, bit his lip,

looked around for help. He knew there was more money to be had, but how to get it? 'Well,' he said.

'So be it,' the *flic* said. 'Your papers, right now.'

'No, no,' the driver said. 'Nothing happened.'

The *flic* looked him over. 'Go home, Philippe,' he said. 'Go to bed.'

The driver staggered back to his van. With great concentration he managed to get the key in the ignition. He started the engine, the van lurched forward, then stalled. The *flic* put his hands on his hips. The driver started up again and drove away, with dark smoke pouring from the exhaust pipe. The *flic* turned to Casson, nodded his head at the truck. 'Will it run?' he said.

'Yes, sir.'

'Then disappear.'

★   ★   ★

Casson drove slowly through the snow-covered countryside, bleak and silent. Now, there was nothing but the work of driving a truck, and it steadied him. As he got closer to Chalon the traffic increased. By cutting France into two countries, the Germans had created choke points at the border crossings — Moulins, Bourges, Poitiers, all the towns along the rivers. For the moment, Casson didn't mind; it felt safe, one truck among many, all of them rumbling north together. But it took longer than he thought it would, and it was six-thirty by the time he found the Quai Gambetta and the warehouse of the Coopérative de Beaune.

Henri was waiting for him. Sitting with his legs dangling off the old wooden loading dock and smoking a cigar. '*Enfin,*' he said. At last you're here. They stood together in the cold evening.

'What happened to Degrave?'

Casson told him.

'*Milice.*' He spat the word. 'Degrave deserved better.'

He was, in military life, a sergeant. Casson had already guessed that by the time he got around to mentioning it. A sergeant — good at getting things done, by the book so long as it worked, by being crooked if that's what it took.

He led Casson into the warehouse; wine in bottles, in small casks and huge wooden barrels. The air inside was thick, a cloud of manure, raspberries, vinegar. 'We don't help ourselves,' Henri confided the smoke of his cigar hanging in the still air. 'Hands off the Romanée. But they always put something out for us, over on the table. When you want to sleep, there's a cot in the broker's office. Can't imagine why he put it there. Naps, maybe. Good for a few hours, anyhow — you look like you could use it.'

* * *

By five the next morning they were on the move, riding bicycles past the docks and warehouses, out to the residential districts. 'We'll go and have a look for ourselves,' Henri said, 'to see how things are. But I suspect nothing's changed.'

They pedaled up a long hill to a staid old neighborhood, plane trees and handsome street lamps, to a park on a bluff overlooking the western side of the city. Henri leaned on an iron railing and the two of them talked casually for a time, making sure they were alone. 'Have a look,' Henri said, and handed over a pair of binoculars.

Casson could see out over the rooftops to Route 75. Parked by the road, a long line of trucks. Under the direction of German guards, the merchandise in the trucks was being searched; mounds of potatoes or coal probed with pitchforks, crates stacked on the ground, counted, and checked against shipping manifests.

He shifted the binoculars from scene to scene: a driver pacing and smoking, a soldier using a bayonet to pry open a packing case, an officer checking an upright piano — the panel above the keyboard had been removed, baring the strings and hammers. All of this overseen by a group of officers, standing beside an armored car, its machine gun trained on the search area. It would have taken only a moment of indecision, Casson realized. Staying on the main road instead of turning off on the streets that led to the river docks.

'Quite a show,' Henri said. 'It didn't used to be like this.'

'Anything we can do?'

'Oh there's a way around it, there always is.'

They rode back down the hill, to a crowded market where they walked the bicycles. 'One thing I have to let you know,' Henri said. 'This is Degrave's operation — he wanted it done, he ran it. And his friends are going to make sure it's completed, we owe him that. But then, my guess is that senior officers won't get involved. So, when it's over, don't be surprised if we disappear.'

★   ★   ★

279

They waited at the Cooperative until 8:20 in the evening. Henri killed time with stories — twenty years in the army, Beirut, Dakar, Hanoi, Oran. Then they backed the truck out of the loading area, drove to the edge of Chalon, and parked by a bridge. There they waited again. Casson stared out at the icy river, slow and gray, watched the girls, two by two, going home from work over the bridge. A policeman rode by on his bicycle, glanced at them sitting in the truck, but didn't care. A tramp went past, possessions in a blanket roll on his back. 'There's the life,' Henri said. 'Sleep under the stars, answer to no man.' Later on it began to snow. Henri was pleased. 'God's on our side tonight,' he said.

From the river, Casson heard the steady beat of an engine. A barge appeared, moving slowly against the current. It slid neatly below the bridge, then throttled back. On deck, a man walked up to the bow, a match flared. Henri clamped the cigar in his teeth and buttoned up his coat.

The barge was carrying gravel, a tarpaulin tossed casually over the middle of the load. Henri drove the truck onto the bridge and the man on the barge pulled the tarpaulin back, revealing a deep pit dug in the gravel. Sweating in the cold, Casson and Henri dropped the crates a few feet down to the man below, who stacked them in the pit. When the truck was empty, they drove it to the end of the bridge and parked.

'Anything in here?' Henri said. 'Papers? Marked maps?'

'Nothing.'

They left the truck, climbed over the railing of the bridge, and dropped to the barge. The last crate lay two feet down, and the three men began to shovel gravel in on top. When they were done, Casson walked to the far end of the barge and leaned against the wall of the pilothouse. A young woman at the helm waved to him through the window. Casson lit a cigarette, his shoulders ached and he was breathing hard.

At the foot of the bridge, the door of the truck slammed shut, the sound sharp in the cold air. Then the engine started up, idled for a moment, and faded away in the streets by the river. Henri appeared out of the snow and handed him a coverall, black with grease and oil. 'We have a cabin below,' he said. 'Put this on when you get a moment. You're a deckhand now, you have to look like one.'

Slowly, the barge got under way.

'We stay on the Saône up to the Burgundy Canal. That takes us north — to Dijon and Tonnerre, and up the river Yonne all the way to Montereau, near Versailles, where we get on the Seine. About three days, if the rivers don't freeze.'

'The gravel goes to Paris?'

'Normandy. They're building like crazy on the coast. Big stuff. Sand and gravel and cement, barged in from all over Europe.'

PARIS. 28 JANUARY.

Hands in pockets, face numbed by the wind, Marcel Slevin waited in a doorway on the rue Daguerre. Across the street, in an apartment owned by his uncle Misch, a Luftwaffe officer was getting ready to go out for the evening. A bomber pilot, a Nazi. Who would not see the sun rise again — if only he would get a move on before his assassin froze to death. *Calm down*, Slevin told himself, *don't let it get to you.*

They had watched the German for three weeks — Slevin and the people who worked for Weiss. Learned where he went, and what he did. At one point, he'd disappeared. He was picked up by a friend at 8:32 and didn't come home that night or the next. Gone to work, no doubt.

That had worried Slevin — maybe some Spitfire pilot had beaten them to it, setting Fritz on fire over Liverpool. *Merde.* But he was also secretly relieved. Lately he couldn't sleep, couldn't eat, maybe he just wasn't cut out for murder. Or maybe just not this murder. For one thing, the German pilot wasn't what he'd expected. Not young, and no blond superman. He was tall and spindly, with sparse hair and a hawk nose, and to Slevin he seemed more like a pilot for Lufthansa than the Luftwaffe.

The first night of surveillance, Slevin thought his prey might be going off to the nightclubs to meet 'Bébé' or 'Doucette,' but who he went to see was Lohengrin. And then, the next night, back for seconds. Ten days later it was *Rigoletto*. He would take the Métro to the Opéra station, join a milling crowd of officers and diplomats, wives and girlfriends, all smiling and jabbering away in that godawful language. He would say hello to this one or that one, then take a seat in the balcony. And, when the opera was over, back he went to the rue Daguerre.

Slevin waited, stamping his feet to keep warm. In his pocket he had a small revolver, bought from a friend in the garment district who loaned out money at a very high rate of interest. He'd taken a long, careful look at his prey and had his escape route well planned out. The streets around the rue Daguerre weren't so different from the Marais, passages

283

and tunnels and alleys — some blind, some not. After the shot he would scoot, a ten-second sprint to a shed where he'd hidden a bicycle. A few seconds more and he'd be just one more Parisian on the street.

Slevin's plan had been drawn up after careful study of the terrain, and depended on a particular feature of the pilot's Métro stop, Denfert-Rochereau. The staircase went down twenty steps, to a landing hidden from the street, then turned back and continued down forty steps to the platform. That landing, once the crowds thinned out after 7:00 P.M., was invisible from above and below. The pilot would, for a moment, be alone and unseen. And then, no more Lohengrin.

Hurry up.

Slevin stared angrily at the door across the street. He was scared. He didn't want to do this. Weiss and the guys in the FTP were tough — worth your life to fuck around with them — but he wasn't, not really. He was all talk and he knew it. Well, now look what he'd talked himself into.

The pilot came out of the apartment and stopped for a moment as the door swung closed behind him. Topcoat, white silk scarf, tuxedo. He looked up at the sky and took a deep, satisfied breath, glanced at his watch, and strolled off toward the Métro.

Slevin waited a moment, then followed, moving among the last few shoppers and the merchants rolling down their shutters for the night. The pilot took his time, obviously enjoying the street life.

Denfert-Rochereau was a large, busy station, a major *correspondance* where several lines came together and riders could transfer from one to another. But this was not the main entry — the staircase simply led to the end of the platform, useful if you wanted to ride in the last car.

The pilot dropped a *jeton* in the turnstile and headed for the staircase. He was one of those people who run down stairs, letting their momentum do the work, sliding a hand down the banister.

'Hey.'

The pilot stopped on the landing, turned halfway around. *Yes?* A young Frenchman behind him. Short, a real monkey. What did he want?

Slevin drew the revolver from his pocket and fired. Down on the platform, a woman screamed. Slevin and the pilot stared at each other. *What?*

Slevin pulled the trigger again but this time, click, nothing at all. The pilot's reflexes kicked in and he turned and ran, flying down the stairs toward the platform. Slevin took off after him, cursing under his breath, tears in his eyes. He skidded around the landing, ran halfway down the staircase, now in full view of the passengers below. They saw the pistol, some screamed, some ran, some went to the floor. The pilot leaped over them, head down, running with long, loping strides. Slevin steadied himself, aimed, pulled the trigger. The shot echoed up the tunnel, a tile in the wall beside him shattered as the cylinder was blown into it.

Slevin stared at the pistol, stared *through* it.

He turned and ran back up the stairs. Out the entrance, down a narrow passage between two high walls, and into a weedy yard behind a workshop. He reached into the shed, grabbed the bicycle, and pedaled for his life, throwing the pistol over a wall into somebody's garden. He stood on the pedals, racing down a cobbled lane and out into the avenue. A few people were riding along in a group. He drew even with them and slowed down. Just then, the sirens started up.

The bicyclists looked around to see what was going on. A fire? An accident? Always something, around here.

★ ★ ★

286

Hour by hour, the barge pushed its way north. It wound through fields, always, it seemed to Casson, distant from houses and people. The sky stayed heavy, with thick, tumbled cloud rolling west, and gray light from dawn to dusk. Sometimes it snowed, a January that would never end.

He had almost nothing to do. He read a pile of old newspapers; the Red Army had been repulsed in its efforts to break the siege of Sevastopol. The Wehrmacht was fully engaged in the Mozhaisk sector, sixty-five miles from Moscow, where the temperature was −70° Fahrenheit. Sometimes he talked to Jean-Paul and his wife, who took turns steering the barge. They usually brought the kids, they said, but not this trip. Sometimes he talked to Henri. At night, a bottle or two of sour red wine broke the monotony. 'We fill these up every fall at a little *cave* down in Languedoc. Not so bad, eh?'

They had gone through the German border *Kontrol* just north of Chalon. Twelve barges had to be processed, and the Germans didn't get around to them until midnight. Then another hour, while the border guards poked around and looked under things. A German corporal drove a steel rod into the gravel, tried three or four places, and that was that. The barge was doing Third Reich business — the load en route to a French contractor working for the German construction authority — so the papers got a fast once-over and they were sent on their way.

Ten hours upstream, in Dijon, they docked for an hour and refueled. Jean-Paul went off to buy bread and *haricots blancs*, a little oil, and a newspaper. They turned west on the Langres plateau and then north, the next morning, toward Montbard, barges hauling fuel — Casson could smell it — headed south on the other side of the canal. 'Gasoline,' Jean-Paul said. 'Going across the Mediterranean, for Rommel's tanks.'

At night, Casson slept on a burlap mattress stuffed with straw in the small cabin he shared with Henri. There was no heat, and, as tired as he was, the cold kept waking him up. Finally he went out on deck. No stars, just dark fields stretching out to the edge of the world, and willow trees along the bank, their branches hanging limp in the frozen air. He stared out into the night and thought about his movies, about Citrine, about Marie-Claire. His old life. Finished, he thought, he couldn't go back. He'd played the part of someone else for too long, now he was someone else. He thought about Hélène, about the things they did together in his hotel room.

He got up and walked back toward the pilothouse. Jean-Paul's wife was heating water on the woodstove. 'Come in,' she said. 'At least it's warm. I'm making chicory, if you'd like some.'

He waited at the table, lighting a candle and reading the newspaper they'd bought in Dijon. *Attack in Paris Métro*. An attempt on the life of a German flying officer had failed. In reprisal, a thousand Jewish doctors and lawyers had been deported.

31 JANUARY.

The Seine, south of Paris. A hard, bright dawn, the sun on frost-whitened trees. Factories and docks and sheds, half-sunk rowboats, workers' garden plots — stakes pulled over by bare vines. The Michelin factory, one end of it charred, windows broken out, old glass and burnt boards piled in a yard. Bombed, and bombed again. The smell of burned rubber hung in the morning air.

The river *Kontrol* was at Alfortville, just upstream from the madhouse at Charenton. Very brisk, dozens of soldiers with machine guns, Casson could feel the tension. The Germans weren't fooling around, but they

289

had no interest in gravel barges that morning. A sergeant waved them through after just a glance.

The *quai* at Ivry, and far enough. Even there, in the chaos of docks and factory streets, Casson could feel the life beating in the city. The barge was tied up to a wharf, Henri went off to the porte d'Italie, among the thieves and the produce merchants, and returned late that afternoon with a truck — the smell of earth and rotting vegetables almost overpowering when they opened the rear doors. Painted on the side, the name of a wholesaler.

After dark they dug the crates out of the gravel and loaded them in the truck. Jean-Paul went to buy something for dinner and came home with a piece of bright red meat wrapped in newspaper. His wife put it in a pot with salt and wine and cooked it for a long time.

'What is it, do you suppose?' Henri said.

'I didn't ask,' Jean-Paul said. 'It's fresh. *Filet de Longchamp*, maybe.' Longchamp was the race track.

'It was an ox,' Jean-Paul's wife said.

After supper, Casson lay down on his mattress to rest and went out like a light. The next thing he knew, a hand was on his shoulder. 'Yes?'

290

Henri, his coat buttoned up, leaned over and handed him a key. 'For the truck,' he said.

Casson sat up.

'So,' Henri said. 'From here on . . . '

'Are you going?'

'Yes.'

They shook hands. 'Good luck to you,' Henri said.

Casson wanted to say something, *thank you* or *see you soon*, but Henri melted away into the darkness.

★ ★ ★

At daylight, he nursed the cold engine to life and drove around the neighborhood until he found a garage. The owner helped him back the truck into a wooden stall — the garage had been a stable only a few years earlier — then said a month's rent would be a thousand francs.

'A thousand francs?'

'You're paying for peace of mind,' he said. 'There's somebody here at night. And a couple of dogs, big ones.'

Casson paid. He walked for a block or two, then saw a taxi with one of the new wood-burning engines mounted on the back.

'Where to?'

'The Hotel Benoit.' He watched as the city went by. He got out at the hotel, went to his room, and slept for twenty hours.

★ ★ ★

Call Hélène. He was barely awake, still trying to figure out where he was. He'd had powerful dreams; a woman, a boardwalk by the sea. She pulled her dress up, put her foot on a bench and fixed the strap on her sandal. He kicked his way out of bed and struggled to stand up, then he went to the window and moved the curtain aside. Gray winter Paris, nothing more.

★ ★ ★

'*Agence Levaux, bonjour.*'
'*Bonjour. Mademoiselle Schreiber, s'il vous plaît.*'
'*Un petit moment, monsieur.*'
Casson waited. At the hotel desk, a fiftyish couple was checking in. He looked at his watch, 10:30 A.M.
'Hello?'
'Hello, it's me.'
'Thank God you're back.'
'What's wrong?'
'*Merde.*' She switched to a professional

292

voice. 'I believe it sails the ninth, monsieur, from Copenhagen.'

Casson waited a moment. 'All right now?'

'Yes.'

'Will you meet me for lunch?'

'The little bar on Marigny, just off the boulevard. One-fifteen.'

'I'll see you then. I missed you.'

'I'm sorry, here we go again,' she said. 'Certainly — I'll have it in the mail this evening.'

'One-fifteen,' Casson said.

★ ★ ★

He stood on the corner of the rue Marigny and watched her coming down the boulevard, walking alongside a short, dark-haired girl and a blond woman with a bright red smile; shoulders braced, head held high. Victorine? Very tightly wound, he thought. A high forehead, blue veins at the temples, they would pulse when she was angry.

'See you later!' Hélène called out as she left the other two. They waved and continued down the boulevard.

When she spotted Casson her face lit up. As they embraced she said, 'Did you see her?'

'The blonde.'

'Yes. The other one was my friend Natalie.'

They went into the bar and sat at a small table. 'There's been all kinds of trouble,' she said. Casson ordered a carafe of wine and beet soup, the only dish on the blackboard.

'What happened?'

'Well, first of all, Degrave.'

'You know?'

'They told Laurette.'

'How is she?'

Hélène shook her head.

'You're spending time with her?'

'When I can.'

'Not much else you can do.'

'No. You can't just sit there, so you say things, but . . . ' A waiter brought the carafe, the soup, and a basket with two small pieces of bread. 'The bread's for you,' he said.

'Then, a few days ago, Victorine called me into her office — she's the supervising agent now.'

'The job you gave up.'

'Yes, and I thought that was the end of it.' From Hélène, a rueful smile. 'She was quite concerned, she said. About me. I wasn't doing so well. Letting things go, not keeping up with my correspondence. I would simply have to try harder. Or else. She didn't say that, but she didn't have to.'

'And you said?'

'I crawled. Agreed with her, promised to do better.'

Casson nodded. 'No choice,' he said.

'A day went by, then another. I kept out of her way and did my work — if she wanted everything perfect, that's what she'd get. I thought, she's just letting me know who's boss. But then she called me in again. This time I was really scared, but she was pleasant enough. She asked me some questions about a client, I told her what she wanted to know, and then we chatted. She went on for a while, something about her mother needing medicine, how life was getting harder, everything so expensive. I was nodding and smiling, wondering when she was going to let me go out of there, and then she said, 'Hélène, I'm afraid I must ask you to lend me a thousand francs.' '

About half a month's salary, Casson guessed. 'What did you do?'

Hélène shrugged. 'What could I do? I gave it to her. Went to the bank at lunchtime and cleaned out my account. And then, a week later, she asked again. I said I couldn't help her, I didn't have it. She didn't say anything right away, but she was angry. I'd seen it before — she doesn't stop smiling but you can sense some kind of rage inside her. She has it under control, but not for long. After a while she looked at me and said, 'I'm sure your people can help you, Hélène. You'll just have to swallow your pride and ask.' '

'Your people?'

'That's what she said.'

Casson thought for a moment. 'She's going to turn you in.'

'I know.'

'When I was at Degrave's house, in Cassis, he gave me a name — a man who can help you get out of the country.'

'Degrave is gone, Jean-Claude.'

'Even so, we have to try.' He paused, then said, 'How much does she want now?'

'Another thousand.'

'I'm going to give it to you. She has to have it *today*, after lunch. It will keep her from going to the police, she won't do that until she's sure she's got everything you have.'

'Jean-Claude,' she said, 'I'm sorry. I didn't mean to drag you into this.'

He reached under the table, took her hand and held it tight. 'And when you give it to her, be casual. You know the game, you don't mind playing it, you and she are in this together.'

★ ★ ★

296

They went that evening. He'd looked up the name in the telephone directory, found several de la Barres but only one in the 7th — *André, Textes de Médecine Anciens.*

A maid let them in and led them down a long hallway lined with bookcases that rose to the ceiling. In the room that served as an office it was the same. De la Barre was in his late seventies — at least that, Casson thought — bent by age into the letter *c*, so that he looked up at the world from beneath thick, white eyebrows. 'How may I help you?' he said.

Casson was direct. He told de la Barre that Hélène had to leave France, and that they had come at Degrave's suggestion. Casson wondered if he knew who they were. *Have you been told it's a favor for a friend?* De la Barre listened intently, but his face could not be read. When Casson was done, the room was very quiet. De la Barre looked at them for a full minute, making up his mind. Finally he said to Hélène, 'Is it urgent, madame?'

'I'm afraid it is,' she said. Briefly, she explained her situation.

He opened a drawer and studied a list of some kind, then ran a hand through his hair. 'I can't promise,' he said. 'We can only send a few people, and even then . . . '

'I have to try,' Hélène said.

297

'Of course,' de la Barre said gently.

Again, he consulted the drawer. 'We will help you to cross into Vichy, that much is easy, and you can continue on to Nice. From there, you will have to sail to Algiers — still French territory, but you can find your way to neutral ports. The ship is Italian, the *San Lorenzo*, a small freighter that carries twenty or thirty passengers — it's up to the captain. The next sailing is *scheduled* for a week from today, the eleventh of February, but it is always delayed. The weather turns bad, or the engines break down, or the shipping authority in Nice delays all departures for military reasons. Of course, working in a travel agency, you're familiar with the situation.'

Hélène said she was.

'And speaking of that,' de la Barre said, 'I wonder if you could do me a small favor? The agency must use a great variety of forms, is that right?'

'All sorts — for steamships and railroads and hotels. Of course they're not valid until they're stamped by the Germans.'

'No,' de la Barre said. 'Of course not.' The edge of irony in his voice was so finely cut that Casson wondered if he'd actually heard it. 'Even so, I would greatly appreciate it if you'd select a few of each, whatever you have, and make a small package for us. And while you're at it you might include some stationery.'

'With pleasure,' Hélène said.

'On your train ride down to the Unoccupied Zone, someone will open the door of your compartment and say, 'Any room in here?' They'll look directly at you when they ask, but you don't have to answer. Later, go out into the corridor and give the package to that person. Don't be furtive, simply hand it over.'

Hélène agreed.

'Now what you'll need to do at work is ask for some time off — we don't want you to disappear suddenly. Do you have some vacation days you can take? Good. Explain the request as a family emergency. Is there any reason why travel documents into the Unoccupied Zone shouldn't have your name on them?'

'Not that I know about.'

'Good. Before you go, give me your identity card and I'll copy off the information. You'll need to travel south on the Monday night train, stop by here at seven or so and we'll give you the permit.'

Hélène handed over her identity card. While de la Barre was writing, Casson walked around the room. *Phrénologie. Physick. La Théorie de l'Alchimie de Jehan le Breton*, in

299

wood boards. 'I should mention,' de la Barre said, 'that you'll need enough money for an extra week in Nice — not for a hotel, you'll stay in an apartment. But sailings are at ten-day intervals, and if we can't get you on the first one, we can try for the next.'

★ ★ ★

Afterward they went to a café. Hélène was flushed, excited. Casson ordered Ricon.

'My God,' she said. '*Monday.*'

'I know,' Casson said. 'We have the weekend.'

★ ★ ★

On Thursday morning he took a train to Melun and left a message for Kovar. Late that afternoon, a response was dropped off at the hotel desk — a meeting at 9:30, same place.

He went out to the Gare du Nord quarter and found the office building. On the second floor, behind a set of double doors, was the Madame Tauron School of Ballet and Modern Dance. He could just make out the measured notes of a piano as he climbed the stairs. What *was* that? He paused for a moment and listened. Erik Satie, *Gymnopédies*. He could hear the shuffling of feet and a voice that echoed in a vast room. 'Yes, and yes, and three.'

The third floor was dark, and deserted. Except for Alexander Kovar, behind somebody else's cluttered desk. 'Welcome,' Kovar said. Casson was pleased to see him.

'Still at it?' Kovar said.

'Yes,' Casson said. He could hear the piano on the floor below.

Kovar took a slightly bent cigarette from his shirt pocket, carefully tore it in two, and gave Casson half. 'Maybe you have a match?' he said.

Casson lit their cigarettes. 'The guns are in Paris,' he said. 'So I need to contact the FTP.'

'A success,' Kovar said.

'So far.'

'I'll talk to my friend.'

'And you — you're surviving?'

'As usual. I think, the last time I saw you, I'd just quit my job at Samaritaine. Now I'm back to my old tricks, writing for the risqué weeklies.'

'*Vie Parisienne?*'

'Oh yes, and *Le Rire*. Under several pseudonyms — each one has his specialty. For example, the story of Mimi, the dance-hall girl. Adrift in the backstreets of Pigalle, innocent as a lamb, and headed full speed for debauchery.'

'But, somehow, never quite gets there.'

'No. Something always comes up. One week the *frites* catch fire. Next installment, a surprise visit from Uncle Ferrand.'

'Wicked Uncle Ferrand.'

'So it turns out — poor Mimi. When I get bored with that, I write 'The Inquiring Reporter.' I ask men with beards, 'do you sleep with it over or under the sheet?' Then I did one on 'my favorite recipe for *Lapin du Balcon.*''

'Guinea pig?'

'Yes.'

'You actually do it — go around and inquire?'

'Are you mad? Half the world is looking for me. I barely go out in the street.' He laughed. 'Actually, it's not so bad. I've been on the run for a long time, eventually you get used to it.'

Casson tapped out his cigarette in a saucer on the desk. 'There's something I want to ask you,' he said. 'What do you think will happen here?'

'The war will go on. For a few years, anyhow, until the Americans get organized. Then, probably, civil war.'

'Here?'

'Why not? The right is finished, what with Pétain and Vichy. So, after the Germans leave, the Gaullists and the communists will fight it out. For myself, I plan to be somewhere else.'

'When the war ends.'

'Sooner. Maybe a lot sooner. I may see you again, Casson, but there's a good chance I won't. In a day or two you'll be in direct contact with the FTP. They'll ask about me — how we met, and where. Please, don't tell them. Not about Melun, and especially not about this office. Can I depend on you for that?'

'Of course.'

Suddenly Casson realized that it was his fault, that Kovar had to leave because of what he'd done. He started to say it, then didn't.

They stood and shook hands. '*Bon courage*,' Kovar said.

★ ★ ★

They decided to spend their last weekend in the country. Casson told himself he didn't care about the money, and they could go to a hotel where travel agents got a discount. Friday after work they took the train up to Vernon, across the river from Giverny, and a taxi down a poplar-lined road to an inn where the *paysagistes* used to stay while painting the valley of the Seine. In the room, blue Louis the Fourteenths bowed to blue courtesans on the wallpaper, and through a tiny window under the eaves they could see, if not the Seine at least the Epte, its tributary. There was a fireplace with a basket of sticks, and a sepia photo of Berthe Morisot, hung slightly askew to hide a hole in the plaster.

They walked by the Epte, had the Norman omelet supper — obligatory for the *demi-pension* — went upstairs to drink the bottle of Algerian wine they'd brought from Paris. Took off their clothes, walked around naked in the firelight, made love.

A little broken, both of them, Casson thought. But that couldn't be permitted to spoil things. The idyll at the country inn was like meeting for a drink or going to a dinner; you knew how to do it, you were good at it. Away from the husband, the wife, all the vengeful smiling and chattering of Parisian existence, stripping the blanket down to the end of the bed and getting to the urgent sixty-nine with all passionate speed. Once upon a time a cure, he remembered, a cure for almost anything, but different now — more had to be forgotten. There had been a moment, Hélène sprawled luxuriant across the quilt, her colors pale and dark rose in the firelight, when desire suddenly fled and what he saw struck him as fragile, vulnerable.

He wasn't alone; she was also, sometimes, adrift, he could sense it. She was certainly adept, knew everything there was to know, and if the fire inside her was low she would make sure it was blazing in him. They managed, they managed, enough art to get to pleasure, the gods of the country idyll victorious in the end. She flopped back, her head off the bed and upside down, which made her voice a little strangled. '*Enfin*,' she said. 'Something that felt good.'

They stared into the fire for a time. It was quiet on the river at the end of the road, only the old beams of the inn creaking in the winter air. He turned to look at her, saw tears in her eyes.

'Are you all right?'

She nodded, not trusting her voice.

'Scared?'

She was.

'I'll miss you,' he said.

Again she nodded.

'When you reach Algiers, I want you to write me a postcard. So I know you're safe.'

'I will. To the hotel?'

'Yes. And just to be on the safe side, write one to Natalie too. Did you ask for vacation?'

'I had to go to the office manager, but he's always been nice to me. And then to the dragon herself. At first she was suspicious, but I told her I was going to see an old family friend. I didn't actually say it, but she got the idea he was rolling in money — nothing he wouldn't do for me.'

'Good.'

'Maybe I'll send *her* a postcard.'

Casson laughed. 'Maybe you should.'

'Will I ever see you again, Jean-Claude?'

'Yes.'

She took a deep breath, let it out slowly. Swung her feet over the edge of the bed, crossed the room, and put a piece of wood on the fire. Her silhouette against the firelight was slim and curved.

'Lovely,' he said.

LUNA PARK

Life came down to money. Something he'd always known and never liked. He'd even tried, for a time, insisting that it wasn't true. Age twenty, a student at the Sorbonne, he had left home, where money ruled with an iron fist — they had it, they lost it, it didn't matter, it did — and taken a room under the roof in the 5th Arrondissement. A classic room, the aesthetic sensibility of a thirteenth-century thief, so perfect of its type that his mother wept when she saw it. His father took one step inside, looked around, and said, 'If you're not happy now, Jean-Claude, you never will be.'

On 9 February, 1942, life came down to one thousand, two hundred and sixty-six francs. He laid it out on the bed and counted it twice. What he'd managed to save from his work with Degrave was pretty much gone. He'd given Hélène a thousand francs for Victorine, and another five thousand for the trip to Algiers. He had a cheap watch, a few books, and the Walther pistol, probably worth a few hundred francs but difficult, and dangerous, to sell.

Cold. He shivered, rubbed his hands, and walked around the room. Winter could be mild in Paris, but not this year. And the Germans had set the coal ration at fifty-five pounds per family a month, enough to heat one room for two hours a day. At the Benoit, that worked out to a few feeble bangs from the radiator at four in the morning and a basin of tepid water in the sink.

He counted the money once more — it hadn't grown — withdrew a hundred and fifty francs from the account and slid the rest under the mattress. He combed his hair, put on the glasses. A café over on the place Maillart had a wood-fired stove. You couldn't get all that close to it — a flock of letter writers and book readers occupied all the best chairs, but even over by the wall it was warmer than his room. A fairly genial atmosphere in there — on his last visit he'd shared a table with one of the regulars, an appealing blond woman who wore eyeglasses on a cord and read Balzac novels.

As he passed the hotel desk, the clerk called out to him. 'Monsieur Marin?'

'Yes?'

'Could you step in to the *propriétaire's* office for a moment?'

He liked the woman who owned the Benoit. Pretty and fading. Sympathetic, but nobody's fool. An adventuress, he guessed, in her younger days, and apparently good at it.

'A small problem, Monsieur Marin. The monthly rent?'

'Madame?'

'The deposit has always been made directly into our account at the bank, on the twentieth day of the month. But, according to our statement, there was no payment in January. I'm sure it is an oversight.'

'Of course, nothing more. The mails perhaps. I'll have to see about it. However, just to make certain, it is . . . ?'

'Six hundred francs.'

'I'll stop at my bank today.' He looked grim — damn the inconvenience.

'Thank you. These things happen.'

'If this is going to take a few days, it might just be simpler to pay you in cash. Tomorrow, madame?'

'Whatever suits you, monsieur.'

★ ★ ★

He never reached the café. On a side street near the hotel a young woman appeared out of nowhere and fell in step beside him. 'You are Marin?'

'Yes.'

She was no more than nineteen, very thin,

311

with silky colorless hair. 'I am called Sylvie, monsieur. Do you mind if we go inside for a minute?'

'No, I don't mind.'

'Are you followed?'

'I don't think so.'

She led him into the hallway of an apartment house and handed him a piece of paper. 'Please memorize that,' she said. 'It's my address and telephone number. I've been assigned as your liaison with the FTP — all contact is to go through me. Nobody else will know where you live.'

They left the building and walked together for a few blocks, then took the Métro for one stop, crossed over to the other side of the station, let one train go by, and took the next one back to the station they'd started from. They went into a large post office, stood on line for five minutes, and went out another door. On the street, Casson saw two men, at a distance, standing in front of a café and looking in their direction.

'Don't worry,' Sylvie said. 'Their job is to watch us.'

They walked to a street off the avenue des Ternes. 'You see the automobile parked in front of the pharmacy?'

'Yes.'

'You will be getting into it. In the front

seat. Walk to the car as quickly as you can, but don't run.'

Casson started to say good-bye. 'Go,' she said. 'Right now.'

The car was a nondescript Renault, one of the cheaper models from before the war, dented and dusty. Casson slid into the front seat. He had barely closed the door when the car took off, not quite speeding.

The driver was tall and pale with a Slavic face and a worker's cap. Suddenly Casson realized he'd seen him before. In May of 1941, his screenwriter, Louis Fischfang, had decided to go underground. They had met in an empty apartment, on the pretext of wanting to rent it. Casson had said good-bye and given Fischfang as much money as he could. But Fischfang had not come alone. The driver had been with him, a protector, a bodyguard. The driver had also recognized him, Casson saw it in his eyes. But neither of them said a word — they weren't supposed to know each other and so they didn't.

The man in the back seat leaned forward so Casson didn't have to turn around.

'I'm called Weiss,' he said. 'Let me ask you right away, is the meeting to hand over merchandise from the *Service des Renseignements*? Or something else?' The voice was

313

educated, and foreign.

'The guns have been brought into Paris,' Casson said. 'Six hundred MAS 38 sub-machine guns, a thousand rounds of ammunition for each.'

'Where are they?'

'In a garage near the porte d'Italie.'

'Take us out there,' Weiss said to the driver.

*　★　★

As they left the garage, the driver was in the truck with Casson. Weiss took the Renault. They drove for a long time in the midday traffic, circling east just beyond the edge of the city, then turning north into the Montreuil district. Casson followed the Renault into a cinder yard behind a brick building — dark, windows boarded up, perhaps a deserted school. 'This is it,' the driver said. 'You can give me the key.'

Two men were waiting for them. One of them was short and round-shouldered and spoke with a Spanish accent. The other was young, not long out of school, with steel-rimmed glasses and the severe haircut of a man who doesn't like to give money to barbers. A *polytechnicien*, Casson thought. He knew the type from his days at the

Sorbonne, serious, square-jawed, wearing a suit meant to last a lifetime. Probably an engineer.

At Weiss's direction, Casson and the driver moved the sardine boxes to one side, dug down into the load, and set one of the unmarked crates on the floor of the truck. The engineer produced a flashlight, a screwdriver, and a small wrench. He used the screwdriver to pop the boards free, then folded back the sheet of oiled paper. Once again, Casson saw six submachine guns side by side in a beam of light.

The engineer picked up one of the guns and wiped the Cosmoline off it with a clean rag. He studied the gun for a moment, raised it to a firing position, worked the bolt. Next he laid it on the truck bed and disassembled it. This took, to Casson's amazement, less than thirty seconds. His long fingers flew as they spun the barrel out of its housing. One after another the parts came free — a spring, a slide, a bolt — each of them examined, then set down in a row. Without missing a beat he said, 'Meanwhile, maybe somebody could get me the 7.65.'

Casson brought the crate over, broke it open, and took out a box of ammunition. The engineer used a pair of small pliers to open one of the bullets. He smelled the powder, rubbed a few grains gently between his fingers, and dusted it off with his rag. 'It's good,' he said to Weiss. 'And the guns haven't been used.'

'Or tampered with.'

'They're right off the factory line. Of course, I can't really guarantee anything until I do a test-firing. Three or four magazines at least.'

'Can they be shortened? To fit under a jacket?'

The engineer shrugged. 'A wooden stock, all you need is a saw.'

The engineer laid the gun back in its crate, Weiss turned off the flashlight. 'We have a little house in Montreuil,' he said to Casson. 'Just a few minutes from here.'

★ ★ ★

The house stood at one end of a row of cottages. Weiss took a large ring of keys from his pocket and flipped through it twice before he found the one he wanted. He had to ram his shoulder against the door to get it open. Inside it was musty and unused. Cold air rose from the stone floor. At the far end of the room, a window looked out onto a tiny garden — soot-dusted snow in the furrows, sagging poles, and a dining-room chair, left outside far too long to ever be brought in again.

They sat on couches covered with sheets. Weiss put his briefcase aside and made himself comfortable. Outside, the sky was low and the afternoon light had darkened. 'Going to snow,' he said. He had the face of an actor, Casson thought. Not precisely handsome, but smooth, and composed. He could be anyone he wanted to be, and what he said you would likely believe. He leaned forward and smiled. 'So then,' he said. 'What happens next?'

'I don't know.'

'We expect to be asked for something, of course.'

'It's up to the people in Vichy,' Casson said. 'They may come back to you, they may not.'

'They'll be back,' Weiss said. 'You should contact Sylvie when that happens, she'll put you in touch with *Service B*. Meanwhile, make sure she knows where you are, in case we need to talk to you.'

'*Service B*?'

'The FTP intelligence unit. We call it B, the second letter of the alphabet, rather than *Deuxième*. *One Deuxième Bureau* was more than enough for us.'

They were silent for a time, then Weiss

317

said, 'I understand you were in the film business.'

'I was, yes.'

'Hope to go back to it, after the war?'

'If I can. It's changed since the Occupation.'

'You'll find a way,' Weiss said. Something he remembered made him smile. 'I imagine it was different here, but where I grew up anybody who'd actually *seen* a movie was something of a celebrity.'

'Where was that?'

Weiss shrugged. 'A small town in central Europe. My father was a shoemaker. First time I ever went anywhere else I was seventeen years old.'

'The war?'

'Yes. And on the wrong side — to begin with, anyhow. I was a conscript, in the Austro-Hungarian infantry. On the eastern front. Eventually my regiment surrendered, and I became a prisoner of war in Russia. So I was there in October of '17. The Red Army needed soldiers and they recruited us — they were going to change the world, we could help them do it. Not a hard decision. Most of us had grown up in villages, or workers' districts. Czech, Polish, Hungarian — it was all pretty much the same. Some days there wasn't anything to eat, we'd see people

318

frozen to death in alleys. We figured we might as well join up, why not? They made me an officer — that never would have happened in Austria-Hungary.'

Weiss stopped, and looked at his watch. Casson got the impression he'd said a little more than he meant to. 'Now,' he went on, all business, 'when you talk to your people in Vichy, there is one point I'd like you to bring up. Over the last eighteen months, the SR has arrested quite a few of our operatives, they're in the military prison at Tarbes. We'd like them out, at least some of them.'

'Arrested for what?'

'They're communists. Accused of working against the government, which is what they're under orders to do. In general it's for leaflets, illegal printing presses, agitation — strikes and labor actions. I'm not saying some of them weren't involved in secret cells, spying, or sabotage, but if they were, it had to do with operations run against the war effort.'

'Technically crimes, according to French law.'

'Crimes against Vichy. To us that means Germany. Look, we know the SR has to function under the eyes of the Germans, it can't just sit there and do nothing. But, in our case, it's been a little too successful. So, maybe they could arrange to leave a few doors open, let a few people walk away.'

Casson nodded, it made sense.

'We have a lot to offer, Casson. Help with field operations, intelligence — but they have to ask. From the first contact we felt that no matter how hard we've fought against each other in the past, we now have a common enemy, so it's time for us to be allies.'

'War changes everything.'

Weiss smiled. 'It should, logically it should. But the world doesn't run on logic, it runs on the seven deadly sins and the weather. Even so, we have to try to do what we can.'

'And it helps,' Casson said, 'to have machine guns.'

'It does.'

'I expect I'll be reading about them in the papers.'

'Maybe not next week, but yes, you will.'

★ ★ ★

Why not next week? But that wasn't up to him. He called the contact number for the SR about an hour after he left Weiss, using a public telephone at the Gare d'Austerlitz. And did his best — reported that the guns had been delivered, reported what Weiss had suggested.

And heard it rejected. That was, at least, his

impression. The voice on the other end of the phone was polite, and businesslike. *Pure deflection*, Casson thought. He knew in his heart that if he ever called again the phone would not be answered. 'Thank you for letting us know,' the voice said. That was it — nothing about the future. Henri had told him he was out of a job, the telephone call confirmed it.

That afternoon he paid his hotel bill. It would give him at least ten days more at the Benoit. Meanwhile, he'd better start looking for a job. He bought a *Paris-Soir*, which had more *petits annonces* than any other paper, and took it to the café on the place Maillart.

He felt alone and abandoned, and couldn't stop thinking about Hélène, due to leave in a few hours. Of course she had to go, he told himself. But, whatever else was true, a love affair was over. He had said he would see her off at the station, but she'd turned him down. She wanted to remember their last time together in the country hotel, she said, not pushing through the crowds at the Gare de Lyon.

The café was jammed, Casson had to wait for a chair. The unaccustomed warmth had put some of the patrons to sleep, but nobody bothered them. Casson ordered a coffee and read the newspaper. The French liner

Normandie, now a war transport for the USA, was shown burning at its pier in New York. The accompanying story was sly, but suggested German sabotage as the cause of the fire. On the next page, a photograph of an Afrika Korps platoon lounging around a white fountain, a few camels in the background. *In Libya, victorious troops take a break from the fighting after capturing the town of Derna.* Below that, a headline: *ANTIDRAFT RIOTS IN MONTREAL — À BAS LA CONSCRIPTION!* No news from the Eastern Front, Casson noted, which probably meant a Russian offensive was under way.

He read everything, trying to make the newspaper last — the horoscope, the births and deaths — and fooled with the crossword puzzle while his patience held out. But, finally, he had to turn, pencil in hand, to the help-wanted columns. Wanted: mechanics, electricians, bakers. *Merde*, it was an encyclopedia of things he couldn't do.

This is not going to work. He'd sensed it that morning, when his remaining funds were laid out on the bed. The employment ads in the newspaper seemed remote, mysterious — Fischfang used to say the editors wrote them. In Casson's life, work came through friends. Didn't he know somebody who could help him? All those years of making films, churning up money for casts and crews — there had to be someone in the city who felt gratitude, somebody who would pay him to do something.

Wanted: a room-service waiter at the Bristol. Wanted: an experienced salesman of luxury automobiles, must speak German. Probably Bruno, he guessed, his former wife's live-in boyfriend. Where was it? Avenue Suffern. No, Bruno was on the Champs-Elysées.

Wanted: bicycle messenger. Machinist. Exotic dancer.

* ★ ★

In a room on the rue St.-Denis, *SS-Unterscharführer* Otto Albers sat on a sofa in his underwear and waited for the show to begin. A young woman wearing spectacles and a ragged cardigan sweater made herself busy dusting a lamp, then a table, with a handkerchief. He had discovered her on a corner in the red-light district, clutching a Bible, looking scared. The mouse — as he thought of her — now appeared as The Maid in his weekly drama.

He yawned and leaned back, the waiting was not unpleasurable. Albers's day had begun at dawn. He had stood for a long time in front of the urinal in the hotel where SS men were billeted. A long time. On the wall, somebody had written:

Vorne Russen
Hintern Russen
Und dazwischen
Wird geschussen

Obviously, Albers thought, somebody transferred to Paris from the Russian front. 'Russians ahead/Russians behind/And in between/Shooting.'

Not so funny, the little poem. And if what he heard from other soldiers was true, a rather polite version of what really went on. Not only the *partizan* sniping mentioned in the verse, but midnight raids — Mongolian cavalry armed with sabers, emerging like phantoms from the ice fog, riding silent to the edge of the encampment, then war cries, somebody sliced just about in half, screams, shots, havoc.

At dawn, Soviet punishment battalions attacked with NKVD machine-gunners aiming at their backs. Since they couldn't run away, since they were going to die, they might as well take you along. Thousands of them. They just kept coming.

Waiting in front of the urinal, Albers had shivered, remembering the stories. That wasn't for him. He preferred Paris, and the mouse. *Ach!* What pleasure she gave him. He didn't mind at all that he had to pay for it. What he did mind was the other thing she'd given him, which made him stand so long in front of the urinal. He would have to get that taken care of, and he would have to be rather clever about how he did it. But he'd always been rather clever — thus he found himself waiting for a private exhibition, and not for Mongolian cavalry.

Again he yawned. A long day, the Gestapo worked hard. He labored in a chilly basement, in charge of a platoon of clerks, fetching dossiers, stacking them on metal carts, distributing them to offices all over the building. Then, picking them up at the end of the day, back on the carts, back on the shelves. *In the proper sequence.* Woe betide the careless soul who filed *Boudreau* behind *Boudret* — they might never find poor Boudreau again!

A knock at the door, sharp and authoritative. Oh! The poor maid had been startled. 'Yes?'

'Open up. Be quick about it.'

Timidly, the maid opened the door. Enter,

The Mistress of the House. Not a professional, Albers thought, an old friend of the
mouse. Always he imagined her at work in an
office, then home in one of the better
neighborhoods. Small and fair, tight slacks, a
thin, angry face. 'Well, have you cleaned up
the room? It doesn't look very clean to me.' A
thumb swiped across a tabletop. 'What's this?'
A tiny voice. 'Dust.'
'So!'
'Oh madame, please forgive me. Please.'
A cheek taken between thumb and
forefinger. 'Always I forgive you. This time, I
think not.'
It went on — why hurry? The director Otto
Albers was not loath to let a scene develop as
it should. For a moment, it seemed the
mistress might relent — the maid was down
on her knees, hands clasped, she would do
better next time.
But no. The maid was lazy and deceitful,
she had neglected this, that, and the other
thing. The mistress — a little overheated
— peeled down to black corset and stockings.
'Right over here, you. You know how it's
done.' Poor maid, bent over the arm of the
sofa, skirt up, panties down, white skin
glowing in the lamplight, peeking horrified
over her shoulder as the mistress punished
her.

326

At this point, both women glanced expectantly at Albers, because it was just about here that he usually took an active role. But not tonight. Until he felt better he had no desire to participate. 'Continue,' he said, and settled back in his chair. When they were done, the two women got dressed and shared out the hundred-franc notes stacked on the night table.

Albers had always suspected that the mistress went home to some grim husband, who looked up sharply from his newspaper when she came through the door. 'Well, what's for dinner?'

⋆　⋆　⋆

Casson got up every day and looked for a job. He read the *petits annonces* and underlined the best possibilities, then set off for the morning search. But he immediately ran into problems. For one, Casson might have found a job, but Marin couldn't, because Marin didn't have a past. 'And where have you worked, monsieur?' He tried various answers — his own business, a job abroad, but the eyebrows went up and Casson looked for the door.

Once or twice he came close. He applied to be a salesman in the toy department of the

327

Bazaar de l'Hôtel de Ville, the BHV. The manager was sympathetic. When Casson started to tell stories, he held up a hand. 'Please,' he said, 'I understand.' Just what he understood Casson could only imagine, but when he returned to the store that afternoon, the manager told him his candidacy had been vetoed at a higher level.

To save money, he stopped taking the Métro. The weather turned furious in the last days of February, broken clouds rolling like smoke above the rooftops, the western sky black and violet at sunset. Casson walked head down into the wind, one hand clamped to his hat.

He tried hard for a week, then went back to see Charne. Charne had a scarf wound tight around his throat, his eyes were red and watery. 'I'm sick as a dog,' he said. Casson sympathized, then said he needed to find work.

'What I used to do, if I needed money between pictures, was go to a café near Luna Park. The ride operators had a wall where they pinned up notes, *help wanted*, whatever they needed. In fact' — he smiled at the memory — 'just before we made *The Devil's Bridge* I was running a Ferris wheel out there.'

Casson tried it the next day. He found the

café, read the notes on the wall, and went to see a man called Lamy. 'I own the Dodge-em cars,' Lamy said. 'I need a bookkeeper, maybe two mornings a week. Can you do it?'

Casson said he could. A strange little man. Lamy sat behind his desk in a soiled homburg and an overcoat with a velvet collar and told Casson stories. Born in Paris but traveled the world. He'd made and lost fortunes, served in the Rumanian navy — by accident, he swore it! Sold wind-up toys on the streets of Shanghai. 'Come in tomorrow morning,' he said. 'We'll see how it goes.'

Casson showed up at eight and went to work. The money wasn't much, but he figured he might just be able to squeak through on it if other opportunities came his way. He decided to leave the Benoit and move into a cheaper hotel, a Gothic old horror out by the Saint-Ouen flea market.

He made contact with Sylvie, the FTP liaison girl, and let her know his new address and the number of the pay phone by the downstairs desk. Then he packed his belongings: an old shirt, a razor, toothbrush, underwear, pencils, a tattered copy of Braudel, the Walther.

He worked in Lamy's office, writing long neat columns of figures, using an adding machine for the totals. Just outside the window was the Dodge-em ride. As the drivers — mostly German soldiers — stomped on their accelerators, showers of blue sparks rained down from where the cars' rods made contact with the copper ceiling. The cars bounced and shivered as they hit, the drivers spun their steering wheels like the great Nuvolari, their girlfriends screamed and hung on tight.

That evening, Casson returned to the office to finish up his work. At nine, a flight of British bombers passed over the city. The air-raid sirens wailed and, as usual, the power was cut off. The rides went dark and the cars coasted to a stop. Casson stared out the window — something so strange about the scene he couldn't look away. The German soldiers sat patiently in the dead bumper cars, one or two of them lit cigarettes, while airplane engines droned overhead.

Fifteen minutes later, the all-clear sounded, the little orange lights strung around the Dodge-em ride went back on, and the cars clattered around the floor.

★   ★   ★

The first day of March. Payday. Thank God, Casson thought, he was down to his last fifty francs. He went out to the park and looked for Lamy. 'Come back this afternoon,' Lamy said. 'I'll have it for you then.'

That left him with several hours to kill. He took the Métro over to the Benoit, and asked at the desk if he'd received a postcard. No, nothing had come, but he could leave a forwarding address. He said he was still looking for a permanent place to stay, and left the hotel. Where was Hélène? By now she should be in Algiers. Could he go see de la Barre, ask for news? Maybe once, he thought. It wasn't time for that yet. Inter-zonal postcards were slow, he had to wait.

He walked across the city, headed for Saint-Ouen. It took him an hour and a half — the streets glazed with ice — and he was tired by the time he got there. He trudged up the stairs and saw that the door to his room was padlocked. For a time, he stood and stared at it. Then he went back down to the desk.

'I'm in Room 65,' he said. 'It's locked.'

The clerk looked up from his newspaper. 'Rent due by noon on the first day of the month.'

'It's two-thirty.'

'Yes, that's right.'

'I get paid this afternoon,' Casson said.

The clerk nodded. Everybody in the world

had money coming. Mostly, in his experience, it didn't come.

'Isn't there some way?'

Apparently not. 'We must all pay to live, monsieur.'

★ ★ ★

Over at Luna Park, Lamy was in his office. Casson told him he'd been locked out of his room. 'Once they get to know you,' Lamy said, 'they ease up a little.' He took a metal cash box from the bottom drawer, wet his index finger, counted the notes, and fanned them out on the desk. Then he put the coins on top. 'Everything cash at Luna Park,' he said with a smile.

It wasn't enough.

Casson could pay two weeks' rent and eat for a week, but he'd run out before he got paid again.

'We'll see you Thursday morning,' Lamy said.

Casson thanked him and put the money in his pocket. 'Is there something else I can do?' he said. 'I could use the money.'

Lamy thought it over. 'There might be, remind me next week.'

Casson returned to the hotel and paid the clerk, who climbed the stairs and took the padlock off the door. Casson sat on the sagging bed. *This can't go on.* Maybe it was time to see his old friends. Would they help? He wasn't sure. If they were living as they always had, it was costing them a fortune. The coal and food and clothing they were used to was available on the *marché noir*, but getting more expensive every day. Parisians lived on nine hundred francs a month — if they did without. Lately, it cost nine hundred francs for two kilos of butter. No, he thought, leave the friends alone. Think of something else.

He reached under the mattress and pulled out the Walther. Its presence had worried him since his return to Paris. Under Occupation law, the ownership of weapons was a serious crime — somebody might find it and turn him in. What could he get? A thousand? A few hundred? At least he'd be rid of the thing, and whatever he made would help.

He put the Walther in his belt and left the hotel.

★ ★ ★

He walked north, through Clignancourt, most of it boarded up in the late afternoon. Saturdays, before the war, he used to come here. He never bought anything but he liked the feel of the place, dusty drapes and crackled varnish, postcards of Lille in 1904.

Out past the *antiquaires'* stalls of Serpette and Biron there was a different market, this one jammed with people. The streets were lined with pushcarts and rickety tables piled with old clothes, rusty pots and pans, shoes and dishes and sheets. The narrow aisles were packed; the crowds shifting and pushing, somebody stopped to bargain, somebody going against traffic. A vendor called out to Casson, 'You could use a new tie, monsieur.' He stood by a cart full of spotted horrors, some with painted scenes. 'Take a look, anyhow,' he said. He had a beret pulled down over his ears and stamped his feet to keep warm.

'I need to sell something,' Casson said. 'Quietly.'

The man blew on his hands. 'Quietly,' he said. 'Papers? Ration coupons?'

'No. A gun.'

The man looked him over. 'Keep going,' he said. 'To the end of the row, then right. You'll see the people you need to talk to.'

He turned right at the end of the aisle and found another market. Hard to see at first, the same carts and tables, the same crowd, poking at clocks and lamps. But, in among them, a different group — hands in pockets, restless eyes.

By a table stacked with army blankets he saw a young man in a leather coat, belt pulled tight. Casson caught his eye and walked toward him. Then somebody — Casson never saw who it was — hurried past and whispered '*Rafle.*' Roundup. It happened so fast Casson wasn't sure he'd heard it.

The man in the leather coat had vanished. Somewhere ahead, a sudden commotion — shouts, a dog barking. Then, police. They swarmed through the crowd, shoving people aside with batons, grabbing others and demanding papers.

The gun. He backed up, working his way around the table, took the Walther from his belt and slid it into the pile of blankets. Then squeezed between carts into the next aisle, jammed up against two women with shopping baskets who were blocked by the crowd. He stood still and watched, a bystander. The police were everywhere, thirty or forty of them. He saw a couple — foreign-looking, the man bearded, the woman in a head scarf — questioned, then led away. A kid, maybe fifteen, tried to run for it. The *flics* chased him down, he broke free and crawled under a table. Casson heard the batons as they landed.

He felt a hand close on his elbow. When he

turned, the *flic* said, 'Get your papers out.' As Casson reached under his coat, the man glanced at somebody behind his back, a question in his eyes — *is it him?* He got his answer, took Casson's identity card without bothering to read it, and slid it in his pocket. 'This one,' he called out. Casson was surrounded. One of them jerked his elbows together, another snapped handcuffs on his wrists.

★ ★ ★

They were taken to the far end of the market, Casson and ten others, shackled to a chain and led off to the Saint-Ouen police station. The men were separated from the women and pushed into a holding cell — yellowed tile, the ammoniac reek of Javelle water, a bucket in the corner. The bearded man he'd seen arrested paced around the cell for a few minutes, then squeezed in next to him, sitting with his back against the wall.

He was balding, heavy in the shoulders, and smelled of woodsmoke and clothing worn too long. 'Listen, my friend,' he said. He had a thick accent, Polish or Russian, stared straight ahead and barely moved his lips when he spoke. A prison voice, Casson thought. 'We can't stay here.'

Casson made a half-gesture — nothing to be done.

'This is a little police station, not a prison. One door and you're out. We can take the guard when he comes in — I'll do it. You grab his keys and open the cells. Let everybody go, will give us a better chance to get away.'

'They'll shoot us,' Casson said.

'Maybe not.'

'It won't work.'

'*Listen* to me.' The man leaned hard against Casson, his shoulder was like a rock. 'We started running in Lithuania in '40 — we didn't come this far to die here.' He paused. 'You know what happens next?'

Casson didn't answer.

'Do you?'

'No, I don't.'

'I know. We saw it done.'

Casson heard footsteps, the man beside him tensed. A *flic* stood at the barred door of the cell, a key in his hand.

'Jean Marin?'

'Yes?'

From the man beside him, a fierce whisper. 'Don't be a fool!'

'Come to the door,' the *flic* said.

Casson stood up. So did the bearded man.

'Not you,' the *flic* said. 'You sit down.'

The flic turned the key in the lock. As Casson walked to the door, he looked over his shoulder. The bearded man saw he wasn't going to try it, sat down, let his head fall back against the wall.

Casson stepped into the corridor, heard the door slam shut behind him.

'Straight ahead,' the flic said. He took the shoulder of Casson's coat and shoved him forward. To the desk, and beyond. Down a long hallway to the end, then a second hallway to a heavy door in an alcove. The flic let him go, and faced him. 'Back in the market, somebody got rid of a pistol in a pile of blankets. That was you.'

Casson was silent.

The flic leaned close to him. 'Perhaps you'd like to tell me, what would this Monsieur Marin, the insurance adjuster, be doing with a Walther pistol?'

No answer.

'You better tell me something,' the flic said, his voice low. 'There are forty agents in this station — some of them would be calling the Gestapo right now.'

But you aren't one of them. 'You know what I am,' Casson said.

The flic watched his eyes. Truth or lie? He handed Casson his identity papers, went to the door, ran the bolt back, and pushed it open. It was dark outside, Casson could see a long alley that ran to the street. The *flic* looked at his watch. 'End of shift,' he said. 'Things to be done.' He turned abruptly and walked down the hall.

CORBEIL-ESSONNES. 1 MARCH.

At 11:30 A.M., Brasova, Weiss, and Juron met in the FTP safe house. They worked their way through several points on the agenda, then Brasova said, 'The Center's transmission of 27 February transfers the case of Alexander Kovar to the French section of the Foreign Directorate.' That meant Juron.

Weiss had seen the message. He didn't like it. He met Brasova's eyes — *any chance?* They'd known each other for a long time, since Weiss's service in the Comintern in the 1930s. 'Can we be absolutely sure we won't need him again?' he said.

'It's up to the Center,' Juron said. 'Their decision is final.'

'I have to agree,' Brasova said. 'Of course,' she said to Weiss, 'Casson will remain your responsibility.' She meant, you got half of what you wanted, don't be greedy.

Weiss turned to Juron. 'What do you plan to do?'

'He's become a liability,' Juron said.

To Weiss, Brasova said, 'It's my understanding that the last time we met on this subject, you promised Colonel Antipin your cooperation.'

'I did,' Weiss said.

'Do you know Kovar's whereabouts?' Brasova asked.

Weiss started to say that the investigation was ongoing.

'We know,' Juron said impatiently. 'Casson was followed to an office on the rue Pétrelle. Kovar goes there at night.'

Weiss gave up. 'Is there anything else you need?'

'Tell your people I have a job for them.'

Later, after Juron left, Weiss said to Brasova, 'It's wrong to do this, Lila. He acted against the Germans, nothing more.'

'I know it's wrong,' Brasova said. 'I'd guess that Antipin did the best he could. He horse-traded — saved Casson, gave up Kovar. So that's the way it has to be.'

Weiss drummed his fingers on the table.

Brasova's voice softened. 'Let it go,' she said.

HOTEL DU COMMERCE

Marie-Claire was waiting for him, a little way down the street from the doorway on the rue de l'Assomption. She'd thrown a fur coat over a pair of pajamas. '*Mon Dieu*,' she said, when she got a look at him.

She took his arm and led him around to the side of the building, using the service entry meant for deliveries and adultery, avoiding the eagle-eyed concierge in her loge in the front hall. They took the stairs up instead of the elevator. Not the first time Casson had come this way. But then, not the first time for Marie-Claire, either.

She opened the door, Casson stepped inside. His old apartment — producer's fees from Paramount for *Night Run*, development money from Pathé for *The Man from Cairo*, which was never made. That, and some very dire months when the bills sat in a desk drawer and steamed. But, back then, a love nest, so it didn't matter. The dinner parties came later. And all the rest of it.

Casson took off his coat. Marie-Claire never faltered, hung the awful thing in the hall closet. 'What about Bruno?' he said.

'In Rome. He's getting the dealership for the Alfa Romeo. The 2500, I think. Is there an SS model?'

'Yes.'

'So there he is, wining and dining Mussolini's nephew — somebody like that — to get an export permit. Anyhow, he's not here.'

She shrugged off her coat, revealing cherry-red lounging pajamas, stepped out of her shoes, and put on matching slippers. 'Jean-Claude,' she said, shaking her head in mock exasperation. 'What *time* is it?'

'A little after six.'

She fell back on the sofa, covered her eyes with her hands. She was the same, he thought. Maybe a little blonder than usual, but the same. Not beautiful. Narrow eyes, thin lips — spite and meanness promised, though not all that often delivered. Then what, he'd always wondered, made her so deeply *appetizing*? She lived in clouds of perfume, sat close to you, touched you. But that was simply *parisienne*. There was more to her, and here he didn't have the word. Indomitable? Strong, anyhow. And driven by *grandes ardeurs* — if she wanted something, she was on fire to have it.

'A shower?' he said. 'Any warm water?'

'All you want. We have to pay the

344

black-market prices, but Monsieur Krajec — you remember, the coalman — has been a magician.'

'I would like a shower,' he said.

'I'll tell you what, just leave everything in the bathroom, and when Rosine comes in, we'll try to do something with it. Jean-Claude?'

'Yes?'

'Why do you wear that little mustache? I had to look twice to make sure it was you.'

'It's me.'

'It's horrible.'

'I know.' He went into the bathroom and undressed. There was a full-length mirror on the inside of the bathroom door. He shuddered at the sight of himself, thinner than he realized.

Marie-Claire was standing on the other side of the door. 'Jean-Claude, when you disappeared, last June — what happened to you?'

'A long story.'

He turned on the taps in the shower, let the water run down his head, his arms and back and chest. The soap was scented. The glow inside him swelled until he burst into a helpless laugh.

The bathroom door opened a crack. 'Are you all right?'

'Yes.'

He forced himself to step out of the shower, and dried off with a large white towel. On the knob of the door, Marie-Claire had hung a pair of slacks and a shirt. 'Thank you,' he called out.

He put on the clean shirt, big and soft. Then the slacks — Bruno, he thought, was fatter than he'd realized. He held them up and stepped into the bedroom. Marie-Claire was lying on a chaise longue. She moved her legs to make room for him. 'Come and sit,' she said.

'What time does the maid get in?'

'Eight. Should I send her away?'

'It might be better if she didn't know I was here.'

This was, he could see, slightly annoying.

'She doesn't gossip.'

'Even so.'

She nodded. 'A day off then,' she said. 'Did you know that your actress got married?'

'Yes, I read about it.'

'Local opinion had it that you had some sort of *crise*, a breakdown. Over her. But then, we had Germans in suits coming around and asking about you. They were nice enough — they're very tender where their French friends are concerned, and they consider Bruno a friend. Still, I didn't think unrequited love was the sort of thing they investigated.'

It wasn't unrequited. Casson smiled and shrugged.

'Your lawyer friend Arnaud thought you'd jumped in the river. Of course, I know you too well for that. You might have jumped in the river — but then you would have swum to the other side.'

'And you?'

'What did I think?'

'Yes.'

'Oh, I don't know. That you'd found a way to get involved in the war. Possibly gotten yourself shot.'

'The first part is true.'

'I thought it might be. One of the resistance groups?'

'Yes.'

'I kept telling myself, he'd never do that, but I knew you would.'

'Did you tell anyone?'

She shook her head. 'No, my love. Not me.'

'You liked the idea.'

Her expression said she did.

'Then how — forgive me for asking, Marie-Claire, but how can you live with somebody like Bruno?'

She laughed. 'He's not so bad. Just ambitious. And greedy. He wants to climb,

Jean-Claude, and he was busy doing just that when this very inconvenient war broke out. Now he's determined that it mustn't *spoil everything*. What he's doing is collaboration, of course, but he doesn't want to hurt anybody, he just means to hang on to all he's worked for.'

'And you?'

'I don't like the Germans. I never did like them and I like them even less since they took the country. There was a time when Bruno was bringing them here, for cocktails and dinner parties. Well, I put a stop to that. Maybe it doesn't get me a statue in the park when the war ends, but it's better than nothing.' She paused for a moment. 'And, truth be told, there might even be a little more than that.'

'Really?'

'Nothing much. A favor for an old friend. The use of the guest room for a few days.'

'Who was the guest?'

'No idea. A woman, on her way someplace.'

'And the old friend?'

'He's with de Gaulle. Rather high up, I would guess. When I discovered what he was doing, I told him to ask if he ever needed a favor.'

'You *discovered* what he was doing?'

She smiled — she'd shocked him and she was enjoying it. 'Jean-Claude, my dear long-lost husband, if it goes on in this city, in this arrondissement, among people I've grown up with, had dinner with, gone to bed with, and will lie next to in the cemetery, I know about it.'

That was true. She came from a prominent family in the 16th, old and mean and reclusive. With staggering hauteur. They'd certainly never approved of him, in fact they'd never approved of each other. But people on that level knew what went on. And, whether she liked it or not, Marie-Claire was one of them. He stood up, wandered over to the window, and stared out at the Bois de Boulogne; bare trees in the gray morning drizzle. He looked over at Marie-Claire, now lying curled up, her head propped on her hand, watching him with cat's eyes. 'And, once you found out what he was doing, he admitted it?'

'He did.'

'Why?'

'Courtship. He wanted to go to bed with me, so he puffed himself up like a pigeon, told me how terrifically important he was, that he lived in constant danger.'

'And, did you do it?'

349

'No. Ech.'

'Do I know him?'

'Mm, maybe.'

'Is it somebody I . . .'

She cut him off. 'Jean-Claude, you are very tired. I think you ought to sleep, we can talk later. When Rosine comes, I'll give her money for a taxi and tell her to go home. For now, we won't worry about clothes or anything else.'

She was right. He went over to the bed and lay down on the tumbled quilts and sheets.

'Under the covers.'

He pulled a quilt over him.

'Now, Jean-Claude,' she said, a laugh in her voice. '*Nu comme un ver.*' Naked as a worm. He took off the shirt and pants, dropped them on the carpet by the bed. The room swam around him, he could smell soap and Marie-Claire's perfume and all the nice things in life that went on in that apartment. He turned on his side, the quilt cool and light against his skin. Heard a click — opened his eyes. Marie-Claire had turned off the lamp, leaving the room in twilight. He drifted off, heard footsteps coming toward him. He felt her lips on his forehead for just a moment, then slept.

350

He woke up to a series of refined, rather contented little snores from the woman next to him. Well, what had he thought would happen? Strange experience, dimly remembered. Somewhere, in the middle of a dream, he was no longer alone under the quilt. Marie-Claire had crept into the bed, then her bare bottom came looking for him. He'd never really woken up, not at the beginning anyhow. A luxurious twenty minutes, sliding around on the exquisite sheets. Like making love to the life he'd once lived, he thought, smooth and soft.

Very slowly, he swung his feet over the edge of the bed and stood up. Walked to the bathroom, got back in the shower. Today was apparently his day to have everything, he'd better take advantage of it while he could. He stared absentmindedly at the water beading up, then running down the tiles. He was going to have to do something with his life — what? *Maybe this.*

The bathroom door opened. 'Like the old days,' she said, pink and white and smiling.

She stepped under the water, handed him the soap.

At the kitchen table, an omelet, real coffee, bread. *Butter.* Marie-Claire, back in her red pajamas, was pensive. 'Jean-Claude, why did you telephone?'

'When you live day-to-day, sooner or later you run out of luck. I got myself arrested — was in the wrong place at the wrong time. They let me go, but I knew it couldn't go on like that.'

She thought for a moment. 'So, you came to me for money.'

'Yes.'

She smiled, bittersweet — *at least you're honest.* 'About two years ago, when Bruno moved in here, he said this would happen, that you'd come around looking for money.'

'Bruno was right,' Casson said. 'I am looking for it. But then, the fact is, you don't have any money. At least you never had any when we were together.'

'True.' She drifted for a moment. 'There was a ghastly scene, back then. I never told you about it. We were trying to buy this apartment. I went to my father.'

'Marie-Claire,' he said. They'd agreed not to do that.

'I know, I know what we said. But I thought, well, why not? They had plenty. We were having a hard time — they knew it, they'd had the *pleasure* of knowing it.'

Casson sighed. 'I only thought, perhaps Bruno gave you money to run the household, maybe he wouldn't miss a few hundred francs.'

'Ha!'

'No?'

'No.'

'Well then, just the, the respite. More than enough, believe me.'

She was silent for a time, off in her own world. 'All right,' she said, resigned. 'Tell me what you need.'

'Two or three months. To find a place to stay. To find work, some kind of life that can be lived in wartime. What I was doing before, it's over. Now, I have to figure out a way to exist on my own. I can do it, but I need a few weeks.'

She nodded, resigned to some private decision. 'I suppose the time has come,' she said. 'I knew it would.'

★ ★ ★

She threw on a sweater and a skirt, left the apartment for a few minutes. Perhaps went down to the cellar, he thought, to the land of steamer trunks and broken chairs. God only knew what was hidden down there, in the spiderwebs and coal dust.

353

She came back, face flushed, a small cotton bag in her hand. She moved the omelet plate to one side, untied the strings of the bag, turned it upside down. A necklace fell out on the tablecloth. '*Tiens*,' Casson said. Was it real? He picked it up, felt the weight of it in his hand. For the opera, or some grand celebration in a ballroom. Tiny diamonds, small emeralds.

'Bruno?' he said.

She shook her head. 'He has no idea.'

'How'd you get it?'

'It came to me.'

'Came to you?'

'So to speak.'

'Do you wear it?'

'Oh no, there's no way I could do that.'

Casson smiled. During the time they'd lived together, the world had thought *he* was the rogue, and she was long-suffering.

She took the necklace from him, turning it so it caught the light. 'When my grandmother died — I was sixteen — we all went immediately to the apartment, on the avenue Ranelagh, over the gardens. Vast confusion, my father giving orders, lawyers appearing from nowhere, weeping maids, my mother shouting at the doctor. Poor Nana, the only one of the whole crew with a good heart. She once told me to look in her bureau if she died, in the corsets. I looked, and this is what I found. It was meant for me, but I knew if I took one step into the parlor it would be snatched away from me and I'd never see it again. So, down the front of my underpants it went. And not a moment too soon. One of the maids showed up just after I did it, looked at me, looked at the bureau. Said something, 'how we shall all miss her,' something like that, and gave me a look of pure hatred. By then I was sorry I'd done it, because I was going to get caught, when they read the will, and there was going to be hell to pay.

'Only, there wasn't. Nobody knew about it. Nothing in the will — oh, the jewelry went to various people, but everything else she owned was terribly simple and discreet. And nobody mentioned it — and I began to understand that she'd never worn it. This thing was, I realized, a lover's gift. If my grandfather had given it to her she would have worn it, but she didn't. Can you imagine? A married woman, well off, from a stuffy old family. Sometime in the 1890s, probably. And, you know, she had that figure, buxom and rosy, all hips, like a Renoir lady getting in the tub. She must have done something — quite wonderful. This is *gratitude*, Jean-Claude. A night a man would remember all his life. That's what

I like to believe, anyhow. Do you think it's possible?'

'What else?'

Slowly, she put it back in the bag. 'I never really knew what to do with it. Of course there were moments, when you and I were starting out, when we couldn't pay the bills, and I would say to myself: very well, Marie-Claire, it's time for Nana's necklace, but then, I couldn't do it. I just couldn't, and a day would go by, then a week, the *huissiers* about to take the furniture, and then, all of a sudden, from the sky, money. You would come home, with perfume or flowers, and I'd leave the necklace where it was.'

She handed him the bag. 'Do you know how to sell such a thing?'

'This is worth tens of thousands of francs,' Casson said. 'I can't take this.'

She shrugged. 'It's the war.'

'What if,' Casson said, 'what if I sold it, took, say, five thousand francs for myself, I can live on that for three months, and gave you back the rest?'

'You can live for three months on five thousand francs?'

'Of course.'

She was heartbroken, he saw. He started to give it back — they could find something else in the apartment, there had to be something.

356

She read his mind. 'No, no. It's done,' she said. 'Just take it up to Vendôme and get the best price you can.'

'Where on Vendôme? Karabeghian?'

'Of course. Where else?' It was where the Parisian upper classes had always taken their business in troubled gems.

'I mean still, after all these years?'

'Yes, still. Nothing ever changes here, Jean-Claude.'

'All right. I'll go this morning.'

'Jean-Claude?'

'Yes?'

'If you can get Swiss francs . . .'

★ ★ ★

He didn't do as well as he'd hoped — everybody selling, nobody buying. The jeweler was apologetic; his eyes were, at least. After all, there wasn't much to say: old wealth was heavy on the market, from Jews, from fugitives of all kinds, trying to find a way out of the country. And then, there were others; a senior German officer, coming out the door as Casson entered, gave him an extremely polite little bow.

In the event, the jeweler agreed to pay in Swiss francs. Casson took some of them to the back room of an umbrella shop on the rue de la Paix — used traditionally by barmen and waiters at the hotels frequented by tourists — and converted them into French Occupation francs. The rate was so good it surprised him. 'Market's going up,' the woman said. 'We'll take all you have.'

He returned to Marie-Claire's, where they spent the day together, and, also, the night, why not. Old love, as good as it ever was, maybe a little better. 'I love doing this with you,' she said, lying next to him. 'I always did.' They smoked together in the dawn, really not much to say, odd how happy some things in life made you.

* * *

He left the apartment at midmorning. Fine weather — a springtime wind, brilliant, sunny light — a good day to start a new life. He would find a better hotel, move his few things. He stopped for a newspaper, found a café, and ordered coffee. 'Real, if you have it.'

* * *

Then he looked at the news. ITALIAN FREIGHTER SABOTAGED. *SAN LORENZO* EXPLODES AT THE DOCK IN NICE HARBOR. RESISTANCE TERRORISTS SUSPECTED IN

DAWN ATTACK. EIGHT DEAD, MANY INJURED.

He went first to the Benoit, but there was no postcard. Next he headed for de la Barre's apartment, then changed his mind and walked down the Champs-Elysées to the travel agency. 'I'm here to see Natalie,' he told the woman at the *réception*. She showed him to a desk in a small room, and Natalie appeared a moment later. 'I'm Hélène's friend,' he explained.

'Oh,' she said. 'I couldn't imagine who Monsieur Duval was.'

'Is she alive?'

For a moment, she hesitated.

'I know where she was going,' he said. 'She told me she would send you a postcard when she got to Algiers.'

'She was on the ship that burned,' Natalie said.

'Is she all right?'

'Yes. She telephoned, from Nice. She was afraid to speak openly, but she let me know she'd survived — 'a bad accident.' '

'Did she say anything about trying again?'

'Yes, in a way. She said she'd be staying in Nice for another two or three days. Then she told me I mustn't worry, that she would see me soon and tell me the whole story.'

'See you in Paris?'

'That's why she called. She may have to stay with me if her landlady won't let her have the room.'

'You said she could?'

'Of course. And she'll be coming back to work.'

'Not here.'

'Yes.'

'They'll let her do that? She's been away three weeks.'

'Well, they think she's been in Strasbourg — a family emergency. And then, the big surprise, Victorine's been a saint. Hélène is welcome to her old job. No problem.'

Naturally, Casson thought. A thousand francs anytime she felt like it — no problem.

'At least she's not hurt,' Casson said.

'Thank heaven. She'll be here by the end of the week, she wasn't sure exactly when.'

'I'll come by in a day or so and leave a phone number,' Casson said. 'Tell her to call me as soon as she can.'

★ ★ ★

A quiet evening on the rue Pétrelle; closed shops, buildings deserted. Ivanic and Serra watched the windows for a time, but the only lights were on the second floor. The third floor, where Alexander Kovar used a friend's office, was dark.

'What does he do up there?' Serra said.

'Who knows? Writes books, or pamphlets.'

'In the dark?'

'Why not? Perhaps it suits him.'

'A friend of mine used to read his book. In Spain.'

'I don't know it,' Ivanic said. *Why make it personal*, he thought. Juron had told them what to do. And Weiss had been very specific about how he wanted it done. That was all Ivanic needed. He checked the time, 8:30. No cars about, no people. 'Let's get it over with,' he said.

Ivanic used a skeleton key to open the simple lock on the building door. As they entered, they could hear music, a scratchy old record of a single piano, the melody slow and sad. It grew louder as they climbed the stairs and came, they discovered, from the Madame Tauron School of Ballet on the second floor.

A woman's voice — somehow hopeful and weary at the same time — rose sharply above the piano. '*Allons* — Bernadette? This is the afternoon of a *faun*, my dear, yes, *that's* right, so light, so delicate . . . '

Ivanic gestured up the staircase, took the automatic from his leather coat, worked the slide.

'Won't they hear it, from upstairs?' Serra said.

'They'll stop what they're doing, for a moment,' Ivanic said. 'Then they'll pretend it didn't happen.'

They climbed to the third floor, turned left, walked slowly and silently to the office at the end of the hall, then stood on either side of the door. Serra took a revolver from his belt. He held it casually, like a familiar tool.

Very carefully, Ivanic leaned close to the pebbled glass window in the upper half of the door. But the music from the floor below made it hard to hear the small noises people make when they are alone, the sound of a chair, or a newspaper. He signaled to Serra that he couldn't hear, then pointed to a place just below the keyhole.

'Typewriter?' Serra mouthed the word.

Ivanic shook his head.

Serra stood in front of the door, raised his leg. Ivanic gestured with his gun, Serra drove his foot against the door. A second time, a third, the glass cracked and the door flew open.

Ivanic went through the door in a crouch, turned left, then right. Nobody. Serra came in behind him. 'Easy does it,' Ivanic said. 'He's not here.'

They searched the dark office, there were

cigarette stubs in the ashtray, a typewriter, a few pages of scribbled notes, but no Kovar.

'Where could he go?' Serra said.

They had seen him enter the building at 7:30. As far as they knew, there was only the single door to the street, and they had watched that for an hour. Ivanic rested a finger on the receiver of a telephone on the desk. 'Warned,' he said. 'Otherwise, he would either be here, or he would have gone out the door to the street.'

'Still in the building?'

'He could be.' Ivanic thought it over. In the ballet studio? In some other office? Hopeless, he thought. 'We can look on the roof,' he said.

They climbed the stairs to the roof, looked over the parapet into the empty street. Went down to the fifth floor, walked the endless labyrinth of hallways with titles lettered on the glass door panels; importers, detectives, matchmakers. Then, to be able to report that they'd done it, they searched all the other floors.

'The ballet studio?' Serra said.

Ivanic considered it. 'Better not,' he said. 'We couldn't do it there, even if we did find him.' He checked his watch. 'We're supposed to be out of here by 9:20, we'll just go see Weiss and tell him what happened.'

'Perhaps he went to another office.'
'Maybe. Let Weiss worry about it.'

★ ★ ★

Kovar waited until 10:20 before he left the building.

He'd been hard at work at 8:15, when the telephone rang. This had never happened before — *wrong number*, he thought. *They'll hang up*. He let it go; ten, eleven, twelve rings. What if they heard it downstairs? He picked up the receiver, a man's voice said 'Kovar.'

The voice was measured, and without emotion.

It was a voice he didn't recognize, certainly not Somet. It told him to leave the office immediately, to go to Room 408, the door would be unlocked. He was told to stay there until 10:00 P.M. Told he should not return to the office, told he should find a new place to live, not in Melun. 'Kovar,' the voice said, 'do you understand?'

He said 'Yes,' the connection broke, the dial tone hummed. On the door of Room 408 it said JOUVET, below that, PROMOTIONS EXTRAORDINAIRES. Inside, there were photos and press clippings on the wall. Later, he heard footsteps in the corridor, then saw a

364

shadow on the glass. It paused a moment, then moved away.

★   ★   ★

Casson tried one hotel, then another, then a third. Hotel du Commerce, on the avenue Daumesnil, behind the Gare de Lyon. He was getting rather good at it now, he thought. A particular combination of seediness, anonymity, and old age — you had to develop a taste for it. *Perfect — nobody would ever stay here.* Except that every room was taken. He had to wait a day to get in.

4 March, a spring gale; rain blown sideways, the window rattled all night. Casson stayed awake until dawn, reading battered mysteries from the stalls on the Seine. He'd bought a radio, it crackled and hissed, but he could listen to piano concertos, sometimes jazz. A new life. *Monsieur Marin, of the Hotel du Commerce, went out only rarely . . .*

★   ★   ★

The next morning he walked to the railroad station, called Natalie and told her where Hélène could find him. Then — finishing up old business — he tried the contact number for the SR. As he'd expected, the phone was not answered. Just to make sure, he dialed a second time, but he knew what would happen.

Which left him with one last telephone call, and that would be that.

But the liaison girl at the FTP contact number wanted him to meet her at a newsstand in an hour. Twenty years old, he guessed when he saw her, maybe younger. Earnest and intense, prepared to die to change the world. And, Casson thought, it would probably turn out that way. 'I am called Emilie,' she said.

They walked through the 12th, up to Bastille, then into the dance-hall area around the rue de Lappe. Entered a nightclub by a cellar door at the bottom of a flight of steps. Strange in midmorning, canvas flats on a tiny stage, scenes of *la vie parisienne*: Eiffel Towers, *flics* blowing whistles, their cheeks puffed out.

Weiss was waiting for him at a table in the back.

'The way it looks right now,' Casson said, 'I don't think I can be of further use to you.'

'No? Does that mean that Vichy doesn't want to talk to us?'

'Not through me.'

'Is this final?'

'Nothing's final,' Casson said. 'But that's

366

the way it is right now.'

'Was it what we asked? To let our people out of prison?'

Casson shook his head. 'I was wondering,' he said, 'what became of Sylvie?'

Weiss didn't answer immediately. 'You can contact us through Emilie,' he said. He paused a moment, then went on. 'If it should happen that you get back in touch with your contacts in the SR, I want to make sure they know we are still very much in the market for weapons — that above everything else.'

'And the MAS 38's?'

'We're glad to have them, but there are still a number of cells that need to be armed. The way we saw it, the first delivery was a test of good faith. On both sides.'

'I've been reading the newspapers, but nothing's mentioned.'

'They've been used. Well used.'

'In Paris?'

'Up north,' Weiss said. 'And in Paris. Remember, what the Nazis permit the newspapers to print is what they want them to print.'

'Well, yes, that's true.'

'Casson,' Weiss said. 'I need guns. Thousands of them. Ammunition. Hand grenades. I want you to know we're willing to take on any kind of operation if we can get them. Almost anything — I hope you understand me. Of course we'll take the blame; bloodthirsty Bolshevik beasts and so forth. People see us that way, after all, so it almost doesn't matter what we do. And then we are held responsible for the reprisals. Somebody must see how very useful that can be.'

Casson nodded.

'Talk to them, Casson. For the moment, the real war behind the lines is in the Ukraine and in Poland. We have to make more happen right here. We don't want these Germans walking down the streets of Paris smiling and laughing, we don't want them walking down the street at all. We want them on special buses, with motorcycle escorts, going off to some wretched cultural program staged just for them.'

'I'll try,' Casson said. 'I'll do what I can. But please understand my part in this is probably over.'

'It may be,' Weiss said. 'If it is, I want you to know we appreciate what you've done.'

'There is one favor I want to ask,' Casson said.

'Yes?'

'I have a friend, a Jew. She needs to get out of France. Can you help?'

'I'm sorry,' Weiss said. 'There are escape lines, some of them run by the British, but it's not something we do. From time to time, we'll move somebody — a senior officer, a special operative — but mostly our people stay here and fight.'

'If you think of something, you'll let me know?'

'I will.' Weiss looked at his watch. 'I have to be on my way,' he said.

They stood, shook hands.

'Another meeting,' Casson said.

'Yes. Then, another.'

'It never ends,' Casson said.

'No,' Weiss said. 'It never does.'

Casson walked toward the Metro. No help from the FTP, he thought. That leaves de la Barre.

★ ★ ★

He took the Métro to the 7th and headed for de la Barre's apartment. When he reached the street, there was a Citroën *traction-avant* parked at the corner, the driver behind the wheel. Casson glanced at him, then looked away. He walked down the block, went past de la Barre's doorway. At the other end of the street, a man was standing on the corner. Casson's heart sank.

He went to a café and called de la Barre's number. A woman answered. 'Monsieur de la Barre, please.'

'One moment.'

A man came on the line. 'Yes? This is de la Barre.'

Casson couldn't be sure. It was the voice of an older man, maybe it was de la Barre, maybe not. 'I'm interested in eighteenth-century texts,' Casson said. 'Particularly physiognomy and anatomy.'

'Anything in particular?'

Casson improvised. 'The illustrator Matinus, in Montpellier.'

'The best thing for you, monsieur, is to come and take a look at what I have. Do you know the address?'

'I do.'

'And you are?'

'Monsieur Brun.'

'When would you like to come, Monsieur Brun?'

'Perhaps this afternoon.'

'I look forward to meeting you.'

Casson hung up. Walked away as fast as he could. A *trap*, he thought. They would trace the call.

★ ★ ★

The following morning he went out to Luna Park and worked on the books. Lamy sat with him, telling him stories about the Shanghai tong wars of the 1920s. Then he said, 'I think I can help you out, Marin. I'd like to spend Thursday afternoons with my girlfriend — I could use somebody to keep an eye on things here. It isn't hard. Collect the money at night, just make sure nothing goes wrong. An extra six hours a week, maybe a little more. Want to try it?' Casson said he would.

* * *

Some people went to church, Casson went to the movies. It took him most of the afternoon to decide what to do — a monologue in bits and pieces. He sat through the German newsreel, straight from the propaganda *Abteilung* in the Hotel Meurice. Rommel's Afrika Korps bouncing over the sand dunes of Libya, then taking Benghazi. A shot of a British tank on fire, a shot of a sign that gave the distance to Cairo. Then, the film. Three girls from Paris take their summer vacation at the beach, each of them, it seems . . .

He sat in the comforting darkness, amid the coughs and the steady whirr of the projector, pretending to wonder what to do. He knew, of course. He just kept telling himself he was a fool. Not a realist, not shrewd. The first article of faith in French society: *il faut se défendre*. Gospel. You must take care of yourself, first and foremost. Because, if you don't, nobody else will. Marie-Claire had baited him, telling him about her friend who worked for de Gaulle. Maybe if she hadn't said anything — no, that wasn't true. He would have found another way. On the screen, young Maurice, too shy to reveal his love, leaves a bouquet of wildflowers on the doorstep. What's this? The milkman's donkey. Oh no, he's eating them!

How had they found out about de la Barre? Probably interrogated the passengers after the ship burned in the harbor. One of de la Barre's fugitives, papers a little wrong, a forced confession. Casson looked at his watch. Twenty minutes more, he might as well see how it ended.

Why me?

He didn't know. It didn't have to be that way — here was Lamy, offering him a way out. A nice little job, soon enough, for *Monsieur Marin of the Hotel du Commerce.*

The final shot, a beach in the moonlight. *Not so bad,* he thought. Long white waves rolling into the shore, breaking gently on the beach.

The movie theatre had a telephone; he called Marie-Claire.

★   ★   ★

She met him at a café, just after five. Bruno was back, she explained, they were having dinner at nine. Celebrating his victory. From now on, German officers, crooked bureaucrats, butter dealers, any of the suddenly rich, would be able to buy an Alfa Romeo.

Casson ordered Marie-Claire her customary Martini Rouge, with lemon. 'You don't seem in the mood for a celebration.'

'I'm not. It's beginning to bother me, all this.' She made a face he knew all too well.

'He is what he is,' Casson said, sympathetic.

'Yes, he is.' She paused a moment. 'Our part of the world, up in Passy, is coming apart, Jean-Claude. That's really what's going on. Half of my friends listen to de Gaulle on the radio, the other half keep portraits of Pétain on the piano. Somehow, Bruno and I wound up on different sides.'

'That's not so good.'

She looked sorrowful. 'And it's not just the couples, it's everywhere, even in the same family — between sisters, between fathers and sons. It's terrible, Jean-Claude. Terrible.'

'I know,' Casson said. 'Marie-Claire, I would like to talk to the friend you mentioned. The one who has ties to the French in London.'

'Did I tell you who it was?'

'No.'

She gave him the look that meant *I know you too well, Jean- Claude, you're not going to like this*. 'It's Jacques Gueze,' she said.

'Oh no.'

'That's who it is.'

Casson knew him, had sat across from him at a dinner party back in the old days. After that, a handshake two or three times at some *grande affaire*. Casson hated him. Short and wide, prosperously fat, with thick glasses and tight, curly hair. He floated on waves of *amour propre* — boundless conceit, in measures rare even in France. He described himself as an ethnologist, no, there was more to it than that, it was *better* than that. Socio-ethnologist? Psycho-ethnologist? Anyhow, a hyphen. Now he remembered — gods, something about gods. He'd written a book about them.

'So,' Marie-Claire said, one eyebrow raised. 'That's it for you and the *resistance?*'

'Jacques Gueze? Did you think he was telling the truth?'

'Yes. I believed him.'

'All the time trying to get you in bed.'

'Trying hard. Puffed himself up like a pigeon, as I think I told you, but I declined. It seemed to me he would probably fuck like a pigeon.'

Casson laughed. 'All right,' he said, a sigh in his voice. 'Can you let him know?'

'Let him know what?'

'That I want to speak with him. You can say 'confidentially.' How can de Gaulle tolerate him?'

'De Gaulle does not exactly undervalue himself, Jean-Claude. I don't know, but to him Jacques Gueze may seem perfectly normal.'

★　★　★

A message was left at the hotel the following day, a meeting at 8:20 by the St.-Paul Métro station. 'We will go to dinner,' Gueze announced. 'To Heininger. A *choucroute*, I think, for this weather.'

Casson was horrified. 'I might see people who know me,' he said. 'Maybe not the best idea.'

'Don't be absurd,' Gueze said. 'You're with me.' The idea of doing without his *choucroute* was beneath consideration.

They walked a few blocks toward the place

Bastille, to the Brasserie Heininger. Famous, infamous, a vast marble palace, glowing wood, golden light, waiters in fancy whiskers and green aprons, and *scandale*, as fragrant in the air as the grilled sausage.

'Table fourteen, *jeune homme*,' Gueze said to Papa Heininger, not at all a 'young man,' who accepted the courteously rude appellation with a genial nod. Of course it was available, held nightly for customers powerful enough to know about it. Table fourteen — a small hole in the mirrored panel where an assassin had fired a machine gun on a spring evening when the Bulgarian headwaiter was murdered in the ladies' WC. The table where an aristocratic Englishwoman had once recruited Russian spies. The table where, in the first months of the Occupation, the companion of a German naval officer had taken to shooting peas at other diners, using a rolled-up *carte des vins* as a blowpipe. The table where, a year earlier, Casson — in the last days of life as himself — had dined with a German film executive and his friends.

A waiter appeared, Gueze rubbed his hands. '*Choucroute, choucroute*,' he said with a smile. 'Beer, do you think?' he asked Casson.

'All right.'

'Alsatian,' Gueze said to the waiter. 'Dark.

Two right away, then two more — keep an eye on us and see when we're ready.'

Casson looked around the room — a number of Germans in uniform, and at least two people he knew, both of them very busy talking and eating.

'So then,' Gueze said. 'Marie-Claire tells me you're thinking of joining up with us. *Les fous de Grand Charles.*' He laughed merrily at the name — Big Charlie's lunatics.

'Maybe,' Casson said. 'I'm not sure what I could do.'

'Don't worry about *that*. There's plenty to go around.' A small cloud crossed his face. 'You don't want to go to London, do you?'

'No, it hadn't occurred to me.'

The cloud vanished. 'Good, good. People show up at the office, they all want the big desk. I was back in August — a real circus. Where we need help, of course, is right here.'

'What kind of help do you need?'

'As a government in exile, we've had to start from the beginning. That includes what we call the BCRA — *Bureau Centrale de Renseignements et d'Action*. Essentially, we're de Gaulle's intelligence service. The money comes from the British, along with lots of advice, most of it useless, and sometimes an order, which we usually ignore.'

'And the Americans?'

'A sore point. The people in the State Department don't like the general. Nothing new there, all sorts of people don't like him.'

Gueze turned gloomy for a moment — de Gaulle's personality didn't make his life any easier — then smiled. 'In May of '40, when de Gaulle went up to Belgium, Weygand got so mad at him he threw him out! Threatened to have him *arrested* if he didn't leave the front lines.' Gueze paused to enjoy the scene. 'But all for the best, all for the best. We're rid of that now, it's in the past. What we are, my friend, is the future.'

The waiter arrived, carrying a tray with two glasses of beer, dark brown, almost black, a thin layer of mocha-colored foam on top. 'Ah-ha,' Gueze sang out. *'La bonne bière.'* The good beer — real, honest, ancient, like us peasant French. Gueze beamed at the idea, pleased with himself. *Even so*, Casson thought, he's no fool.

Casson's father had taken him to the park on Sunday afternoons. Neither of them knew what they were supposed to be doing there, but his mother insisted and so they went, sitting on a bench in the Ranelagh gardens until they were allowed back in the apartment. Once, Casson remembered, his father had stared a long time at a horse and carriage. 'A noble head on that animal,' he'd said at last. 'But, Jean-Claude, do not underestimate the value of his backside.'

They drank the beer, cool and thick and bitter. All around them, the brasserie was getting louder as the evening went on. 'This is good,' Casson said. He paused, then, 'There is something I wanted to mention, it may not be of interest, but I leave that up to you.'

Gueze raised his eyebrows.

'For some months,' Casson said, 'I've had to live underground. During that time I came across an old friend, and he asked me to help him. The work we did was political, and covert. In the process, I had conversations with people who are involved in the direction of the Communist Party. The FTP, to be exact. With jobs maybe not so different from yours. We had several meetings, some of their views became clear over time. At the last meeting, I was told they needed weapons, thousands of them, with ammunition, and hand grenades. Would this interest you? Because, if it does, there's more. They are willing, in return, to undertake specific operations against the Germans.'

'Interesting,' Gueze said. 'No doubt about it. Tell me this, are you a believer? I don't care if you are, I happen to be a socialist, but if you look around this restaurant, at the

379

German uniforms, you'll see where political divisions have gotten us.'

'No,' Casson said. 'And they knew that from the beginning.'

The dinner arrived. *What war?* Casson thought. Warm sauerkraut, thick bacon on its rind, a pork chop. And a *saucisse de Toulouse* — he filled the bowl of a tiny spoon with hot mustard and ran it down the burst, blackened skin.

'Not too bad for a cold March night,' Gueze said.

Casson agreed. No, not too bad.

'Of course I can't give you an answer straight away,' Gueze said. 'This will be pawed over by a committee, but something has to be worked out. Naturally we talk to the communists in London, then wait until they wire back to Moscow for permission to blow their nose. It's terribly slow. However, if we patch something together in Paris it's on-the-ground, not binding, but at least something will come of it. *That's* the attraction of what you've told me.'

Gueze picked up the empty bread basket and looked around. A waiter swept it away and returned a moment later with a full one, rounds of fresh bread piled high.

'The fact is,' Gueze said, 'we are making an effort to get all the resistance movements

— at the moment we count fifteen or so — going in the same direction. At least now and then.' He ate a forkful of sauerkraut, washed it down with beer. 'You said you had to live underground?'

'I got into trouble with the Gestapo, June of '41. At that time, I had some contact with the British special services.'

'Which? The people who blow things up? Or the people who steal blueprints?'

'Blow things up.'

'Well, they're a lot easier to deal with, that much I can tell you. We do both, in one service. So, the Gestapo wants you. How badly?'

'I wouldn't know.'

'We'll have to find out. If they're really hunting for you, you can't be of much use to us. One thing I should say is that if you come to work for us, we'll pay you. Not a lot, but enough. Marie-Claire seemed to think that your existence has been, well, day-to-day.'

'It has.'

'You'll have plenty to worry about, with us, but not that.' He went back to work on the *choucroute*. 'She is, you know, a very attractive woman.'

'I know,' Casson said.

'Do you regret, the, ah . . . '

'No. We just couldn't get along. You know how it is.'

'Oh yes. Unfortunately, she lives with that awful man.'

They ate in silence for a time. 'Communists, you know,' Gueze said, 'turn out to be crucial. The British have to bleed the Germans to death — they can't absorb the number of casualties the Russians can. Their strategy is to shut down the power stations, the rail-roads, the phones and the telegraph, keep the important metals away, blow up the tool-and-die works. It's not easy, because the Germans are ingenious, they wire it all back together, and they've learned to put things underground. But, if you're going to deliver the explosives by hand, rather than by plane, you need the railwaymen, the telephone workers, the lathe operators. That's the working class — labor unions, communists. And they've been in clandestine operations for twenty years.'

'One thing did occur to me,' Casson said. 'What if we help the FTP to get arms and then they don't do all that much. They simply wait till the end of the war. They're armed, and well organized. They demand a share of the government — or else.'

Gueze shrugged. 'That's what we're doing, why shouldn't they?'

Later, Casson mentioned Hélène, and the *San Lorenzo*. Gueze was waiting for the tarte Tatin he'd ordered. 'Tell me what happened,' he said. Casson told the story in detail, from the beginning. Gueze listened attentively. 'I'm not sure how we can help,' he said at the end. 'But there may be something we can do. Let me think it over.'

★ ★ ★

Hélène called him at the hotel in the late afternoon — she'd arrived in Paris at dawn, and gone to work. Casson offered to take her out to dinner and they met at a restaurant. As she came toward the table, he could see a dark bruise on one side of her jaw, and when he embraced her she winced.

'You're hurt,' he said.

'Not much, a little sore.'

She sat next to him on a banquette, he ordered a bottle of red wine. The trip down wasn't bad, she said, a few identity checks and the train was cold. She'd spent two weeks in Nice, de la Barre's people had arranged for her to stay at an apartment in the old city. 'Day and night,' she said. 'We were not permitted to leave.'

She didn't get out the first time. 'The next sailing was delayed but, finally, they let us on board. I was in a cabin on the deck, with eight other passengers. It was after midnight, nobody said a word, we just waited to get under way. Then there was an explosion below deck — maybe more than one — it was like a wind hit the floor. The lights went out, we heard people screaming that the boat was on fire. Everybody ran, somebody pushed me out of the way and I fell flat on my face on the steel deck, but I got up, and a sailor grabbed me by the elbow and led me down the gangplank. Then we all just stood there, watching the ship burn.'

She paused a moment. Casson poured wine in her glass and she drank some. 'Finally,' she said, 'the police came and took everybody to the station. We were questioned most of the night — the police were Italian, but the people asking the questions were German. Later on we heard that somebody had been arrested.'

Casson told her about his attempt to see de la Barre. 'We'll just have to find another way.'

'I don't know,' she said. 'We'll see.'

Back at Casson's hotel, she folded her skirt and sweater over the back of a chair and lay down on the bed in her slip. There were bruises down one side of her leg. Casson stretched out next to her. 'How was work?' he asked.

She shrugged. 'It doesn't change.'

'Victorine?'

'We talked about Strasbourg. She went once to Buerehiesel for dinner, she always tells me what a good time she had.'

'Did she — '

'Not today. Let's not talk about it.'

Casson stubbed out his cigarette and put his arms around her. 'Where are you staying?'

'Same place. Today it felt like I never left — maybe I'm fated to be here.'

'Don't say that, Hélène.'

'I could find another job. In a shop, perhaps. I just have to live quietly, I'll be all right.'

As gently as he could, Casson said, 'We have to try again.'

She didn't answer. Casson told her about Lamy and his stories, about the Dodge-em cars. Then they were quiet for a time, and Casson realized she had fallen asleep. Carefully, he slipped off the bed and covered her with a blanket. He sat by the window and read for a time. She called him softly when she woke up. 'Is it curfew yet?'

'In about an hour.'

'I should go back to the room. Tonight, anyhow.'

'All right. You know you can stay with me, as long as you like.'

'I know.'

She sat up, held her face in her hands.

'I'll take you back to the apartment,' he said.

They rode the Métro together in silence. He kissed her at the door of her building, then waited while she went upstairs.

★ ★ ★

For SS-*Unterscharführer* Otto Albers, it was perhaps the worst day of his life. One of them, anyhow. There had been the time he was caught stealing rolls from the baker, the time caught cheating in school. He'd had the same knot in his stomach.

But he was no child now, and what had happened was his own fault. Another corporal worked alongside him in the basement vaults of the Gestapo headquarters on the rue des Saussaies, Corporal Prost. Prost had been in Russia, had fought there, had barely escaped with his life. He was missing an eye and most of a foot, and more than that, to hear him tell it. 'I don't care about it anymore,' he told Albers sadly. 'It just doesn't come to me.'

He was a good storyteller, Prost. He'd seen

386

action around Nikopol, in the Ukraine, with a Waffen-SS unit. They'd beaten back days of Soviet counterattacks, then dealt with *partizans* — shot most of them, hanged the ones they caught alive. But it didn't seem to matter — there were always more. Prost was wounded when a rigged mortar shell was set off in the latrine. Then the *partizans* stopped the hospital train and burned it with kerosene. Most of the wounded died, Prost crawled away. As the *partizans* withdrew, a little boy, maybe eleven, shot Prost in the face. Because the shot was fired at an angle, Prost survived. 'Do whatever you need to do,' he told Albers. 'But don't go to that place.'

Albers didn't want to go. But the problem he'd picked up from his 'mouse' on the rue St.-Denis was getting worse. He'd considered going to the infirmary, but the penalty for catching a venereal disease was immediate transfer to the eastern front. So he asked a friend for the name of a doctor and was sent to a wretched old man out in the northern suburbs. He muttered something in French, which Albers couldn't understand, then resorted to sign language, explaining how to apply the precious ointment. Albers returned to Paris feeling enormous relief — thank heaven *that* was over.

But it wasn't. Over lunch ten days later, in

a café near Gestapo headquarters, a young man rather boldly sat himself down at Albers's table. He was apologetic at first — Albers thought he might be a student, but he was a few years too old for that. A fair-haired Frenchman, with cold eyes. The young man finished his soup, then leaned over and said, '*Unterscharführer* Albers?' Shocked, Albers nodded. 'Here is a little something for you.' Excellent German, clipped and confidently spoken. Then he was gone, leaving an envelope on the table.

Albers was almost sick. They had his medical record, knew the doctor, knew everything. His choice: do what they said to do, or his superiors would be informed that he'd had a venereal disease. The letter said he had to signal his intentions immediately. If he put the envelope back on the table and left it there, he would cooperate. If he left with it, he might as well show it to his boss.

Albers looked frantically around the room but all he saw were people eating lunch. He left the envelope on the table, the waiter swept it away with the dishes. The waiter! Yes? he asked himself. Just what would he do to the waiter? It would only get him in deeper.

He spent the day frozen, terrified, trying somehow to find the courage to carry out their orders. He took no satisfaction that afternoon in the soothing rhythm of his work, rolling the metal cart up and down the endless rows of files. He replaced twenty-eight folders, took out forty new ones.

Just names, Albers told himself. French names — it took some time to get used to them, with their strange accents — and Jewish names, with difficult Polish spellings. Maybe life wouldn't be so good for them tomorrow, or in a week, whenever the people upstairs got around to arresting them, but that wasn't his fault.

He worked in a fury. How could he have allowed these sneaky Frenchmen to get power over him! Hitler was right, they had no sense of fair play — no instinctive, no *Aryan* sense of justice. You could never trust them. Albers returned the files of *Levagne, Pierre* and *Levi, Anna* to the shelf. The people upstairs were done with them.

He heard Prost, clumping along in his special shoe, as he came around the corner, pushing a file cart. He gave Albers a smile. 'So, Otto, what's for you tonight?'

'Nothing much. Tired, lately.'

'It's the cold weather. But spring is coming, soon you'll be bounding around like a new lamb.' He laughed.

Albers joined in as best he could. But then, Prost was right. If he took care of this, he could stay in Paris, go back to his Parisian pleasures. The mouse, cured of her malady, her friend, maybe another friend — a new character for his little theatre. Prost slipped a file back into the *D* section — just the end of it on the top shelf, *Dybinski*, a few others — then he went around the corner. 'Klaus,' Albers called out, following him.

'Yes?'

'If you're going down that way, could you take care of this?'

Prost looked at the folder Albers had given him. *Vignon.* 'Be happy to do it,' he said.

Albers listened to the wheels of the cart, rolling over the cement floor, headed off to the other end of the alphabet.

Now.

Cascone, Caseda, Casselot, Cassignier, Cassignol.

Casson. There were several, what he needed was —

Casson, Jean.

As he'd practiced: undo three buttons of the shirt, take the dossier, slip it inside, then around under the arm, hidden beneath the uniform jacket. Button the buttons. Now, keep it there for thirty minutes, then it was time to leave the building. That wouldn't be a problem.

Done, he thought.

MONSIEUR MARIN

28 MARCH, 1942.

The apartment was in the 7th, on the avenue Bosquet, above a small and very expensive restaurant. It was well used; smelled of Gauloises and wet overcoats, and too much time spent indoors with the windows shut. 'It belongs to a wealthy family,' Gueze explained. 'They've left the country, but we can use it for as long as the war goes on. The best way to come in is down the hallway from a door inside the restaurant, then up the stairs.' He paused, then said, 'We think it's safe, but look around before you enter the building. It's like everything else.'

He had a sheet of paper in front of him, which he tapped with the end of his pen. 'We got hold of your dossier. Not too bad. They want to question you again, but there's nothing about an escape.'

'How is that possible?'

'Apparently they've protected themselves. The Gestapo is unforgiving — in their view, accidents don't happen. So, they called you in for questioning, then you left.'

393

'A man chased me. Fell off the roof into the courtyard.'

'If it happened, it isn't in here. They may have reported it separately, as an accident, or a suicide. There is a cross-reference to the files of the SD, the SS intelligence service, we don't know what's in there. It seems to us that the case against you is obscure, not appealing to most investigators. You were certainly suspected of involvement with the British, but so were a lot of other people. And now the dossier is missing, perhaps misfiled.'

'So then?'

'You're just as well off as Marin. You can't be rehabilitated. Not now. Major Guske, the officer who called you in for questioning, is still in Paris. I would, if I were you, try to avoid him.'

'I'll try.'

They both smiled. 'As I said, we're all new to this. We've suffered losses, but we're learning as we go along. I think I may have to concede that perhaps the Brasserie Heininger wasn't such a good idea after all. When you went to the WC, a man came over — I knew him slightly — and asked if you were the film producer Jean Casson.'

'What did you say?'

'That you were an insurance executive.'

'Claims investigator, is what my papers say.'

'Yes, but I wouldn't be having dinner with somebody like that. Anyhow, you can stay in Paris for the time being, but you must be careful.' He paused, cleared his throat, put his notes away. 'Now,' he said, 'the British have come to the London office with a problem. Of course we agreed to help, and it's up to us, to you and me, to show them we can do it.

'According to their intelligence, during the period January-February of this year, fifty-five hundred tons of gasoline and aviation fuel went from France to Rommel's Afrika Korps in Libya. A war in the desert is a war of gasoline — for warplanes, for the tanks. In this kind of expanse — thousands of square miles — whoever can cover more ground, whoever can stay in the air longer, wins. What they want is for somebody to slow down the fuel deliveries. Some of it moves by rail, a good deal of it goes south on the rivers and canals, from the refineries in Rouen. Some of it must be coming from the Toulon refineries in the south, but the tonnage is well beyond what they produce. That's more or less the situation, do you understand?'

'Yes.'

'Good,' Gueze said. 'Now do something about it.'

* * *

395

5 APRIL.

3:40 A.M., raining hard. The dockyards at Ablon, just south of Paris.

The union office was in a wooden shack — a few desks and chairs, a cold woodstove with a zigzag pipe to the roof. Weiss flinched as he entered, water dripping on him from the doorframe. Inside, the two men in *bleu de travail* grinned. 'We've been meaning to do something about that,' one of them said.

His friend laughed. 'Comrade Weiss doesn't care.'

Weiss smoothed his hair back and wiped the water off his forehead.

'We have what you want,' the first man said. He produced a sheaf of paper, a handwritten manifest.

The oil lamp was turned down to a glow, Weiss peered at the columns of tiny script. 'Maybe if I had my glasses,' he said.

'We have eleven fuel barges waiting to go. Looks like a convoy. There may be more coming down today, from Rouen.'

'What is it?'

'Just plain gasoline. Not the fancy stuff for planes. That's what the manifest says, anyhow.'

'What time does it leave?'

'Sometime around six-thirty this morning.

Lots of Germans around, though. That usually slows things down.'

'Any idea what they're after?'

'Who knows? Sometimes they hear something.'

Weiss thought for a while, staring at the darkness outside the window. 'We want these barges to burn,' he said. 'Can you take care of it?'

'Not here.' The man laughed, though nothing was particularly funny. 'They'd kill every last one of us.'

'What about a little way downstream?'

'I suppose it's possible, with explosives.'

'What happens if you put a bullet in it?'

'Not much. We tried that during a strike in '37. Somebody put four shots right in the tank and nothing happened — it spilled a few pints of gasoline, somebody else was beaten up, and a couple of people who had nothing to do with it were fired.'

'Is the manifest complete — bargeloads, names, and numbers?'

'It's all there,' the man said, a little relieved.

* * *

Casson was waiting in a hotel room near the docks. Weiss hung his wet coat on the back of a chair. 'Fuel barges all over the place,' he said. 'Up in Ivry, and Choisy, and eleven down here. They're being very careful.'

'What are they worried about?'

'Hard to say. It's a big war, some damn thing goes on in Copenhagen or Odessa and a message shows up on the teleprinter in the rue des Saussaies.'

'Anything we can do?'

Weiss exhaled, rubbed his face. He was tired. 'I'm out of ideas. This thing was organized in a hurry — I'm not complaining, you understand, it's what we asked for. But we usually work slowly, find out what we need to know, plan every step.'

Casson wondered what he could offer. Gueze had given him a briefcase full of hundred-franc notes, but Weiss and the FTP didn't work that way. 'We'll think of something,' Casson said.

Weiss brooded, took a well-creased road map of France from the pocket of his coat and spread it out on the bed. 'It's hard, with the waterways. You can't blow up a river.'

* * *

Later that day, riding a local train south to Troyes, Casson found a leaflet on the seat from the resistance group *Liberation*. The lead story: a heroic attack by three RAF

Beaufighters on a barge convoy at Elbeuf, in the curve of the Seine south of Rouen.

... their 20 MM cannon firing thunderbolts of destruction, crewmen leaping off the decks and swimming for their lives. A hard blow, and daring, in full daylight, engines screaming as they dove, lower, lower, leveling out just a few feet above the water, machine guns blazing. Then, bombs released, the planes roar away. A huge blast — windows tremble in Rouen, hearts tremble in Berlin. Four bargeloads of coal sent to the bottom of the river. No tank turrets will be forged with that coal!

Coal, Casson thought. *Merde.*

He met with Weiss as planned, at a café in Troyes, and told him what he'd read. Weiss shrugged. 'Could as well have been turnips,' he said. 'Last I heard, Rommel was running panzer tanks, not locomotives.'

'Were they after the gasoline?'

'What else? The problem is, doing this kind of thing with airplanes is very hard. They miss, they hit the wrong building, the wrong *part* of the building, the wrong town, and, yes, it's happened, I promise you, the wrong country. So, in this case, they hit the wrong barges.' They were silent for a time, the rain slanting down beyond the steamy window. 'There is one thing we can try here — a lock, on the canal south of the town. The countryside looks flat but actually it isn't, the barge traffic has to move uphill.' He looked at his watch. 'I have to sleep,' he said, 'it's been forty hours.'

'You have a place to go?'

'Yes, and you better come along. I don't want you in hotels today — if there's one thing the British did with their raid, they woke the Germans up. It's typical of the British — they'll try an air attack and a sabotage operation on the same target. If one doesn't work, maybe the other will.' Weiss rubbed his eyes. 'Let's get going,' he said, 'before I fall asleep on the table.'

The woman in the small cottage was not pleased to see them. Her husband mumbled something or other as they came through the door but she wasn't having any. She was big and broad-shouldered, stood over a huge pot with an iron spoon in her hand and glowered at them. Five kids in the house, at least as far as Casson could count, and her husband invites his pals for dinner.

Weiss stretched out on a sofa in the tiny parlor and fell sound asleep. Casson slept in a chair.

'You could have stayed in Paris, you know,' Weiss said to him later. 'This is only going to get harder.'

'I know,' Casson said. 'But I tried that once. It was a disaster. We were making *The Devil's Bridge*, shooting on location — a bridge over the Sambre, way up north, almost on the Belgian border. I think the Germans blew it up in '40. 'Why not stay in Paris?' the director said. 'When the problems come, you're right there in the office to solve them.' Well, the problems came, all right, oh how they came. First, the usual problems, then the problems that came from not having a producer on location. I went up there on the next train but it was too late — started out badly and it was going to stay that way.'

'But you made the movie.'

'We made something.'

Just before dark, a woman knocked on the door. Weiss introduced her as Jeanne. She acknowledged Casson with a glance, her hands thrust deep in the pockets of an oilskin field coat. Casson offered her a cigarette and lit it for her. She nodded her thanks as she inhaled, her face drawn with fatigue. 'This wasn't easy,' she said to Weiss, 'but we found somebody, the uncle of a teacher at the *lycée*.

He has a barge called *Le Zephyr*, docked about thirty miles upstream. He promises to be in Troyes by eleven tomorrow.'

'That's the first good news today,' Weiss said. 'Will he do what we want?'

'Perhaps he will — he *says* he will. If he doesn't show, we'll have to find somebody else.'

'No time.'

'All right,' she said, 'I'll steal a barge and do it myself.'

* * *

The *Zephyr* was north of Troyes a little after noon. The teacher's uncle, its captain, had already stoked up his courage: the sour smell of wine hung around him like a mist. 'What must be done must be done,' he mumbled, as much to himself as anybody else. As arranged, they'd met him on the riverbank, about five kilometers from Troyes, where he'd tied the barge to a willow tree. 'I am ready, monsieur,' he said to Weiss.

The lock system was on the other side of the town. Weiss and Casson bicycled there and found a patch of woods where a street turned into a dirt path. Weiss swore when he saw what was going on. A German officer was standing with the lockkeeper in his small hut

402

to one side of the gates. A string of barges had just gone through the lock, white water was foaming out of the downriver spillway, and a line of barges waiting to enter had tied up to posts on the far bank.

It seemed a long time, a half hour or more, before they saw the *Zéphyr*. Moving quickly for a barge, its stern engine hammering away in a haze of blue smoke.

Casson watched the German officer. Tall, hands clasped behind his back, a sharp profile below the visor of his cap. He rocked back and forth as he watched the *Zéphyr* approach.

'I don't care for this German,' Casson said.

Weiss agreed. 'No, he's taking it very seriously, whoever he is.'

'What's our captain going to think, when he sees him?'

'We'll find out,' Weiss said. 'If I'd known he would be here, I would have called the thing off. I thought this would be a French affair — catastrophe as daily bread and all that. But now . . . ' He didn't bother to finish.

The last of the water spilled from the downriver gate and the lockkeeper thrust his weight against a huge iron wheel. As it turned, the two gates began to move toward each other, an inch at a time, until they met. When the lockkeeper looked up, there was the *Zéphyr,* headed full speed for the closed gates of the lock. On the tied-up barges, people were shouting, waving their arms. The lockkeeper did his best, ran to the other end of the hut and turned the wheel frantically, trying to get the gates open, but they parted only a foot or so. He saw he couldn't do it in time, ran out of the hut and along the stone wall that held the gates, and signaled violently with both hands: *run it into shore!* But the Zéphyr never wavered, headed directly for the lock.

The sound of the collision was not dramatic, a muffled thud as the wooden prow hit the gates, then the sound of metal on metal as they bent backward. A chain snapped, an ancient iron pulley fell into the canal with a splash. That was all.

The *Zéphyr*'s stern swung around in the current and the side of the barge bumped against the crushed gates as the captain shut off his engine.

For a moment, silence. On the barges, people stared in disbelief. Casson wanted to laugh. There was something comic about it, slapstick, you saw it coming but there was nothing anybody could do.

Weiss's voice was so quiet Casson barely heard it. 'Oh no,' he said.

The German officer came tearing out of

the hut and ran onto the stone wall, brushing past the lockkeeper. Lean and graceful, he ran hard, and Casson now saw what Weiss had seen a moment earlier: something about the way he was running made it clear what he was going to do.

The captain of the *Zéphyr* stumbled out of the wheelhouse and threw his arms wide, palms up to heaven. *Oh Lord, now look what's happened.* The officer never missed a step. He leaped onto the barge, grabbed the captain by the shirt, and threw him to the deck, the man's feet flew up in the air as he landed. He started talking, some of the words drifted over to Weiss and Casson, shrill, whining. The officer waited, the barge captain never stopped. The officer's arm swept up from his side, pointed out straight, and a flame came out of his hand, the sound flat and hollow on the open water. The man on the deck thrashed for a time, Casson thought he heard him saying something. The officer put his pistol away, vaulted back up to the stone wall and returned to the hut.

8 APRIL.

The town of Coligny, on the Briare Canal. Weiss had a room over a café on the main

405

square. It was quiet in the evening, farm country in Burgundy, people played cards and drank wine in the café. The telephone in the room rang from time to time. Weiss listened, said a few words, hung up. He made one brief call, then another. 'The news is not so good,' he told Casson. 'They're saying in Troyes that the canal will be back in operation in a day or two. If we get a sixty-hour delay out of this I'll be surprised.'

'Maybe it's just a rumor.'

'I don't think so. We got word in Paris, about an hour ago, that one of the foundries in Metz has a complete stop-work order — to set up for an emergency job. Somebody will try to get a look at the drawings, but I would bet they're going to make a new set of lock gates. What that means to me is intervention at a very high level, so we have to assume the Germans pretty much know what we're doing. By tomorrow, they'll probably have a couple of infantry companies at every lock on the inland waterways, and we'll be out of business.'

He paced the room for a time then sat in a swivel chair by the desk. 'What we're doing tonight,' he said, 'is maybe our best chance. It's improvised, but at least we're depending on our own people.'

The waiting was hard. Casson walked

around the room. The town outside was dark and silent, farm dogs barking somewhere in the distance. The phone rang again, Weiss let it ring a second time, then answered. He looked at his watch and said, 'Just after eight-thirty,' and hung up.

A knock at the door and two men entered: the pale Slav who'd been with Weiss the day the guns were delivered, and a man who Casson thought, from his accent, might be a Spaniard. They both nodded to Casson.

'Ready to go?' Weiss said.

The two men exchanged a look. After a moment the Spaniard said, 'I don't know this explosive. They use it in the mines, but not where I come from. It's been in the rain, I think.'

'That won't matter.'

'No, the man who brought it said it wouldn't.'

'What kind of fuse?'

'Detonation cord. Also damp, but I cut off a small piece and it worked.'

'You have enough people?'

'Escobar. And three others.'

'It's scheduled for eight-thirty,' Weiss said. He turned to the other man. 'What about the power station?'

'I have somebody from the local office. It won't be a problem.'

'Good.'

The two men said good night and left.

'We can't get the right explosive,' Weiss said. 'What we're using now is Ammonal, powdered aluminum and TNT, mining explosive. We get it from the Poles who work the iron pits up in Nancy.'

'What do you need?'

'C4. Likely the English have something even better.'

'Do this tonight,' Casson said. 'And they'll give you whatever you want.'

8 : 30.

Serra and Escobar were waiting in the shadows at the Coligny lock, on the edge of town where the Briare Canal met the river Loing. The Germans had lit the area with two powerful searchlights — which created a fine hiding place just beyond the beams. The lock had been built in 1810; heavy gates on either end of a long *barrage*, a dam of dry-masoned set stone that measured several hundred feet from end to end, large enough to hold thirty barges.

Serra had packed the Ammonal into a metal drum he'd found outside a workshop in Coligny. He'd punched a hole in the side and set the end of the fuse between two packets of explosive.

'A lot of people on the barges,' Escobar said.

'Yes. They're waiting to go through in the morning.'

They could smell smoke from cooking fires. Somebody laughed, a woman called out to a friend.

'Who is at the power station?'

'Ivanic.'

'Then we don't have to worry.'

'No,' Serra said.

'And the guards?'

'Four of them. Gendarmes, in the lock-keeper's hut. They stay in there most of the time, people here say they go to sleep after midnight. I don't think you should be worrying about them, somebody's covering that side of the dam. They have a machine gun, the gendarmes will not argue with it.'

8 : 44.

The searchlights flared brilliant white, then died away.

Serra closed his eyes and waited for the afterimage to fade. It was very dark now, a power failure in Coligny. A half-moon and a few stars showed through the scudding cloud, just enough light to catch the dull silver of the gasoline tanks on the barges.

'In a minute,' Serra said.

Some commotion, a single shout from the lockkeeper's hut. Moments later a whistle, and a man came running low around the stone wall of the dam. 'Serra, are you there?' he called in Spanish.

'Yes. What is it?'

A young man squatted beside him and whispered, 'Do you have any cord?'

'No. What do you want with that?'

'The gendarmes. They say to tie them up, or else the Germans will shoot them.'

'I don't know — use their belts. Certainly there is rope on the barges.'

'Serra, I just want to ask you, will the explosion hit the lockkeeper's little house?'

'Don't worry about it. Just do your job, and we'll do ours.'

The young man gave him a look, then ran off and circled back around the dam.

'Now,' Serra said.

'Look.' Escobar pointed back toward the town.

'What?'

'Something's on fire.'

'That's the power station. Ivanic always burns something.'

★ ★ ★

The barrel of Ammonal went off at 8:46.

Serra had started his apprenticeship in the mines of Asturias when he was eleven years old. By the time he was twelve, he knew how to move rock around with explosive.

The barrel had been set snugly at the base of the stone wall of the dam and blew a great cloud of stone chips and dirt into the air. People on the barges screamed, leaped onto the embankment, and scrambled away into the darkness. Dust and smoke drifted slowly toward the town. The hole in the wall of the dam was only three feet wide to begin with, but the force of the water soon took away one piece of cracked stone block, then another.

The water ran into the backstreets of Coligny and down the grates of the medieval sewers, echoing in the huge vaults below the town. People heard it, opened their windows and leaned out, had a word or two with their neighbors across the street.

'Albert, is your power out?'

'Yes. Something blew up.'

'A bomb?'

'No. Nothing like that, probably those *conards* at the power station pulled the wrong lever.'

'Do you smell smoke?'

411

'Yes.'

'Well, we'll never get to sleep now. Want to play cards?'

'What about Francoise?'

'Nothing wakes her, we can play in the kitchen.'

★ ★ ★

On the dam, the barges sank slowly, it took a long time for the water to run out of the hole blown in the stonework. Just about all of the people on the barges took advantage of it — some had to swim but most of them made their way from the deck of one barge to the next, stepped onto the shore, then stood and watched as the water went down. At the end, the barges bobbed for a moment on the blackish slime at the bottom of the empty dam, then settled softly into the mud.

11 : 25.

In the room above the café, the light went back on. The workers in the power station had apparently rigged up an emergency system. A moment later, the telephone. Weiss waited, then picked it up. He listened for a few seconds, then hung up. 'Four months,' he said.

'Can you be certain?' Casson asked.

'We know what it takes to build things. Thirty barges at the bottom of a well, that's pretty much what's happened. Twenty of them carrying fuel. Another hundred or so are headed south on the canals — they won't be able to get through.'

'Well, then.' Casson didn't know exactly what to say. He was too tired to feel victory.

Weiss smiled. 'I have to go out for a time,' he said. 'An hour, maybe. Then we'll head back to Paris. It's not a good idea to stick around after one of these things.'

Casson stood, they shook hands.

★ ★ ★

He was exhausted, he realized. He turned the light out, sat at the desk, and almost went to sleep. The phone rang. Casson reached for it, couldn't decide whether to answer or not, but it didn't ring again.

Back to Paris. To start again, some new operation. It wasn't going to end for a long time. If they took the night train he could sleep — even that seemed like a luxury now.

One ring. Why? A signal?

No. He was letting his imagination get the

413

better of him, a bad idea. He stood up, walked to the window, looked out over the deserted street below. *Calm down*, he told himself, this is over.

He sighed, but the feeling wouldn't go away. He walked down the stairs into the café and stood at the bar. Normal, another night in the village café. Two white-haired men, heavy sweaters under their jackets, were playing dominoes. A farmer in rubber boots, drinking pastis. A couple of old ladies in the corner. A *fonctionnaire*, peering through gold spectacles at the evening paper. A young woman, smoking, staring into space, by her side a Briard stretched out on the muddy tile floor, dreaming away.

The woman behind the bar came over and asked him what he'd like.

'Could I have a *vin rouge*?'

'You can, monsieur.'

She poured it from a pitcher, wiped the bottom of the glass with a rag, set it on the zinc bar in front of him.

'Some excitement tonight,' he said.

The woman shrugged. 'Yes, I suppose. Some kind of accident over at the canal, the electricity out.'

They both heard it at the same time — people charging up the stairs that went to the room above the café. More than two, maybe three or four. Not quite running, but in a hurry. He heard the door open — its knob hit the wall. He heard them walking around, directly above his head, the old wooden flooring creaked under the weight. He stared at the ceiling, so did the woman behind the bar. He saw that her hand was shaking. In the café it was quiet, none of the little sounds, cups and spoons, and nobody talked. Up above, he could hear voices.

It went on for a few minutes. Then he heard them coming back down the stairs. They threw the door open and slammed it shut. A car started up in the street, and drove away. Casson could hear it for a long time, the driver shifting up through the gears as the sound of the engine faded into the distance.

The woman behind the bar took a deep breath. 'That will be two francs, monsieur,' she said.

★ ★ ★

Monsieur Levaux arrived at his office on the Champs-Elysées punctually at ten on Monday morning. In his perfect suit and perfect shoes, with his perfect shave, he was the local god. On the way to his office he accepted obeisance — 'Bonjour, Monsieur Levaux,' 'Bonjour, Monsieur Levaux' — with profound disdain. A cold, polite face, it gave nothing away. *You are not in favor. Neither are you.* Phones rang, typewriters clattered. At the end of the room, his office. He went in and closed the door. His secretary gave him a few minutes, then knocked discreetly and entered. Levaux told her what he wanted, and away she went.

Life had not always been so easy. His father had been a railroad clerk, he had not shone in school, but he had worked hard, very hard, over the years, and, in time, the Agence Levaux was a place where people went when they needed to travel. By train or ship, to a commercial hotel or a resort, the agency was pleased to suggest the appropriate route, to make the reservation, write the ticket, collect the money. It was not the grandest agency in Paris, but it was not the smallest either. It made money, year in and year out. It made Monsieur Levaux a rich man.

He lived well, belonged to a club, lived in a fine apartment. But this was Paris, where money mattered but wasn't everything. It didn't, for instance, buy membership in the upper classes. It was pleasant to be rich, he thought, and it would just have to be sufficient. To rise any further — one had to be a realist about such things — was unlikely.

Or so he'd thought. Then, one Tuesday

afternoon, a telephone call. A competitor, a man who owned many more offices than he ever would. They'd known each other for years, a distant relationship, a favor this way, a favor that way, one was flattered to be asked. But this call was different — a dinner party, in the 16th Arrondissement, could Monsieur and Madame Levaux possibly attend? Or was it, perhaps, inconvenient?

Oh no, they would certainly attend. *Chez Levaux*, ecstasy. Madame in a flurry, off to the shops. For monsieur, a new suit. They arrived at 8:30 precisely, with damp palms and flushed faces. They talked, they ate, they drank, they were as charming as they knew how to be. And, in the middle of the evening, one of the guests, a *grand personnage* of the Sorbonne — asked of him a small favor. Would it be possible . . . ? Oh yes. He'd been considering it himself, in fact. He had? The *personnage* was pleased, said thank you and meant it.

A knock at the office door. The woman he'd summoned was shown in, he directed her to sit down. She was very nervous, he thought. Was he such a fearsome presence? Well, perhaps he over-did it, but far better to err on the side of authority.

Not unattractive. He'd suspected from the beginning a romantic entanglement lay at the heart of this business, but that didn't matter. Dark, he thought, dark eyes, a generous mouth, seductive. He smiled, she returned the smile. *Calm yourself, he thought, my dear* — he consulted the file — *my dear Hélène*.

He made a show of what he was going to do. Opened her dossier, paged through it, remarked on her years of service. 'What I need,' he said, 'is someone like yourself, who knows the agency, who knows how we do business, and has a good feel for the Levaux clientele.' Someone, above all, *dependable*. Well, how did she feel about that. Good? *Bon*. What he was offering was a job as the assistant office manager, in the Lisbon office. Quite a way from Paris, it was true, but an advancement in salary, and position. Would she consider it? Yes, she would.

★ ★ ★

On an April morning, Monsieur Marin settled his account at the Hotel du Commerce and moved to the Hotel Moncey, on the square of the same name near Nôtre Dame de Lorette. No special reason, he thought, it was simply time to go. Too long in one place, too many nods from the other fugitives in the endless hallways.

He had received, the last week in March,

two unsigned postcards. The first sent from Vera Cruz. 'I'm living now,' it began, 'at the Hotel Alcalà.' There was probably no such hotel — the name from the title of a book by Alexander Kovar — but the message was clear. 'I'm with old friends,' it continued, 'and I am in good health.' The second card, with a photograph of a Moorish garden, came from Lisbon. 'I will never forget you,' it said.

Monsieur Marin spent the day settling in to his new *quartier*. He had one meeting — with a man who'd worked before the war as a surveyor around Caen — then he stopped at a bookstore, and picked up an envelope that held the production schedule of an aluminum refinery in the south.

He woke early the next morning and opened the window, watching the night fade from the Paris sky. The rain had stopped, a few black puddles in the cobbled square, and the air smelled like spring. He heard someone in the corridor, then a light knock at the door.

'Yes?' he said.

We do hope that you have enjoyed reading this large print book.

Did you know that all of our titles are available for purchase?

We publish a wide range of high quality large print books including:
Romances, Mysteries, Classics, General Fiction, Non Fiction and Westerns.

Special interest titles available in large print are:
The Little Oxford Dictionary
Music Book
Song Book
Hymn Book
Service Book

Also available from us courtesy of Oxford University Press:
Young Readers' Dictionary
(large print edition)
Young Readers' Thesaurus
(large print edition)

For further information or a free brochure, please contact us at:
Ulverscroft Large Print Books Ltd.,
The Green, Bradgate Road, Anstey,
Leicester, LE7 7FU, England.
Tel: (00 44) 0116 236 4325
Fax: (00 44) 0116 234 0205

THE FROZEN CEILING

Rona Randall

When Tessa Pickard found the note amongst her father's possessions, instinct told her that THIS had been responsible for his suicide, not the professional disgrace which had ruined his career as a mountaineer and instructor. The note was cryptic, anonymous, and bore a Norwegian postmark. Tessa promptly set out for Norway, determined to trace the anonymous letter-writer, but unprepared for the drama she was to uncover — or that compelling Max Hyerdal, whom she met on board a Norwegian ship, was to change her whole life.

GHOSTMAN

Kenneth Royce

Jones boasted that he never forgot a face. When he was found dead outside the National Gallery it was assumed he had remembered one too many. The man he had claimed to have identified had been publicly executed in Moscow some years before. The presumed look-alike was called Mirek and his background stood up. The Security Service calls in Willie 'Glasshouse' Jackson — Jacko — as they realise that there is a more sinister aspect. Jacko and his assistant begin to unearth commercial and political corruption in which life is cheap and profits vast, as the killing machines swing into action.

THE READER

Bernhard Schlink

A schoolboy in post-war Germany, Michael collapses one day in the street and is helped home by a woman in her thirties. He is fascinated by this older woman, and he and Hanna begin a secretive affair. Gradually, he begins to be frustrated by their relationship, but then is shocked when Hanna simply disappears. Some years later, as a law student, Michael is in court to follow a case. To his amazement he recognizes Hanna. The object of his adolescent passion is a criminal. Suddenly, Michael understands that her behaviour, both now and in the past, conceals a deeply buried secret.

THE WAY OF THE SEA AND OTHER STORIES

Stanley Wilson

Every story in this collection was written by Stanley Wilson with radio in mind. The BBC has broadcast all of them, and many have been used overseas. All have appeared in magazines or newspapers. The stories range the globe and beyond, from India to Canadian backwoods, from an expedition up the Amazon to a hundred years' journey to the planet Eithnan, from the Caribbean to a rain-sodden English seaside promenade, and from a fishing trawler to a hospital ward. There is frustration, there is tenderness, there is horror, there are tears, but there is laughter as well.